THE SHAMING EYES

A NICK DRAKE NOVEL

DWIGHT HOLING

The Shaming Eyes
A Nick Drake Novel

Print Edition
Copyright 2019 by Dwight Holing
Published by Jackdaw Press
All Rights Reserved

ISBN: 978-0-9991468-9-7

Cover Photo: "Leslie Gulch Moonrise " (Owyhee Canyon, Oregon) © 2019 by David Jensen

For More Information, please visit dwightholing.com.

See how you can **Get a Free Book** at the end of this novel.

For my four-legged friends

Reina
Jack
Finn
Rumi

Blame it or praise it, there is no denying the wild horse in us.

— Virginia Woolf

1

S pring finally came to the high desert and anything that grew, flew, swam, or walked shook off the torpor of a bitter winter that had been especially unforgiving for the old, weak, and unprepared. Wildflowers were ablaze, north-bound birds formed mile-long carets in the cloudless sky, and herds of pronghorn raced as if suddenly discovering they were no longer shackled by snow and ice.

Warm air wafted through the canyons of the Snake River. The gentle breezes were blowing in the same direction as I steered my skiff. I was on the final leg of a three-day patrol of a necklace of islands strung along a hundred-mile stretch of water that formed a watery boundary between Oregon and Idaho. Deer Flat National Wildlife Refuge was among the half dozen sanctuaries I'd been assigned to police since taking a job as a US Fish and Wildlife ranger following duty in Vietnam.

I spent the days charting the refuge's riverine islands and tallying the different species of plants and animals. There was no need to flash my badge or make an arrest because I never encountered another soul. In the evenings, I camped on the

bank and fell asleep beneath the stars while listening to the
river.

The gathering waters had begun as snowmelt, some as far
away as Yellowstone, still more borne by the creeks and rivers
that drained the basin and range country of southeastern
Oregon. Knowing the flow was timeless—each drop that passed
was newer than the one it followed but older than the one
behind it—provided solace. After having fought for three years
in a brutal and confusing war, the Snake was a reminder that life
was like a river. Each moment alive was akin to a drop of water.
It carried the possibility of a fresh start, a chance to wash clean
the consequences of the moment it followed, be it a combat
decision that had been made in haste or a decision made too
late.

The sun's position in the cobalt blue sky confirmed my
patrol was nearing its end. The boat ramp where my pickup and
trailer awaited was right around the bend. I wanted to savor a
final moment of peace and freedom, and so I steered into a quiet
elbow in the lee of an island, killed the outboard, and soaked in
the beauty and serenity.

The breeze carried the scent of sage. The shallows were
dimpled by ravenous fry. A pair of western grebes ignored my
intrusion as they continued their mating dance. The waterbirds
were reluctant flyers. They sprinted across the surface toward
one another while making croaks that mimicked the sound of a
ratchet tightening bolts. Upon meeting, the amorous couple
raised their torsos until their heads extended like a pair of
cobras and gently caressed the other's long, slender neck with
aquatic plants clutched in their bills. Pattering on webbed feet
while keeping their stubby wings close to their sides, they
twirled around and around in an aquatic tango before rushing
to a bed of reeds to begin building a nest and life together.

When the newly bonded pair had disappeared from view, I

felt an urge to be home myself. I restarted the outboard, and as soon as I was sure my wake wouldn't disturb the nesters, turned the throttle wide open and was away.

Highway 20 led west from the boat ramp. For the first fifty miles or so, the two-lane followed the Malheur River, one of the many tributaries of the Snake. The Malheur was named by French trappers and meant *misfortune*. The Snake was also named by early explorers, but in error. The Shoshone, who had lived along the river for thousands of years, called it *Yampahpa* for a plant that grew along its banks. When they encountered white men and were asked who they were, they made an *S*-like motion with their hands to signify they were the people who lived by a river filled with salmon. The whites misinterpreted the gesture and called the Shoshone "Snake Indians" and the river that too.

The narrow highway crossed dry gulches gouged from the desert by flash floods and climbed up and down wrinkles in the earth's skin that resembled the pleats in an accordion. Sage-brush and scrubby piñons poked out of the ground. The glint from minerals caused the dun colored soil to look as if it had been sown with precious jewels. I downshifted as I reached a steep grade up the eastern flank of the Stinkingwater Mountains and then stopped at the top of the nearly mile-high pass, not because the Ford's engine was laboring from towing the boat trailer, but because the pullout afforded a view of the heart of Harney County.

Straight ahead was Burns, home to a quarter of the 7,000 residents of the sparse and sprawling county. To the south was a wide valley quilted with patches of desert and grassy fields. Two forks of a river flowing from the north and another coming from the south drained into a broad shallow basin. Called Malheur Lake though it didn't connect to the river of the same name, it was another wildlife refuge. So was Hart Mountain that rose farther south. The pair of federal reserves were the ones I knew best because they were closest to the old railroad lineman's shack I called home on the outskirts of a one-blink town named No Mountain.

As I tried to locate the wooden cabin with its cockeyed black stovepipe, I saw turkey vultures to my left. The big carrion eaters migrated along the Pacific Flyway the same as waterfowl and songbirds did each spring and fall, but it was unusual to see a kettle this large. I counted ten, twelve, fourteen birds swirling in the updraft. Something was dead beneath them, something very big or very many somethings. I turned off the highway and followed a dirt road to see what was attracting so much attention.

Within a mile, a green pickup parked in the road blocked my progress. I was getting out to investigate when shots echoed. I pulled my Winchester from the rack in the rear window and ran toward the gunfire.

A draw nestled between two hillocks lay west of the road. A stream burbled down its middle. A man in a khaki shirt not unlike my own stood over the crumpled body of a wild horse. Six more carcasses littered the ground. He wheeled around at the sound of my approach. His revolver was leveled at me. I recognized the look in his eyes. I'd seen it plenty of times in the eyes of the men in my squad during a ferocious firefight. I'd seen it in the mirror too. It was a mixture of savagery and survival, of horror and sorrow.

"Fish and Wildlife," I said sharply. I stared hard at his pistol, willing him to lower it.

My voice had the effect of a slap across the face. He immediately holstered his weapon. "Sorry," he said. "I had to put two of them down. You have to work yourself up to do something like that even when it's the right thing to do."

"Nick Drake," I said. "Who are you?"

"Clay Barkley. BLM."

The Bureau of Land Management ranger was tall and sinewy. He was in his early thirties and wore a green ball cap. His face had all the etchings of a life spent working in the sun and wind.

"What happened here?"

"Poison." Barkley gestured at a couple of well-licked salt blocks. "If I take those back to my camp and test them, I'm sure I'll find they're laced with strychnine. It wouldn't be the first time."

"Where's your camp?"

"A mile south." He jerked a thumb to where our rigs were parked on the access road. "I was making my rounds when I saw the vultures. Five of the mustangs were already dead. The other two were on the ground and foaming at the mouth. I couldn't stand by and watch them suffer."

"This is BLM land?"

"It is," he said.

"Which office are you out of? Not the one near Burns."

"No, Carson City. I've spent the past couple of years in Nevada assessing the Virginia Range herd. After I turned in my report, I was reassigned to make a similar assessment of wild horses up here."

The vultures were still circling, unwilling to land as long as Barkley and I were there. The magpies showed no fear though. One of the long-tailed black and white birds was perched on the carcass of a dead horse pecking at its eyes. More were strutting to and fro as they staked out their own meals.

I grimaced at the bodies. "You have any idea who did this?"

"A cattle rancher, more than likely. Some view mustangs as competition for graze, what little there is. If I had to choose, the Fannings would be at the top of the list. They run the Seven Fans spread."

"I've met most of the ranchers around here, but not them."

"The Seven Fans is on the eastside of the Stinkingwaters. They lease some BLM grazeland and free range most of their beef. I've had a couple of run-ins with their foreman, Sonny. At least that's what's engraved on the back of his tooled leather belt. He straps the kind of old fashioned six-shooter quick-draw artists wear in the movies and has an attitude to match."

I walked around the draw and shooed away the magpies as I studied each horse. Most were blue and red roans. A sorrel mare made me think of a very special cutting horse that was named to honor Sarah Winnemucca, a famous Paiute leader. I asked Barkley what he was going to do about it.

"Be mad about it. Sick about it. Take your pick. There's nothing I can do. Nobody can. The only law against killing wild horses was passed ten years ago, and it only prohibits shooting them from an airplane."

"But putting out poison? There's nothing to stop a prong-horn or mule deer from licking it. That's against the law on the refuges I patrol."

"Well, if anybody does it in your jurisdiction, I hope you go after them. My hands are tied."

"And the assessment you're making, what will happen with it?"

"Piss people off and most likely get me reassigned again."

I asked him why.

"I recommended they create a management area for the herd in Nevada with protections and guidelines for keeping the number of wild horses in line with what the graze will support."

"And the ranchers were against it?"

"Some, but not all. They weren't alone. There are taxpayers who don't want to foot the bill, animal lovers who know that management means culling the herd from time to time, and then there are the romantics who think the old west is still alive and kicking as long as wild horses run free." The weather lines in Barkley's face deepened as he scowled. "They've never seen a herd starve to death."

"Your job doesn't sound like it makes you very popular."

"And I wasn't the homecoming king in high school either. Seems I always take the rocky road."

"I've come across wild horses plenty of times when I've been on patrol," I said. "If it'd be of help, I could map them for you."

Barkley brightened. "Thanks. That'd be great."

Some movement caught my eye. A skinny filly foal on wobbly legs tottered out from behind a thicket of brittlebush, sniffed the air, and then stumbled toward the body of the sorrel mare. She nosed the dead horse's teats, whimpered, and then collapsed next to what was surely her mother.

Barkley sighed. "Heartless bastards." He reached for his gun as he started walking toward the foal.

Only I didn't see a foal anymore. I saw a little girl crouched and crying outside of a burning hooch as the rest of her family of rice farmers turned to cinders inside.

"Wait," I said. When Barkley didn't, I shouted, "Hold it!"

"The sooner I do it, the better. The poor thing is half dead already."

I hurried after him, grabbed his elbow, and spun him around. "Don't do it. I'll take her to the LZ and put her on an EVAC chopper. They can fix her up at the MASH and then turn her over to the orphanage run by the monks."

Barkley stared at me. "What the—?"

"Don't do it," I said again. "You'll never be able to live with yourself." I was carrying my M16 at port arms. I straight-armed it to block him. "Back off! I got her."

"Hey, are you all right?"

The sun glared. I dipped my head to shield my eyes. Everything came rushing back into focus. I saw the lever action

Winchester in my hands. I lowered it and gulped some air. "I mean, I mean the foal... the foal. I'll take her. I know a horse doctor."

Barkley stared some more. His changing expression showed he was figuring out what was what. "Okay," he finally said. "But you're wasting your time and causing the poor creature to suffer even more. It's best to put her down."

"I'm not asking."

I hustled around the BLM ranger and put myself between him and the foal. She didn't look to be more than a couple of months old, but it was hard to tell considering how skinny she was. Her ribs stuck out. Her breathing was labored. Her coat was dull and matted and her eyes glassy.

"I have a tarp in my pickup," I said. "We can use it as a litter. I have some blankets too. I'll wrap her up and tie her down in the bed."

"She'll be dead before you get to wherever you're going."

"I don't have a choice," I said.

2

No spot along the narrow dirt road was wide enough to turn my pickup and trailer around. Backing up was the only option to reach the highway, but going slowly to avoid bumps wasn't. Time was running out for the stricken foal. I threw it in reverse and gritted my teeth as I bounced backward.

When I hit pavement, I straightened the rig out and sped down the pass, only taking my foot off the gas to coast into the curves. Tires screeched and rubber burned, but the trailer didn't jackknife. If the little mustang was still alive, I knew she had to be terrified. I gripped the wheel tightly and tried to focus on the blacktop ahead and not on the memory of slinging a terrified little girl over my shoulder and firing my weapon while running through the jungle as machine guns clamored, fuel bombs whooshed, and trees exploded in flames around me.

The fifteen-mile-long straightaway that cut across the northside of Harney Valley couldn't come soon enough, nor the turnoff south to No Mountain. I raced past the block of false front buildings that comprised Main Street and clattered over the cattle guard that marked the entrance to the Warbler ranch.

A red Jeep Wagoneer was parked in front of the house. I hammered my horn a couple of times before jumping out to untie the tarp that covered the pickup's box.

The front door banged open and the echo of footsteps on the wooden porch was followed by a gasp as a woman sporting a ponytail and wearing a faded denim snap button shirt reached my side and peered into the bed.

"It's a foal. She's so little," Gemma Warbler said. "Where did you find her?"

"In the Stinkingwaters. Her mother was poisoned along with some others. Strychnine, I think."

"If she's been nursing tainted milk, I—" Air whistled as the veterinarian inhaled deeply. "Oh, Nick, she's barely breathing. Let's get her into the stable."

I freed her from the ties and we carried her across the front yard. Two cutting horses in the adjoining corral watched us, a mare that had the same sorrel coloring as the foal's dead mother and a buckskin stallion. Both horses flared their nostrils. The mare whinnied. The buckskin pawed the ground, shook his mane, and snorted.

"Sarah and Wovoka can smell she's a mustang," Gemma said.

The foal was too weak to stand. We laid her atop fresh straw in a stall and kneeled on either side. Gemma went straight to work, checking the baby horse's airway before inserting a flexible plastic tube into a nostril and stroking the foal's throat to force her to swallow.

"Good girl," Gemma said as she guided the tube through the pharynx and esophagus and down into the stomach. "I'm suctioning but nothing is coming out. That doesn't mean there isn't any poisoned milk still in there. I need to lavage her."

The vet flushed water through the tube and then followed it with a slurry of charcoal and then mineral oil. Anything that was inside the foal's stomach came streaming out. Finally, Gemma inserted a needle into a neck vein, fitted it to a tube from an IV bag, and started a drip.

"She needs lots of fluids to protect her kidneys. I've added a dose of anti-inflammatories as well as some phenobarbital in case she starts convulsing, but honestly, she doesn't look like she has the strength to lift her head."

The horse doctor's ponytail had fallen forward. She flicked it back over her shoulder and frowned. "I don't know if any of this will work. She's terribly weak. Foals start eating solids a week or two after they're born, but they still get most of their nutrition from mother's milk for three months or so."

"A BLM ranger was going to shoot her. I couldn't let him do that."

Gemma placed her hand atop mine. "Of course you couldn't."

"Shoot who?" a voice called from the stable's entrance. Pudge Warbler strode toward the stall. He wore the gold star of a Harney County deputy sheriff pinned above his heart. He pushed up his short-brimmed Stetson with a meaty finger when he saw the filly foal. "Now, if she isn't the cutest. Why was someone gonna shoot her?"

"She's been poisoned," the lawman's daughter said. "Nick found her."

"She get into a field of ragwort?"

I shook my head. "I came across a BLM ranger who'd discovered a herd of mustangs in the bottom of a draw. She's the only one that made it. He thinks a rancher put out salt licks laced with strychnine."

Pudge made a face. "He got any idea who did it?"

"Clay Barkley, that's his name, he said he'd had run-ins with the Fannings."

"Is that a fact? I recently went toe-to-toe with them myself.

That gang of rustlers from last fall has returned now that spring has sprung. They hit the Seven Fans the other night and Darlene and Lester are blaming me for doing squat about it. Well, Darlene is. She does the talking for the pair, if you call shouting and cussing like a sailor a conversation."

"Barkley mentioned their foreman."

Pudge snorted. "That'd be Sonny Stiles. He acts like he's ten feet tall but couldn't reach half that no matter how many extra layers of leather he stacks in his bootheels. Sonny's a jim-dandy, right down to the Pendleton Round-Up Championship belt buckle he bought at a pawn shop."

He looked at the filly foal again. She was quiet, her eyelids closed, her sides barely billowing. "She gonna make it?"

"Only time will tell," Gemma said.

The deputy puffed his cheeks and blew out air. "Killing wild horses is legal, but that doesn't mean I got to like it. I'll make a point of bringing it up next time I stop by the Seven Fans to tell Darlene and Lester what I found out about their stolen stock, which isn't much."

I'd been kneeling next to the foal and stood. "You weren't able to track them?"

"No, but I got a better idea of where the thieves are taking them. They've moved on from the ranches in Harney Valley and are making their way slow but steady eastward. I have a hunch they're running them into Idaho."

"I just came from the borderline," I said. "I spent three days on the Snake."

"I wondered why I hadn't seen you around." Pudge gave his daughter a wink. "There's a lot of wide open country between here and there. Most of it's free range. The big ranches turn their cattle loose until they round them up at the end of summer. Makes it easy pickings for thieves."

"If the rustlers are taking cattle into Idaho, then they have to cross somewhere. Can't the state troopers put up inspection stations?"

"There's too many roads to watch and not enough eyes to watch them. Our best bet is to catch them while they're still in Harney County."

"Let me know if you need help," I said.

"I'm putting the finishing touches on a new plan of attack. Well, me and the college boy are. I'd fill you in, but I got to git right now. Bust'em called and needs me back in Burns pronto." Bust'em was Harney County Sheriff Buster Burton. He gave himself the nickname when he moved from Klamath County to run against then Sheriff Pudge Warbler. The old lawman turned to Gemma. "Good luck with your patient."

The echo of his pickup driving away rolled through the stable's entryway.

I knelt next to the foal again and stroked her withers. "What else can we do for her?"

"Nothing, right now," Gemma said. "It's watch and wait time. I'll start her on colostrum once she's settled. Hopefully, she'll get strong enough to let me bottle feed her."

"If you don't need any more help, I'll—"

"What, leave? You're just going to drop off a sick foal and not say anything to me after three days?" Her ponytail swished as she shook her head. "And to think when I heard all that honking it was you in a hurry to tell me how much you missed me."

"No, it's just that I—"

Gemma laughed. "You should see the look on your face."

I blew out air. "You got me."

Her eyes sparkled when she smiled. "It's still pretty easy to."

"The thing is, I'm already late calling my district supervisor and giving him a report on Deer Flat."

"Since when were you ever in a hurry to talk to him, much less file paperwork?"

"There's a new head of the western region who got hired when President Nixon was sworn in. He's instituted a bunch of policies aimed at reining in field staff. Apparently, he's looking to make an example out of one."

"Well, he won't have to look very far to find him."

"I don't want my supervisor to have to carry my water. If all it takes is for me to pick up the phone, no big deal." I gave the foal another pat. "Why don't you come over later? I'll cook you dinner."

Gemma hesitated. "I should stay and keep an eye on her."

"There's always breakfast."

"Even better," she said.

As I was walking toward my rig, an old woman with a long black braid streaked with gray hairs as fine as cobwebs shuffled out of the ranch house. Despite the warm temperature, she was wrapped in a multicolored wool blanket. It had been a while since I saw her last, and she appeared frail compared to her usual flinty self.

"Good afternoon, *Tsua'a Numudooa Nubabe*," I said in *numu*, her native tongue. It was her Paiute birth name, Girl Born in Snow. Most people called her November, the name the Bureau of Indian Affairs gave her when they put her in a boarding school sixty years ago.

The old woman acknowledged me with a raspy cough. "You brought a sick *pooggoo* here. What disease does she carry?"

"Nothing the other horses can catch. Her mother was poisoned and the foal drank her milk. The mother died and the rest of the herd too."

"Perhaps she will too."

"Gemma is doing all she can to make sure she doesn't. You have powerful medicine. You could help her."

The blanket covering November's shoulders barely rose and

fell as she shrugged. "Not if the *pooggoo* has chosen to join the others on the spirit trail."

"But she's not the one who chose to put out the poison."

"No, but her mother chose to eat it and the *pooggoo* chose to suckle." She coughed again.

"Are you feeling all right?"

"It was a long winter, but I have lived through many winters."

"And may you live many more," I said in *numu*.

The old woman studied me. Her usually piercing eyes were rheumy, the pupils covered with a white film. "You speak our words a little better now."

"I worked on my pronunciation over the winter."

November blinked and when she opened her eyes again, the rheum was gone. "I see you have worked on something else also."

"What do you mean?"

"You are letting others see inside you now." When I shrugged, she said, "Do you know when Deer is in the greatest danger?"

"When he's in a hunter's sights?"

"Right after he loses his antlers." She coughed again. "Be careful you do not lose yours. In the time it takes to grow them back, someone could see inside you and steal your *puha*, your power." November closed her eyes and tilted her face toward the rays of the sun. When she looked back at me, her eyes were cloudy with rheum again. "You will need them, maybe very soon, I think."

Before I could ask her anything more, the old woman shuffled toward the stable. As she passed the corral, Sarah and Wovoka pawed the ground and whinnied the same as when they smelled the wild filly foal.

The old lineman's shack had been built for an abandoned fifty-mile-long railroad that once ferried timber to a mill near Burns. I pulled into the drive and unhitched the boat trailer beside an overhang that shielded a cord of split wood and a Triumph motorcycle. Racing the bike across Harney County's salt flats and down its lonesome roads was my antidote to cabin fever.

I unloaded the pickup and went inside. The shack had only one room, not counting a bathroom that was so cramped picking up a dropped towel required footwork. The kitchen was on one side, a narrow bunk on the other, and a wood stove in the center. I sat at a rickety wooden table and dialed the Fish and Wildlife office in Portland. The district supervisor's questions about my patrol of the refuge's islands in the wide stretch of the Snake River were perfunctory and my replies equally concise. He didn't express any opinion until I told him about Clay Barkley and the poisoned mustangs.

"You say it happened on BLM land? Then let them deal with it. The Bureau manages over sixty percent of all the land in Harney County and has the budget and staff to do it. You're the only ranger I have down there. Keep your nose clean and your eye on your jurisdiction."

"But the words on my badge say fish and *wildlife*. There's nothing to prevent pronghorn, deer, and mountain sheep from wandering off the refuges and getting at those poisoned licks. By definition, mustangs are wild. That makes them my responsibility too."

"No, they're not!" he bellowed, belying his usual bored demeanor honed by thirty years pushing paper. "They're domestic stock that either ran off from wagon trains or were turned loose by sodbusters unable to feed them."

"That was generations ago. These horses don't know their ancestors once pulled a plow or wore shoes. Have you ever seen what strychnine does to an animal?"

He took a deep breath. "I said leave it be. That's an order. And here's another. The new director has ordered every employee to undergo a performance review. Yours is scheduled for 10:00 a.m. sharp next Tuesday. He's going to listen in while I conduct it, so for your sake and mine, call in on time, and whatever you do, don't smart off. Understood?"

The dial tone rang in my ear. I chewed the inside of my lip before setting the heavy black handset back in its cradle. It was clear he was feeling the heat from upstairs, and though I'd been trained to respect the chain of command during my days in the Army's 1st Cavalry Division as a sergeant leading a long-range reconnaissance squad, I couldn't forget the sight of those dead horses and the foal that was teetering on the edge of oblivion. Pudge Warbler and I shared something in common. Killing wild horses might be legal, but that didn't mean we had to like it.

Outside the kitchen window, the sky turned orange and then reddened. The desert floor was turning darkening shades of purple. I twisted the tuning knob on the radio and was able to pick up the college station in Eugene. The DJ was reading the headlines. NASA was readying to launch Apollo 10, a dress rehearsal for the long-awaited lunar landing that was scheduled for the summer. The Department of Defense announced there were now 550,000 GIs serving in Vietnam, the highest number since the war began. The 101st Airborne was engaged in a bloody battle at a place nicknamed Hamburger Hill. California Governor Ronald Reagan had placed Berkeley under martial law and dispatched riot police to quell a protest at a park near the university campus.

I was grateful when the newscast ended. Though I was finished with the war, it was not finished with me. I could smell the stink of fear emanating from the newest crop of cherries as they marched off a transport plane at Da Nang, hear the whoomph of artillery and the swish of bullets scything through the elephant grass as a squad from the 101st sought cover while trying to storm a jungle-shrouded mountain far, far from home.

The DJ announced he'd received a copy of Neil Young's just-released second solo album. "It's called *Everybody Knows This is Nowhere* and he's backed by a far-out band, Crazy Horse. I'm going to play it nonstop until the needle wears a groove in it. Peace."

The cheap radio started to shimmy with reverb as lead and bass electric guitars launched into a long opening riff. The folk rocker's falsetto joined in, and he sang about being in love with a cinnamon girl. I put water on to boil for tea and set about mixing batter for corn bread while a pork chop that had been the sole occupant in the refrigerator's shoebox-sized freezer compartment thawed on the counter.

After dinner I sat at the table, drinking tea and marking places on a map where I recalled seeing wild horses. I tallied my marks. Mustangs were living adjacent to or within the boundaries of three national wildlife refuges, Malheur, Hart Mountain, and Sheldon. Three more herds lived a short gallop away. Seeing it on paper strengthened my resolve that mustangs were wildlife and deserved protection.

I was still studying the map when Gemma arrived. The horse doctor stopped halfway to the rickety table and began to bob. "Are you playing that song on purpose?"

"What song?" I asked.

She started singing along. "Hello, cowgirl in the sand. Is this place at your command?"

The DJ had played the new Neil Young album so many times, I'd all but tuned it out. "Right," I said quickly. "I heard you drive up and cued it."

"Liar." She laughed and then came closer to peer over my shoulder. "What's with the map?"

"Wild horses. I've been plotting where I've seen them to give to Clay Barkley, the BLM ranger. How's the foal?"

"Still alive. She's a tough little thing, I'll hand her that."

"Tough enough for you to leave her?"

"Either she'll make it through the night or she won't. I've done what I can. Now it's up to her."

Gemma's cheek was right alongside mine as we studied the map. It wasn't that long ago I would've recoiled, not only from her touch, but anyone's. The shrinks at Walter Reed where I'd spent six months after returning to the real world, trying to kick heroin, and getting my head straight told me it was a common reaction of soldiers suffering from combat fatigue. Part of it had to do with depersonalizing myself to be able to kill another human being, and part of it had to do with not trusting anyone because they might be trying to kill me. I slid my arm around her waist and gave a squeeze.

Gemma leaned into me. "So, you did miss me. You also missed some herds on your map here. There are wild horses at Palomino Buttes about fifteen miles southwest of Burns, another herd south of there at Warm Springs, and then at least a couple along the Owyhee River. One near Three Fingers Rock and another around Jackies Butte."

"I was at the Owyhee's mouth when I was on the Snake. The confluence is right in the middle of the Deer Flat river islands. I didn't see any wild horses there."

"The Owyhee herds are farther south," she said.

"What about the Stinkingwaters? Are there more mustangs living there or was the little foal's herd it?"

"There's a few. I've seen several different groups when I've passed through on the way to treat patients."

"Does that include the Seven Fans ranch?"

"It was one of the first house calls I made after graduating from vet school in Corvallis. Any illusion I had about ranchers being grateful when I treated their sick stock went up in smoke."

"How come?"

"The Fannings had a dairy operation in addition to raising beef. I got a call from Darlene that their milk cows were having severe diarrhea. I drove over to examine them and saw some were already showing signs of bottle jaw."

"What's that?"

"It pretty much looks like it sounds, a soft swelling under the jaw. The clinical name is Johne's disease. An edema forms from a very contagious infection akin to TB. Once a cow has bottle jaw, its days are numbered. I told Darlene she needed to isolate the herd, destroy the sick cows, and monitor the rest. When I told her she had to stop milk production immediately, she grabbed a shotgun and ran me off the ranch."

"But you didn't let it go, did you?"

Gemma's eyes flashed with indignation. "Heck no. I called the Oregon Department of Ag right away and they showed up with a livestock trailer and an armed escort."

"That would have been your dad."

"You got it. It was when Pudge was still sheriff, before he got shot trying to break up a husband and wife fight. That was the first of many earfuls he's gotten from Darlene."

"And you?"

"After all the Fanning's dairy cows were hauled off, I never heard from her again." Gemma paused. Her eyes softened and her expression changed. "You know, I didn't come over here to talk about sick cows and nasty old women."

"You didn't?" I tightened my grip around her.

She cupped my chin and planted a kiss. "No, I came over for breakfast. You invited me, remember?"

"So I did."

We kissed again and I pulled her onto my lap. "Well, I hope your refrigerator is stocked better than last time," she said.

"I didn't get a chance to go shopping. How does cornbread and coffee sound?" I said between kisses.

"Perfect." She got up and trailed her fingertips along my arm before crossing the shack and disappearing into the tiny bathroom.

I put the map away and built a log cabin of kindling in the wood stove, placed a couple of quartered rounds on top, and struck a match. Then I slid the mattress off the narrow bunk and arranged it on the floor with a sleeping bag next to it.

I was spreading the sheets and blankets over them when Gemma hugged me from behind. I turned around. She was already undressed. I drew her close and we started kissing again. She unbuttoned my shirt and pressed against my chest. We fell onto the makeshift bed as the kindling sparked and the flames leapt. We kept kissing, and soon the stove glowed and the lineman's shack creaked and heaved from all the heat.

THE FIRE CRACKLED AND HISSED. We had the blankets pulled up

and Gemma was curled on her side with her head nestled on my chest. I told her about my time on the Snake.

"If you were a western grebe, I'd've rubbed your neck with waterweed between my teeth," I said.

She poked my ribs. "You may know all the right moves, hotshot, but you really need to work on your sweet nothings."

"Okay, how about this one. If you were a sage grouse hen—"

Gemma mimicked a snore. "I know how the males drum their chests. Remember, I'm the one who was born and raised in Harney County, and you're the one who never talks about his past. I grew up camping. Sleeping on the floor next to the fire here is almost as good."

"Almost?" I said.

"It's hard to compete with shooting stars and spinning galaxies."

I laughed, and that felt pretty good too.

"When did you first know?" she said.

"Know what?"

"You know what. When did you finally know you were going to lower that wall you'd put up and see if I lowered mine too?"

"You sure you don't want to hear about the grebes again?"

"Come on, fess up. Strong and silent only gets you so far."

"If you insist. It was the time we rode Wovoka and Sarah out back of your ranch and it was snowing. I realized it was going to be a long winter."

"Smooth talker, comparing me to a pair of long johns and a scratchy wool blanket."

"I don't mean *winter* winter. I mean continuing to live like I had been, where it's always dark and cold."

"Oh, so now you're a poet. You've been listening to folk music along with rock and roll, haven't you? Don't tell me it's Sonny and Cher."

"What about you, when did you know?"

"That's easy. The first night you showed up at the ranch. Pudge and you arrived in his pickup. He had your motorcycle in the back. You coasted it backward down a plank without even looking over your shoulder. And then you basically ignored me while I was telling you off. You roared away and I went back inside, slammed the door, and kicked the couch for good measure. I knew I was a goner."

"You sure fooled me."

"Not really."

"Yes, you did. I didn't think it was until, you know, that night."

"And what night was that?" she asked coyly.

"You know, the first time you slept over."

"I hate that saying. It makes it sound like kids having a pajama party."

"Funny, I don't remember any pajamas."

She laughed. "That night. It was *some* night, wasn't it?"

"They've all been."

"All? Come on, there haven't been that many."

"What, you've been counting?"

"I mean, between me shuttling from ranch to ranch and you traveling between all the refuges, it's a wonder there was even a second night, much less..." She held out her hand and started counting with her fingers. "Let's see, one, two, three..."

"Funny," I said. "Real funny."

"Just saying."

We listened to the fire some more. "What do Paiute call snoring anyway?" I said.

"Dream talking."

"What are the words in *numu*?"

She told me. Gemma was fluent. November had taught her. It was part of the old healer's promise to Gemma's mother who November tried but could not save from cancer. As she lay dying, November vowed to her she would move to the Warbler's ranch and raise her daughter. She made sure Gemma's upbringing would include learning the Paiute ways so she could benefit from both worlds.

"I ran into November after leaving the stable this afternoon," I said. "How long has she been sick? She seems a lot older."

"She's been fighting a really bad cold. It's probably walking pneumonia. I tried to talk her into getting a chest X-ray, but you can imagine how that conversation went. Don't tell her, but I've been slipping antibiotics into her meals."

"She warned me not to lose my antlers."

Gemma sighed. "She did, did she? Well, that confirms it. She's becoming more determined than ever that someone beside her be responsible for me, not that I need someone to, nor want anyone to."

"I know that," I said.

She snuggled closer. "That's what I like about you. At least you try to understand."

"Why is she thinking that way?"

"I wasn't sure at first. She didn't act like this when I went away to college or even the six months I was married and lived at my ex's ranch. She is getting up there in age and she did catch something over the winter. I started to think, oh no, she sees the end of her time in this world coming." Gemma shivered and so I hugged her a little tighter.

"I finally asked her what was going on. We've never had any secrets. I've told her about us, how we've agreed to take it slow, keep it simple, and let what happens happen. November told me she's been having visions of her husband trying to tell her something."

"Wait, November has a husband?"

"Had. He died, along with their daughter."

"I didn't know she was ever married. What happened?"

"It was a long time ago. November fell in love with a Shoshone man from the *Tussawehee* band, that's White Knife in English. The Shoshone and Paiute have always intermingled. Winnemucca, the Paiute war chief, was born a Shoshone. When he married a member of the *Kuyuidika* band, he became a Paiute according to tribal custom.

"Anyway, November married Shoots While Running, who traced his line back to Chief Washakie, a great Shoshone leader. They had a daughter. Her full name was Breathes Like Gentle Wind, but everyone called her Gentle Wind. One day, Shoots While Running got word that his mother was on her deathbed and wished to meet her granddaughter before she left for the spirit world. The family agreed they would travel to visit her at the Shoshone reservation in Fort Hall, Idaho. Travel in those days was difficult. Few Paiute had automobiles, but there was a bus.

"The morning they were to leave, November awoke with a blinding headache. Shoots While Running said they should delay their trip, but November wouldn't hear of it and said she could catch another bus when she was feeling better. After her husband and daughter left, November fell into a deep sleep. She had a terrible dream and when she awoke, she discovered her dream had become real. The bus carrying Shoots While Running and Gentle Wind had a blowout on a bridge crossing the Snake River. It crashed through the guard rail and plummeted into the water below. Everyone drowned."

The words hung heavily over us. I got up and put more wood on the fire as if the flames and heat could shoo them away. When I returned to bed, I said, "Is having lost a daughter why November wanted to take care of you after your mother died?"

"I'm sure it had something to do with it, but I'd like to think it wasn't the only reason. November and I, well, she is like a mother to me, but she's always been careful to tell me things about my mom. November believes people only die when others stop telling stories about them."

"What is it her husband has been trying to tell her?"

"Either she doesn't know yet or, more than likely, doesn't want to tell me. My worst fear is, he's calling her to join him and Gentle Wind in the spirit world." She paused. "I don't know what I'm going to do if she dies."

I stared at the ceiling and listened to the fire snap and pop as I wondered about the vision November had that led her to warn me not to let down my guard. After a while, I let the soft sounds of Gemma dream talking chase the bad thoughts away. I had slept outdoors plenty of times too, and though I could not see shooting stars or watch the moon as it passed between the constellations from inside the lineman's shack, none of those times had felt as good as right now lying beside Gemma.

Not even close.

4

Clay Barkley's camp was located in a saddle of the Stinkingwater Mountains a short distance off the access road. I recognized his green pickup but not the white Volvo with Vermont plates parked next to it in the pullout. The boxy station wagon was covered in dust and sported a "Save the Mustangs" bumper sticker. The BLM ranger was seated at a folding camp table in front of a large canvas tent that looked as if it had been purchased at an Army Navy surplus store.

"Morning," I said.

He was writing in a notebook. The black and white speckled cover reminded me of composition books they handed out in high school English class. "How's it going?" he said.

"I brought you some information on the location of other herds of wild horses, including the ones around the national wildlife refuges."

"Thanks. What happened with the foal?"

"I got her to the horse doctor, but it's still too early to tell."

"You sure were set on trying to save her. I hope it was worth it, for both of your sakes."

"It was."

He pondered that for a moment and then said, "You served overseas, didn't you?" I nodded. "I figured, you know, with what you said about the, well, the foal and all."

"I've been back a year and a half, but sometimes I forget to forget."

"You don't have to explain. I know others who went to 'Nam. Not all of them came home."

I looked around his camp to break off the conversation about a subject I still had trouble talking about. He'd picked a nice spot for it. There was a view of the ridgelines running north and south, and the Harney Basin below. He'd fashioned an outdoor shower by placing a clear plastic jug with a hose and sprayer on top of a post so the water would be warmed by the sun. Near the tent was a ring of rocks, their faces blackened by wood smoke. An iron grill supported by two flat stones occupied the middle of the fire ring. A coffee pot and cast iron frying pan rested on the grill. A plastic tub for dish washing had been turned upside down. Set out to dry on it were a pair of green enamel mugs, two matching plates, and knives and forks.

"I hope I'm not intruding," I said.

"What do you mean?"

I nodded at the Volvo wagon.

He looked in its direction, paused, and then said, "No, it's okay. That's Lily's car."

"Who's she?"

"You don't know Lily Calla? I thought everybody who lived around here did, especially people who work in the field like you and me. Lily is a wild horse person."

"Where is she from?"

"The East Coast. She was going to college in Vermont and read a short story in an English literature class about a woman and wild horses. Lily told me she couldn't get the story out of her mind and so she dropped out and drove all the way across country to be near horses. She's rented a place in Burns and devoted herself to trying to save the herds around here. Stick around and you can meet her." Barkley pointed his pen toward the northside of the saddle. "Lily hiked up there looking for horses."

"Does she know about the poisoned herd?"

"I told her."

"What did she say?"

"Damn the Fannings to hell, or words to that effect. Lily can get pretty emotional, but she has a big heart and it's in the right place. You can't help but like her for it even if she is pretty single-minded."

"What about you?"

"You spend enough time around mustangs, you grow to admire them. Have you ever seen a herd thunder across the plain or a couple of stallions go at each other over mares, rearing and boxing with their front hooves like a pair of prizefighters? Muhammad Ali and Sonny Liston got nothing on them." The BLM man grinned. "What about you?"

"I have to admit I'm pretty green when it comes to horses."

"Do you ride?"

"I did for the first time last fall."

"You'd never been on a horse before?"

"Not unless you count the ones on a carousel."

He laughed. "How did you like it?"

I thought back on the first time I rode Wovoka. The cutting horse got spooked by dogs and took off at a full gallop, but didn't throw me. "To be honest, it made me feel the most alive since I got back from Vietnam."

Barkley mulled that over and then jotted something down in his notebook before closing it.

I handed him my notes with the coordinates of where Gemma and I had seen herds of mustangs. "You can match them up on your map. I'll continue to watch for horses and try to get population counts too."

He put my notes on the table and placed a chisel-tip hammer to keep them from blowing away.

"That's some paperweight," I said.

"It's a geologist hammer. I've been rock hounding since I was a kid. Doing field work in this part of Oregon is like hitting the mother lode. I've uncovered thunder eggs and sunstones by the dozens. Jaspar and agates are downright common. And opals? I've cracked some open that look like they got fire trapped inside."

"Do you look for fossils and arrowheads too?"

"Sure. I've found points and scrapers made by humans that go back ten thousand years. Lots of fossilized plants too. What I really want to find is evidence of a prehistoric equine. The horses you see in Oregon descended from ones brought over by the Spaniards in the 1500s, but their ancient relatives roamed around here forty million years ago before going extinct."

"That would be some find," I said.

Barkley grinned again. "I'll keep looking. By the way, your notes on the mustangs are going to be a great help. I only have until the end of summer to conduct my assessment, but it's pretty clear from what Lily has been telling me that there are lots of herds and they're spread all over. I'd need a lot more time than what they gave me to complete the study."

"Will you recommend creating a management area again?"

"What other solution is there? If the herds are left on their own, they'll always be at risk of starving or being rounded up and slaughtered. The difference between Oregon and Nevada is there will need to be multiple areas here. That's going to be a challenge, but luckily that's not my job. I do the field work and leave the policymaking and politicking to others in the Bureau. I'm not too good working inside an office and playing the game."

"I know what you mean," I said.

We sized each other up. I liked what I saw. Barkley and I had a lot in common.

"Wide open spaces, no other faces," he said.

"Roger that," I said.

Rocks shuffled. We turned toward the noise.

"Here comes Lily now," Barkley said. He smiled as we watched her cutting switchbacks on a deer trail and triggering mini rockslides "That girl's always in a hurry."

Lily Calla's cheeks were flushed and perspiration beaded her forehead when she reached us. She was full figured and wore her hair cut level to the nape of her neck.

"Hi," she said. "Are you with the BLM too?"

"Fish and Wildlife," I said.

"I hope you're doing something about the slaughter that took place here. Seven horses were murdered."

"Nick knows," Barkley said. "He's the one who tried to save the foal I told you about."

Lily reached out and clutched my forearm. "How is she? Clay said she was at death's door."

"She still is, but a veterinarian is with her now. She's got a chance, at least."

"I need to see her. She must be so scared. I can help comfort her. Is the vet in Burns?"

"A half hour south on a ranch in No Mountain. Her name is Gemma Warbler, but you should give her a call before driving down there. She's away a lot because she treats livestock all over Harney County."

Lily let go of my arm and turned to Barkley. "I couldn't see any horses from up there, but I could see the Seven Fans ranch." She turned back to me. "There are some really awful people who live there. They hate wild horses and won't stop until they've killed them all."

"The sheriff's office knows about the poisoned ones," I said.

"But they won't do anything about it." Lily's voice cracked and tears welled. "I can't believe it. It's like no one cares."

Barkley gave me a see-I-told-you look.

"It sounds to me like Clay is doing a lot to help them. I'll do what I can to make sure mustangs are protected if they're on refuge land," I said.

"Will you? I've been trying to convince Fish and Wildlife to take a stance. I've sent loads of letters to the agency director in Washington DC, but he's never written back."

"Keep at it," I said.

"I will. When it comes to wild horses, I won't rest until they're all saved. Each and every one."

"Look, it was nice meeting you, Lily, but I got to get going." I nodded to Barkley. "I'll swing by again with a population count for you."

"Take it easy," he said.

I glanced in the rearview mirror as I steered back onto the access road. The mustang lover and BLM ranger were standing shoulder to shoulder watching me drive away. I pictured the pair of matching plates and cutlery set out to dry and the still wet spot beneath the outdoor shower. It looked like I wasn't the only one who hadn't eaten breakfast alone that morning.

I'D REACHED Barkley's camp by cutting east from No Mountain and catching the access road at its southern terminus near the no stoplight town of Crane. I continued north on the access road toward Highway 20. The route took me past the draw with the dead horses, and once again a pickup blocked my way. The driver was out of the cab, leaning against the hood and watching vultures tear rotting flesh from the carcasses. He wore a black cowboy hat with a slouch crown and touched the brim with his finger as I got out of my pickup.

"Good day to you, sir, and a good day it is. Any day with one less four-legged pest is a good day. A day with seven less, makes it a good week." When he laughed, his voice took on a high pitch.

His short stature, oversized belt buckle, and long-barreled pistol strapped low on his hip told me everything I needed to know.

"Admiring your handiwork, Sonny?" I said.

Saying his name prompted him to take notice of the Fish and Wildlife badge on my chest.

"Shucks, and here I thought you was with the Bureau of Land Mismanagement. You're only a zookeeper." He gave another cackle.

"Why did you use poison? Why not shoot them?"

"Who said it was me who done it? And even if it was, I sure wouldn't waste good lead on those nags." His hand was a blur as he drew the six-shooter and mimed fanning the hammer. "Bang, bang, bang, bang, bang, bang, you're all dead." He blew imaginary smoke from the tip of the barrel and then twirled the gun on his trigger finger a few times before sliding it back into the holster.

"Keep handling a live firearm like that and one of these days you're going to shoot yourself in the foot."

He bristled. "I'm a pro, zookeeper. Mind what you say or you could wind up like them."

I looked at the carnage at the bottom of the draw. Feathers flapped as the vultures and magpies scrummed over a bloated string of entrails. The machine gun-like *wock, wock, wock-a-wock* squawking of the smaller black and white birds set my teeth on edge.

I turned back to Sonny Stiles. "Try doing that at a national wildlife refuge, and I'll put you behind bars."

He squinted at me. "You must be new around here to think you can talk to me like that."

"The name's Nick Drake," I said. "I live in No Mountain. I'm easy enough to find. Now move your rig out of my way."

The Seven Fans foreman tried a glare off but gave up. He got into his four-by and backed onto the narrow road's shoulder. I slowed as I passed, our open driver's windows separated by the widths of our side mirrors.

Sonny put his fingertip to his hat brim again and grinned. "See you around, zookeeper."

"Kill another horse anywhere, refuge or not, and you can count on it."

5

The Harney County Sheriff's Department occupied a squat pink building on North Court Avenue in downtown Burns. I found Deputy Warbler seated behind a desk in a private office near the front door. That was a switch. Pudge was semiretired after having lost the top job and normally worked at his ranch house, which doubled as a sheriff's substation for the southern half of the county. When he did work in Burns, he had to make do with a chipped Formica table in the coffee room as a desk.

"It looks like you're a regular now," I said as I took a seat across from him.

"Temporarily as of yesterday," Pudge said. "Why Bust'em called me in. We're down two deputies. One's Army Reserve unit got called up to active duty and another went and parked his department vehicle in his living room. The numbskull was drunk and now he's unemployed."

"Two missing out of a force of seven will make for plenty of overtime."

"I suppose that may appeal to the younger men, but I only

agreed to come back full time because I put in close to twenty-five years and I'm not about to turn my back on the department now." Pudge fished a toothpick out of his breast pocket but didn't put it in his mouth. "What brings you here?"

"I ran into Sonny Stiles at the draw with the dead mustangs. He acted like he was at a drive-in movie theater. The only thing missing was a box of buttered popcorn."

Pudge rolled the toothpick between his thumb and forefinger. "Sonny tried bronc busting in his younger days. Getting bucked off scrambled his eggs."

"He's going to need regular reminding not to put out poison again."

"Did you boys have more than words?"

"Not yet."

Pudge sighed. "Do me a favor and leave Sonny and the Fannings to me. I'm used to them. Why did you go back there anyway?"

I told him about stopping by Clay Barkley's camp and giving him a map of the mustang herds I'd seen. "There was a young woman there. She's devoted herself to trying to protect wild horses. She called the Fannings murderers. If she were to meet up with Sonny, it wouldn't go well."

"What's her name?"

"Lily Calla."

"Calla." He pondered the name a moment. "Can't say I know that family and I know everyone in Harney County."

"Clay said she rents a place in Burns. She's from the East and drives a white Volvo station wagon with Vermont plates. It has a save the horses bumper sticker."

"You don't see many foreign cars around here. Wonder where she gets parts and service?" He toyed with the toothpick. "All right, thanks for the heads up. I'll get a bead on Miss Calla's address and have a word with her to make sure she knows she's likely to get bit if she rattles Sonny's cage too hard."

"Since I'm here, do you want to tell me about your plan to catch the cattle rustlers?"

"Good idea, but let me get the college boy in here to do it." Pudge shouted, "Orville, front and center!"

Running footsteps drummed down the hall. Orville Nelson skidded in front of the doorway and slid inside. "Ranger Drake, it is a pleasure to see you again."

"Likewise," I said.

The young man wore a short sleeve white shirt and tightly knotted black tie. "Did Deputy Warbler tell you the good news? I have been accepted to a summer session at Quantico."

"I thought the FBI didn't take recruits until they were twenty-three years old?"

"That is correct, but this is an eight-week preparatory training program for future applicants who already have their baccalaureate degree and law enforcement experience. My internship here qualifies me."

"Will you return to Harney County afterward?"

"While that is certainly my intention, I cannot say for sure. I have heard some attendees are offered temporary positions at other agencies in Washington DC while they wait for their acceptance at the Bureau."

Pudge put the toothpick between his lips. "I'm sure Drake is as proud of you as we are, and will be equally heartbroke when we lose you, but until June fifteen rolls around and you board the Greyhound for summer camp, you got law enforcement that needs doing right here and now. Go ahead and earn your paycheck by giving him the skinny on what we've cooked up."

"Certainly, sir. Sorry about that." The young FBI hopeful slid a file folder in front of me.

"You will find behind the first tab a situation analysis recapping the intelligence we gathered and the actions we took last autumn to apprehend an organized gang of rustlers operating in the county. The gang deployed several two-man teams to locate small groups of cattle on isolated grazeland, load them into trailers pulled by pickups, and drive to a predetermined location where the stolen animals were transferred to a waiting commercial livestock carrier capable of carrying sixty cows. We were unable to track the tractor trailers, nor arrest and charge any culprits."

Orville cleared his throat. "If you will turn to the next tab, you will find a strategy for halting the criminal activity, a tactical plan, and an organizational chart outlining team member responsibilities. Behind the final tab is a foldout map displaying the area of operation."

"Oh Lord, son, you're not in the FBI yet, you're still in little old Harney County," Pudge said. "Let me put it in plain English. We know the rustlers are sweeping east. They hit the Seven Fans, the Big W in the valley next door, and have been plucking cows between there and Warm Springs Reservoir. We're banking on them still using a spoke and hub system for transferring the stolen stock onto carriers. But here's what we're gonna do different this time around."

He grinned around the toothpick. "We got us a secret weapon."

"And what would that be?" I asked.

"Our own air force. A lot of these ranchers pilot planes in order to spare their kidneys from bumping over all the washboard roads. I had a meeting with the Harney County Cattlemen's Association and convinced them to start flying patrols for us."

"But don't the rustlers work at night?"

"Mostly, but these old boys are used to flying in the dark. Some even have their instrument rating. They'll do flyovers along the roads that cut across the eastern half of the county on a regular basis. They spot headlights and see a semi hauling a cow trailer, they radio it in, and we intercept it."

I asked him if it took much convincing to talk the ranchers into it.

"They started griping about who was gonna pay for their fuel, but then I played the ace up my sleeve." Pudge chuckled. "I told them Gemma had already volunteered to lead the charge while she's flying back and forth tending to sick livestock. You should've seen the look on their faces."

"But she's only had her pilot's license six months and isn't instrument rated yet," I said.

"You want to tell Gemma she can't fly when and where she wants now that you two are, um, chummy? Go right ahead. I've spent a lifetime telling her no to things and watched her do them anyway."

A figure darkened the doorway. It was Sheriff Burton. His uniform was neatly pressed and his brush moustache neatly trimmed.

"I was telling Drake about our plan for the rustlers," Pudge said to him.

The sheriff shook his freshly barbered head. "You'll need to shelve that. We have a situation that requires immediate attention."

"What kind of situation?"

"The major kind. Every sheriff's office in the state has been put on alert."

Burton worked his jaw as if trying to find the correct pose for a front page photograph in the *Burns Herald*. "A van transporting three prisoners from the Oregon State Penitentiary failed to keep a scheduled call-in. When dispatch couldn't raise the driver on the radio, they hit the panic button. The state police issued an APB and sent up a fixed wing aircraft. They just located the van parked off a highway." He worked his jaw again. "The driver and guard are still in it."

Pudge sat up straighter, but didn't skip a beat. "Dead." It wasn't a question, but the sheriff nodded anyway.

"The driver was still behind the wheel. His throat was slit. The guard was in the back. Strangled."

"And the convicts have vamoosed." Pudge took out the toothpick. "They either had someone meet them or stole another vehicle."

"Nothing has been confirmed, but either way, they're on the run and they're armed. The guard's shotgun and sidearm are missing. So is the driver's pistol."

"What's this have to do with us?" Pudge said. "The state pen's in Salem. That's two hundred fifty miles from here."

"The van was en route to a state hospital in Pendleton."

The older of the two lawmen mulled over that piece of information. "The fastest route would be the new interstate along the Columbia River. Where did they find the van?"

"Outside of Maupin," Sheriff Burton said.

"Maupin? They turned off the interstate and went south? I would've figured they'd go north, cross the river, and beeline for Canada. Well, Maupin is still a far distance from here. Are we on alert because every county is or is there a particular reason to believe they might come our way?"

Sheriff Burton did his posing for an imaginary news photographer thing again. "Louder Than Wolf Will is one of them."

The old deputy snapped the toothpick in half. "Loud Will. And me the one who put him away."

"Any relation to Tuhudda and Nagah Will?" I asked, naming a Paiute tribal elder and his grandson I'd gotten to know.

"Loud is Tuhudda's only son and the little boy's daddy." Pudge flicked the halves of the toothpick at the trashcan. "Rustlers, horse killers, and now escaped convicts. Looks like I picked a helluva time to come back full time."

The prison bureau sent over a report plus rap sheets for the three fugitives. Orville Nelson stood by the facsimile machine collecting the pages as they spit out. He made copies and rushed them to a meeting room where Sheriff Burton had gathered his remaining deputies. I joined them and we read in silence.

The trio was being transferred from the state penitentiary as part of a plan to reduce overcrowding. The century-old prison was the only maximum security facility in Oregon, but it had surpassed capacity years before. With the civil rights movement and antiwar protests spurring calls for prison reform, the governor promised to build new facilities. In the meantime, some inmates were being relocated.

Old timers and those close to their parole dates were sent to minimum security prisons. Low-risk prisoners were transferred to medium security facilities. A third group were inmates with a history of behavioral problems. That included everything from suicidal tendencies to fighting with other inmates to attacking guards. They deemed mentally unbalanced and transferred to state hospitals. George Roscoe

Banks, Donny Gray, and Louder Than Wolf Will were among them.

According to his rap sheet, George Roscoe Banks was forty-two years old. His mugshot revealed a man with a hatchet face, a receding hairline, and a horseshoe moustache. The corners of his eyes were crinkled with permanent laugh lines. Banks was eight years into a life sentence after having been arrested following a crime spree during which he preyed on older women who lived alone in the Portland suburbs.

Banks's favorite hunting grounds were churches where he would target and stalk his victims. He'd gain access to their home at night by posing as a bereavement officer with the Portland Police Department delivering notification of a fatal accident involving a family member. His victims always opened the door for the man with the kindly voice and shiny badge. Once inside he turned into a monster.

In the beginning, George Roscoe Banks was sated by beating his victims and tying them to their beds. After ransacking their house for valuables, he would gather all the family photographs he could find—pictures of their late husbands, their children, their grandchildren—and arrange them around the bed. Then he would torture and rape the women as the photographs looked on. Some of the victims were so humiliated, they wouldn't report what happened. Others could never face their family and friends again because of their shame.

When Banks was finally captured, he explained why he'd graduated to murder. One of his victims was so ashamed, she begged him to kill her, and so he obliged. One killing became two and then three. He boasted to his captors that he was helping the women by giving them one last fling and then ending their loneliness. The report said he laughed hysterically when he called himself the Grin Raper.

Donny Gray was the youngest of the three fugitives. He was

twenty-one years old and had been in prison for less than a year after pleading guilty to selling a kilo of marijuana to an under-cover detective. Though it was his first offense, he received twenty years. Beneath a mop of blond hair was the face of a terrified boy. His mouth was agape as if he'd been screaming for help while being stood against the wall for his booking photograph.

Louder Than Wolf Will was thirty-five years old. His mugshot showed off high cheekbones, a buzzcut with scars inching like worms through the black stubble, and a nose that had been flattened more than once. Twin tattoos of a broken arrow blued either side of his windpipe. Loud Will's rap sheet dated back to when he was first incarcerated as an adult. A note stated that his juvenile record was sealed, but could be made available upon request. He'd spent time in supervised work camps, county jails, and a three-year stretch in an Idaho state prison. His list of offenses included shoplifting, public drunken-ness, drug possession, auto theft, armed robbery, and assault and battery. Five years prior he'd been arrested for manslaughter. As a repeat offender, he'd been given thirty years with no possibility for parole.

Sheriff Burton stood at the front of the meeting room and cleared his throat. "As you can see, we're dealing with extremely dangerous individuals. While Wasco County Sheriff's Depart-ment is conducting a house-to-house search in Maupin and Oregon State Police troopers are patrolling every road in and out, we will respond as if the three are already on their way here."

"Is there any more information on the van?" Pudge Warbler asked. "Like, did it run out of gas or have a flat or something? Knowing that would help pin down whether or not they were meeting an accomplice or hijacked a vehicle to get out of Dodge."

"Intelligence is still coming in," Burton said. "This is an evolving situation. We can only assume the escapees are mobile."

"They could've split up," Pudge said. "It would help if we knew if any of the three were bunkies who wound up in the same van together. That increases the odds they'll stick together."

"And I said, we will get the information when the prison bureau provides it. End of story." The sheriff took a deep breath. "Let's focus on what we do know. Two prison employees are dead and their killers are at large. Our responsibility is to protect the good people of Harney County, and that's exactly what we are going to do."

"All that's true, Bust'em," Pudge said, "but to do that we need a plan to stop them and another plan for catching them if they get past us. Do you mind?"

The old deputy didn't wait for an answer. He approached the front of the room carrying the state map from Orville's cattle rustling folder and taped it to the wall. "Let's get the timing straight. That way we'll know when we can expect them."

He circled Salem with a red marker and wrote "9 AM" in block letters next to it. "We know that's when they left the state pen. The driver made the ten o'clock call as he left Portland. He made his eleven o'clock as he was nearing Hood River." He circled both cities and marked the corresponding times in red.

"He did not make his noon call. The van was found in Maupin on Highway 197. That means they turned off at The Dalles, which is about thirty minutes east of Hood River." He circled The Dalles and scrawled "11:30 AM" alongside it.

"Now, it's about a forty-five minute drive to Maupin from there. Something happened that led them to kill the driver and abandon the van. My bet is the guard was already dead, killed right when they got loose from the chain that secures their manacles and shackles. Either they had plans for meeting someone there or they stole a vehicle." He circled Maupin and numbered the map with "12:15 PM."

"If you speed," he continued, "you can do the drive to Burns in four hours via Madras and Prineville. If you're trying not to call attention to yourself and stick to the limit, it's closer to five. Let's split the difference and make it a 4:30 p.m. ETA."

The old lawman circled Burns and wrote the time next to it. He made a show of checking the big clock on the wall and then nodded to Sheriff Burton. "We got a couple of hours to get ready for them. What do you want us to do, Bust'em?"

The sheriff coughed before answering. "Put up roadblocks around Burns. We have to protect where the majority of the people in the county live."

Pudge started nodding. "Okay, but there's more roads into town than us even if we can count on help from the Burns traffic cops. We can't call for assistance from neighboring county sheriffs deputies because they're guarding their own front and back doors. Now, these cons could come straight at us on Highway 20 or do an end around and come down 395 via John Day. That is if they don't try to outfox us and loop south and then come up via No Mountain on 205. 'Course none of that takes into consideration all the dirt roads and back alleys that lead into Burns from secondary county roads. Which ones do you want us to roadblock, Bust'em?"

The sheriff thought about it for a minute. "I'll leave the details up to you while I coordinate overall strategy with the state's attorney general. Speaking of, I have a call with him in…" He glanced at the wall clock. "Actually in about thirty seconds. Keep me posted."

Ever the politician, Sheriff Burton strode out of the meeting room, his head held high and no doubt congratulating himself that if his deputies were successful, he would be able to claim the credit, but if things went south, he had a ready-made fall guy in the man he was convinced would run against him in the next election.

Pudge did a poor job masking his disapproval of the sheriff, but he shook it off and got back to business. He stabbed the map with the red marker. "Bust'em is right about one thing. Our first priority is keeping these fellas out of Burns."

He eyeballed the map. "Here's how we're gonna play it. We'll station sheriff's vehicles with flashing lights on either side of town at Highways 20 and 395, another down here at 205 and another at 78. That covers the main highways. We'll check every vehicle coming in. Any that whips a U-turn, we sound the alarm and go after it with sirens screaming. I'll alert the city cops what we're up to and see if they can hold off writing parking tickets for a while and patrol the side streets into town. Orville will man the radio here to keep us all in contact and feed us whatever info gets sent over from Salem."

"What are you going to be doing, Pudge?" a deputy asked.

"I'll shuttle between the roadblocks." The old lawman pointed the red marker at me. "You all know Nick Drake here. He may wear a duck and fish on his badge, but he straps a sidearm like the rest of us. He'll head down to the Will camp and give them a heads up since no one's bothered to string a telephone line out that way."

Pudge paused. "That is unless someone else wants to volunteer for the job." The deputies all found something in the rap sheets worth rereading. "That's what I thought. Okay, everybody move out, except for you, Drake. Hang back a second."

When the room cleared, he said, "Hope you don't mind me volunteering you, but I figured you were gonna do it anyway, seeing how you got friendly with Tuhudda and Nagah Will last fall."

"Leaving the van in Maupin could be a feint," I said. "The

prisoners know we know Loud Will is from here. Maybe they're betting everyone will focus on Harney County and leave them free to double back, cross the bridge at The Dalles, and head for Canada."

"That's a possibility. So is them splitting up. I don't know about the other two, but I bet Loud is coming here."

"Why do you think that?"

"If anybody deserves to be in a state hospital, it's him. He's never been right in the head from the get go. Who knows why? Maybe the belly button cord got wrapped around his neck. Loud's always been angry. I'm guessing he's coming home to settle scores."

"With you?"

"I'm on the list, for sure, but higher up is the judge who slapped him with a manslaughter sentence. Loud was fighting with a fella and the fella killed Loud's wife by mistake."

"What happened?

"It's a long story and I'll tell you about it sometime, but right now we got to stick to our timetable. I need to make sure the boys are where they're supposed to be and you need to warn Tuhudda."

"Loud could bypass Burns altogether and go straight to the Will camp. There are plenty of backroads he could take. You should put a couple of deputies down there."

"And where would I get them? We're already shorthanded as it is. On top of that, the Will camp is on reservation land. Technically, we got no authority there."

"What about tribal police?"

"You ever seen a tribal cop in the year you've lived here? No you have not. That's because when the Paiute reservation was established, the Bureau of Indian Affairs dragged its heels helping the tribe form a council government and police force."

"We can't leave Tuhudda and his family on their own," I said.

Pudge rubbed his jaw, puffed his cheeks, and exhaled loudly. "You're right. So here's what we're gonna do. Tell Tuhudda that Loud is coming and for his family's sake, they need to git. They always take their sheep to Catlow Valley to graze. Tell old Tuhudda to move the schedule up and get down there now."

"And if he doesn't agree?"

"Don't take no for an answer." As I started for the door, Pudge said, "Tell him another thing, would you? Tell him I'll do everything I can to see that no harm comes to his son, but I got to do my job and that means catching Loud and sending him back to prison."

"Hopefully Tuhudda will understand," I said.

The old lawman's silence reminded me what little regard he had for hope.

7

Pulling up to the cluster of single-wide trailers and wood shanties comprising the Will camp brought me full circle. I'd passed by the rutted turnoff to it early that morning when I'd cut across Harney Valley to reach Clay Barkley's. A pair of yapping yellow dogs welcomed my arrival by trying to bite my tires. No one came out to greet me. The family was gathered in a field a short distance away. I told the dogs to back off and started walking.

Nagah Will saw me first. The boy didn't look like he'd grown any since I'd last seen him. He was wearing a two-sizes-too-big brown corduroy jacket. His smile was still shy. "Hello, Mr. Nick. How are you?"

"I'm well. And you?"

He pointed at the field. "Look who came to visit."

Mingling among the Will's flock of sheep was a herd of mustangs. I counted eight, nine horses. "Did your family round them up?"

"No, Grandfather dreamt about them last night and they were here when we woke."

"Are you going to try to break them?"

Nagah shook his head. "The wild ones will only let you ride them if they want you to. They are here for a reason. Grandfather knows why."

"Where is he?"

"There," he pointed again.

I looked past the group of men, women, boys, and girls watching the mustangs. A flash of red caught my attention. It was a headband made from a folded bandana that crowned a mane of white hair. Tuhudda Will was sitting cross-legged in the field as the wild horses grazed around him.

"Grandfather is telling them they are welcome and to eat their fill," Nagah said.

"I need to talk to him alone about something very important. Would it be okay if I walked out there?"

"It is better if I go. The wild ones are used to my scent. Wait here and I will tell him."

The slender boy waded through clumps of knee-high bunchgrass. A white stallion looked up from grazing, but didn't snort a challenge or raise an alarm. Nagah crouched next to his grandfather and then rejoined the rest of the family. A few minutes later, Tuhudda stood, bowed to the stallion, and walked toward me. As he did, thousands of checkerspot butterflies newly emerged from their cocoons fluttered from the blades of bunchgrass and swirled around him, making the old man appear as if he were draped in an orange and black cloak.

"Greetings to you and your family," I said in *numu*.

"And to you," he replied in English in his slow and deliberate manner.

"Your grandson told me you had a dream about wild horses."

"This is so. They were frightened and needed to leave their home because they can trust their grass no more forever. They spoke to the sheep who told them the grass here was safe. I told the stallion they were welcome to share it."

"They're from the Stinkingwater Mountains," I said without hesitation, pointing to the ridgeline that ran alongside the valley's eastern edge.

The red bandana moved up and down. "This is so. Did the stallion speak to you also?"

"I saw a herd up there that had been poisoned. Only one survived. A filly foal. I took her to Gemma Warbler's for healing."

Tuhudda Will's craggy face showed no more surprise than a slab of granite. "The stallion told me evil has come there."

We watched the sheep and horses graze together. Tuhudda said, "Did you see Girl Born in Snow when you were at Dr. Gemma's?" I told him I had. "I have not seen her since the last big storm. She has not come to round dance."

"She's been ill. Gemma thinks she may have pneumonia, but November won't seek help at the hospital in Burns."

"Girl Born in Snow has always traveled her own path. She is winter's child as am I. We were born during the same storm, but I came into this world alongside a fire in my mother's wickiup and was wrapped in warm furs, while she came into this world outside as the snow fell upon her mother and the icy winds blew as sharp as Fox's teeth."

The old man stared into the distance. "We grew up in this land together and have seen much change. We have seen much happiness and much sorrow also. She when Shoots While Running and Gentle Wind passed into the spirit world, and me when my son became lost."

"Louder Than Wolf," I said.

It had the same effect as taking a chisel to his stony visage. A frown grew deeper than the rest of the crags. "How is it that you know of him? He left before you came here."

"That's what I need to tell you. He escaped from prison.

Pudge Warbler wanted you to know. He thinks your son may come here."

Tuhudda shook his head. "Louder Than Wolf knows we cannot welcome him as we do them." He gestured toward the mustangs. "He shamed us and himself when he turned his back on our ways."

I saw no way around it, so I went straight at it. "You can't take a chance he won't. When he escaped, two prison workers were murdered. No one knows who killed them—a pair of inmates escaped with your son—but it doesn't matter. Every city police-man, every deputy from every county sheriff's office, and every trooper with the Oregon State Police is hunting them. If they believe your son is here, they'll storm your family's camp, reser-vation law or no reservation law. They won't care who gets in the way. People could get hurt, even killed."

"My son will not let them take him back, this is so," he said matter-of-factly. "He once spoke to me in a dream. He said being behind bars is worse than being dead. At least in death, he would be able to walk in the spirit world."

"Pudge Warbler asks that you move your family right away. Since you take the sheep to Catlow Valley every year, go now."

"There is no need. My daughters, their husbands, and chil-dren have no reason to fear Louder Than Wolf." He waved his hand toward the group watching the sheep and wild horses and then started walking back into the field.

"Wait," I said. "You don't understand. It's the authorities that are hunting him that pose danger to you and your family."

"Then I will tell them and they can decide for themselves," he said without turning around.

"But what about Nagah? He is only a boy. Surely, you want him to be safe."

Tuhudda stopped midstride. He raised his hands, cupped them, and held them out as if collecting rain. The orange and black checkerspot butterflies began swirling around him again. He lifted his face toward the sky and spoke in *numu*. When he lowered his hands, he turned around.

"I asked the great spirit *Mu naa'a* to guide me."

"Wolf," I said. "The father of creation."

"Yes, you know more about our ways than you did."

"November has been teaching me. Gemma too. *Mu naa'a* created this world and all the people who dwell here, the *nuwuddu*, who are the animals, or the first people, and the *numu*, who are the second people."

Tuhudda bowed his head. "Louder Than Wolf was not our son's first name, but my wife and I changed it when he would not stop howling no matter how much he suckled, how much I tickled him. Our son howled louder than *Mu naa'a* did when he grew angry at his little brother Coyote for tricking him into giving up his bag of stars that he used for telling stories in the sky. Coyote dropped it and the stars spilled out and that is why there are some that tell no story."

The old man's voice lowered. "My wife and I believed once *Mu naa'a* learned of our son's new name, he would silence the child's howls because no one can be louder than *Mu naa'a*, not Coyote, not Owl. It was foolish of us to believe that. My wife went to her death believing *Mu naa'a* punished us for our foolishness by making our son's howls drown out everything to his ears but anger."

I realized the crags in the old man's face were not all from age. A tear bobbed up and down as it fell.

"Did your son ever quiet down?" I asked.

"Only for a couple of years when he was in his teenage years. Right after my wife died, I was so saddened I sent him to live at the ranch of my friend Lyle Rides Alone."

"I know him," I said. "He sold Gemma the two cutting horses, Sarah and Wovoka."

"This is so. Lyle Rides Alone had many horses at one time. He bred the cutting horses for use on his ranch and for sale to other ranchers. He also let wild horses share his graze. Some would even let him ride them. Louder Than Wolf helped out on the ranch and lived in the stable. He liked being with the wild ones the most. Their wildness quieted him. They would not let him approach if he howled, so he learned to stay silent around them. I visited him and saw he had finally found peace."

"Lyle Rides Alone still has the ranch. Why did your son leave?"

"A cowboy came to work there. Lyle Rides Alone did not know him, but he needed more help. This cowboy was full of mean spirit. He teased Louder Than Wolf and then tricked him into drinking whiskey. After two years of no howling, Louder Than Wolf started howling again and the wild horses did not want to be with him no more. He could not hear anything but anger because of what the mean spirited cowboy did."

"It was Sonny Stiles, wasn't it?"

"How did you know that?"

"I met him. He's still mean spirited. He's the one who poisoned the mustangs in the Stinkingwaters."

"My son could stay no longer at Lyle Rides Alone's ranch. He could not stay anywhere. He could not hear me warn him not to drink whiskey and not to take the white man's drugs. He stole things to pay for those things, and because of that he was jailed many times."

Tuhudda paused. He watched the horses graze with his sheep. "In jail, he would not have whiskey or drugs, and he would come out and try not to listen to his anger. He even got married and they had a daughter and then a son, Nagah. But then, he started howling again and was sent to jail. There, he met a Shoshone who could only hear anger also. Louder Than Wolf told him about his wife and children, and when they got out of jail, they came to live with them for a time. But they both still could only hear anger, and so they went to the Shoshone's home across the great river and robbed a store."

The old man looked back at me. "The sheriff in Idaho chased them. My son and the Shoshone stole a car to get away, but it broke down. They took different trails when they ran. The Shoshone got away because he knew the land, but Louder Than Wolf got lost and was caught. He would not tell the sheriff the Shoshone's name. He was sent to prison in Idaho for three years. When he got out, he found his wife was living with the Shoshone as her husband. Louder Than Wolf heard anger and fought with him. The Shoshone had a gun and was going to shoot Louder Than Wolf but his wife ran between them to stop the fight. She took the bullet instead. People heard the shot and called the sheriff."

"Pudge Warbler," I said, "when he was still sheriff."

"This is so. He arrested my son and took him to jail. He told the judge what happened, that it was the Shoshone who killed my son's wife and ran away, that my son had stayed and tried to save her life, but the judge showed no mercy."

"Did Nagah see his mother get shot?"

"Yes."

"What happened to the Shoshone?"

"Lawmen from Oregon and Idaho searched for a long time, but could not find him. Who knows where he is? Maybe he died. Maybe he did not."

"What does Nagah think of his father? Does he hate him or has he forgiven him?"

"He knows there are things in this world that are not always kind, but there is meaning to be found in every unkindness."

"He is a good boy," I said.

"Yes, but his days as a boy are coming to an end. He is of the age to set foot on the path to manhood. That is what *Mu naa'a* told me just now when I asked for his guidance. He told me why Louder Than Wolf is coming. Even though my son turned his back on our ways, he wants to make sure his son is put on the path according to our custom. He wants to be part of the ceremony."

"We can't let him anywhere near Nagah," I said quickly. "It's too dangerous. We don't know what he'll do."

"He will not harm his own son."

I wanted to tell the old man that he couldn't truly know his son's heart anymore, not after years of alcoholism and drug addiction, after spending five years in prison, much of it in solitary confinement, and now having either killed the guard and driver or being an accessory to their murder.

"But you're Nagah's grandfather," I said. "You're the one raising him. You can guide him onto the path to manhood."

"I cannot. While I am his grandfather, Nagah is not of my family as my daughter's children are. When Louder Than Wolf married, he became a member of his wife's family. And Nagah and his sister were born into that family. It is Louder Than Wolf's duty, not mine."

I remembered what Gemma had told me last night. The Paiute were matrilineal, that in marriage, husbands moved into their wife's wickiup and became part of her family and her community, as Chief Winnemucca and November's husband Shoots While Running had done.

"Why didn't Nagah continue to live with his mother's family after she was killed?"

"Because they were saddened over her death and blamed my son. They wanted nothing to do with him no more forever, and that included Nagah and his sister. It did not matter to them that my son did not fire the gun, only that her death was because of him. Nagah came to live with me and his sister lives with one of my daughters as her own daughter now."

"Nagah saw his mother killed. He shouldn't have to see his father killed too, but that's exactly what could happen if your son comes here. What kind of path to manhood will it be if Nagah sees his father die before he can set foot on it?"

The old man grew silent. He turned back to the herd of mustangs grazing with his sheep. The wild white stallion had found a knoll on which to stand and watch over his herd. The other members of the Will family were returning to the camp of singlewide trailers and wooden shanties.

"You will take Nagah with you," Tuhudda finally said. "Take him to the Warbler ranch and give him to Girl Born in Snow. She will know what to do. I will tell the others to take the sheep to Catlow Valley."

"I'm glad you've decided to leave."

"They are leaving. I will stay. Louder Than Wolf is my son. I will tell him why Nagah cannot be here. I will ask for his blessing so that I may perform the path to manhood ceremony for Nagah."

"But your son may not be alone. One of the men who escaped with him has murdered before. He did unspeakable things. He's sick, mad, evil. There will be no one here to protect you from him. Come to No Mountain with Nagah and me."

The old man turned around. His eyes were filled with tears no longer, but reflected the swirling butterflies. Orange checkered his black pupils like flames.

"I do not fear him. I fear no one. I am *Tuhudda*, named for Deer, son of *Tooonugwetsedu,* named for Cougar, grandson of *Padooa*, named for Bear. I run fast, see in the dark, and my hooves and antlers are sharp."

He whipped a knife with a deer antler handle from a sheath concealed in his shin-high moccasin and slashed the air. And then he raised his face to the sun, laid back his ears, and bellowed the grunt-snort-wheeze of a triumphant 12-point buck after defeating a challenger. As the eerie call rolled across the field, the sheep bunched together and quivered, and the mares and foals drew close to the knoll where the wild stallion stood guard. The white mustang reared up on his hind legs and punched the sky as Tuhudda's silver blade flashed like lightning.

8

N agah didn't ask why or argue when his grandfather told him to go with me. We spoke little as I sped across the valley and over the cattleguard that marked the entrance to the Warbler ranch. The pickup kicked up gravel as I pulled to a stop in front of the ranch house. I checked my field watch. The hands pointed to 4:30 p.m. but I saw it as 1630. After my years as a soldier, I couldn't tell time any other way. I pictured the map taped to the meeting room in the sheriff's office and could see the same time scrawled beside Burns in red.

Had the fugitives arrived according to Pudge's schedule? Which road did they take? Did a deputy intercept them and, more importantly, what did he do? I wanted answers, and I wanted them fast.

Pudge's pickup wasn't there. The old lawman wouldn't leave Burns until the fugitives were either caught or killed. If he needed sleep, he'd either lay his head on his desk or fall onto a bunk in one of the jail cells. Gemma's red Jeep was missing too. She'd told me when she left the lineman's shack that morning she was heading to a ranch in Sunset Valley to inoculate calves. I stopped myself when I started imagining her driving home at the same time on the same road as the killers.

"Come on," I said to Nagah. "I have phone calls to make. November's inside."

He had to scurry to keep up with me as I bounded up the steps to the front porch and opened the door. The ranch house was never locked as was the custom in Harney County. I ushered Nagah inside and steered him straight to the kitchen. November was hunched over the stove tending a cast-iron pot.

"You know Tuhudda Will's grandson," I said. "Nagah is going to stay here for a while."

The Paiute woman didn't ask why. All she said was, "You are skin and bones. Does not that old man feed you?" The rheum was still in her eyes and her voice was croaky.

"We eat okay," the boy all but whispered.

She tsked. "You are named for brave Mountain Sheep who climbed the tallest mountain and now shines above us as the North Star, but you speak like *Poongatse*, timid Mouse."

"We eat okay!" he shouted.

November tsked again. "Did Tuhudda teach you no manners at all? Take a knife, a sharp one, and start cutting carrots, not too thick. I am making stew. I do not want to see one of your fingers in it."

"I'll be in Pudge's office," I said.

"So be there," she said.

Pudge's office was his inner sanctum and reflected a life of soldiering and law enforcement. He'd served in the Marines during World War II, and his framed discharge papers and commendations for fighting on Iwo Jima decorated the wall. He joined the sheriff's department right after he mustered out. A glass-fronted cabinet held long guns. Shelves were lined with books. The worn spots in the leather couch were testament to a habit of stretching out to read and, more often than not, dozing off while doing so. A table supported a facsimile machine and a police radio. His desk was buried beneath a blizzard of papers and folders.

I sat on his swivel desk chair and dialed the sheriff's office in Burns. Orville Nelson was manning the phones.

"Have they showed yet?" I asked.

"No visuals of the fugitives or contact with them of any kind," the FBI hopeful said. "Sheriff Burton is coordinating our activities with other law enforcement branches statewide. Harney County deputies are at their assigned posts on the designated highways. Burns City Police has four squad cars conducting sweeps in the outlying neighborhoods. Deputy Warbler is circumnavigating the city limits. The State Bureau of Prisons has provided some new information about the fugitives. If we had a computer like they are now using at Quantico, I could be monitoring everything almost as soon as it happens."

Listening to Orville rattle off facts as if he were reciting a code enforcement handbook from memory, followed by voicing his approval of the FBI for using new machines to help fight crime, made me realize I'd miss him when he left for the summer. His earnestness could be annoying, but it was difficult to fault someone who'd been brought up in a small town by a widowed mother and had big dreams for himself and was determined to achieve them.

"What sort of new information?" I said.

"They are highlights of their personal records while incarcerated at Oregon State Penitentiary. George Roscoe Banks's cellmate hung himself under suspicious circumstances, the suspicion stemming from the fact that he had thirty days remaining until his unconditional release. It was not the first cellmate of Banks's to die in prison. The other one had been found in a shower with his throat slit. Donny Gray has attempted suicide on two separate occasions. Loud Will spent the last two hundred days in solitary confinement. He has been placed in solitary on multiple occasions."

"Anything new about the van?"

"It appears the driver forced a conclusion," Orville said.

"What's that supposed to mean?"

"From what they can tell by skid marks on the pavement and the van's positioning off the highway, he braked the vehicle abruptly, causing it to come to a screeching halt. He managed to turn off the ignition."

"And they killed him for it. Okay, why didn't they push him out and keep going?"

"The driver swallowed the key."

"And they slit his throat trying to retrieve it," I said.

Orville paused. "They were unsuccessful because the incision was made too high, above his thyroid gland to be precise. The key had already lodged in his trachea."

I had witnessed men do unimaginably heroic things in combat. Some were done out of courage, others in panic. Sometimes it was hard to distinguish between the two. I blinked away the image of a corporal in my squad diving in front of a fusillade aimed at his buddies and another image of the van driver stuffing the ignition key into his mouth.

"I need to speak to Pudge about my visit to the Will camp," I said.

"Do you want me to patch you through? He will have his radio on."

"Better if you keep all your lines open. I'm at his ranch. I'll use the radio here. If anything comes up, call me."

"Ten-four," he said. "Over and out."

I pushed the swivel chair over to the table with the police radio. Pudge picked up right away.

"What?" he said. The channel was clear, the reception good, and there was no humming or squawking.

"I'm at your place. I have Nagah with me." I gave him a rundown on my conversation with Tuhudda about the path to manhood ceremony.

He sighed. "That stubborn old man. Guess I shouldn't be surprised he wouldn't go with the others. He comes from a long line of warriors. His grandfather was Red Bear, one of the Paiute braves who rode off to join Chief Buffalo Horn and the Bannocks in the war of 1878."

"Tuhudda says his son won't harm him. He told me about Loud working at Lyle Rides Alone's ranch, how he was calm there until Sonny Stiles came along and got him drunk."

"I'd forgotten all about that. Makes me dislike that half-pint all the more."

"It sure sounds like Loud has always had some sort of emotional problems."

"Mentally retarded, you mean."

"It could be any number of things. When I was at Walter Reed, the doctors had a long list of terms for what they called us. It changed from shell shock to battle fatigue to combat fatigue. I'm sure it'll change again someday."

"Well, all I know is we got three fugitives who were being sent to the state hospital and now they're running loose. Whatever kind of crazy they got, we got to deal with it. I feel for old Tuhudda, but there's nothing I can do about him right now outside of catching his son and the other two. At least you got Nagah and the rest of the family out of there."

"What's your plan if the fugitives don't get picked up at any of the roadblocks?"

"Every minute that goes by with them not showing up here is a minute in their favor. Gives them more time to burrow in deeper if they're hiding, more time to get farther away if they're running. That's the glass half-full part. The half-empty is it gives them more time to acquire weapons and do bad things."

Pudge took a deep breath and let it out in a long sigh. "You served. You know how it is. You're either on offense or defense. Right now we got to stay on defense. The story about the escape is already out. TV and radio are gonna run with it on the nightly news, which starts in about thirty minutes. I'm sure Bonnie LaRue is working overtime to plaster it all over the front page for tomorrow." She was the tough-as-nails editor and publisher of the *Burns Herald*. "That's gonna cause a lot of heartburn among folks. Bust'em is already in a lather. I talked to him a little bit ago. Seems when Bonnie called him for a comment, he spoke first, thought second. He told her he'd come up with a plan to call everybody in Harney County and tell them to lock their doors and be on the lookout."

"A lot of people don't have phones," I said.

"Tell me about it, especially those living on the few-and-far-between ranches. If we don't catch these fellas tonight, we may end up going door to door in the morning. Doing that will stretch our little net pretty darn wide."

I thought of Clay Barkley and his canvas tent set up alongside the Stinkingwater Mountain access road. He wasn't the only one out there who could find himself being in the wrong place at the wrong time.

"I can be in Burns in twenty minutes if I floor it and can help out at one of the roadblocks," I said.

"I need you to sit tight right where you're at. Now that we know why Loud wants to get home, his son just became a whole lot more important. I've lived in No Mountain all my life, and if there's one thing I've learned is, I still have a helluva lot to learn about the Paiute. Maybe Loud can hear as good as he howls. Maybe even better. Maybe he can hear his son's heartbeat. You need to stay alert and stay armed. Expect the unexpected. Plan for the unplanned."

Pudge exhaled loudly into the mike. "Oh Lord, I'm pulling

up to the roadblock on Highway 20 now and it sure looks like one of my men is more interested in keeping his eyes on the latest issue of *Playboy* than vehicles." He clucked his tongue. "What I have to deal with."

I returned to the kitchen. November was holding a wooden spoon to her lips as she tended the pot on the stove. The aroma of sage, wild onions, and mutton filled the air. They were the same smells that drifted through the Will camp. I realized the old woman was cooking something that would make the boy feel at home.

She took a taste, nodded to herself, and put the lid back on the pot. "Show Nagah where to wash up and sit down. It is suppertime."

"It's not even five yet. We should wait for Gemma."

"The boy is hungry. You eat with him now. Gemma can eat later."

As soon as Nagah and I were seated, the old woman pushed through the swinging door that separated the dining room and kitchen. She was carrying the stew pot and a basket woven with a band of black triangles. It was heaped with corn muffins. She ladled stew into bowls that had already been set on placemats.

"Aren't you going to eat with us?" I said.

November wrinkled her nose. "I am not hungry."

She pushed back through the swinging door. As it closed behind her, I heard her cough. It sounded like a baby's rattle.

9

The wild filly foal was still lying on her side as she had been when I saw her last. An IV bag hung from a hook and a clear plastic tube ran from it to a needle inserted into a neck vein and held in place by white tape.

"What's wrong with her?" Nagah asked.

We were both kneeling in the straw next to her. He was stroking her forehead.

"Her mother was poisoned. She may have swallowed the poison while nursing."

"Her mother died?"

"Yes."

"What about her father?"

"I don't know for sure. There were other horses in the herd that died, but it's impossible to know if he was among them."

"I hope he didn't," the boy said quickly. "Maybe he's the white stallion who came to our camp."

I checked the IV to make sure it had no bubbles and the liquid was flowing freely. I knew about IVs. I'd helped corpsman insert them into wounded men on the battlefield more than once. I'd held the bags aloft while hustling litters to EVAC choppers as their spinning blades wrapped us in swirling, stinging cocoons of dirt, rocks, and blood splatter. I'd worn an IV myself in a field hospital after being wounded in an ambush that wiped out my squad. I'd kept my eyes glued to the tube and counted the drips one by one, urging them on to deliver the merciful flood that would ease my pain and silence my guilt for being the only one who'd survived.

"Will she live?" Nagah asked.

"I hope so." I patted her withers. "She deserves to and she's trying very hard."

"I hope she lives too. I hope she grows up big and strong and can run with the other wild ones someday.

"Me too."

"I hope she finds her father and he is alive and they can run together."

We listened to the foal's breathing. Outside, the sun was setting and crickets started sawing their wings like stringed instruments warming up at a symphony. The two cutting horses were also making noises. I had learned how to ride on Wovoka last fall, but the winter had been long and the snow deep and so our outings had become infrequent. It was time to saddle up again.

"How long do you think I will need to stay here?" Nagah asked.

"I don't know. Didn't you like helping November cook supper?"

"I like Dr. Gemma. I'll be glad when she gets here. She comes to our camp to heal our sheep. November scares me."

"She frightens me too."

He smiled shyly. "And the sheriff? Does he scare you?"

"Pudge? No, he'll be your friend if you let him."

The crickets picked up the tempo. Sarah whinnied. Wovoka snorted. "Is the sheriff going to shoot my father?" Nagah said.

"You heard he escaped from prison?"

"I heard Grandfather tell my aunts when I was packing."

"I won't lie to you and tell you everything is going to turn out okay. The truth is, I don't know what's going to happen. All I know is, I'm going to do everything I can to keep you safe."

"My father would never hurt me. He never hurt my mother or me and my sister. He would shout and yell, but he wasn't shouting and yelling at us. He was telling the others to let him be."

"The others?"

"My mother called them that. She said they lived inside him and were always telling him things."

"You love your father, don't you?"

"Of course. I want to see him. It's been a long time since they sent him away. And before then he did not live with us very often. He was in Idaho for a while and before that he was, well, I'm not sure where because he would come and go. The others made him leave. That's what my mother said."

"The others."

"Yes, the others."

Tires crunched gravel outside. I stood quickly. A door slammed. I moved between the boy and the open half door to the stall and drew my gun. A light in the stable turned on. I recognized Gemma's silhouette.

"Hey, you two," she said. "How's our patient?"

Nagah pushed past me and threw his arms around her. "Dr. Gemma!"

She hugged him and tousled his hair. "I'm so glad to see you, Nagah. I hear you're staying with November and me. Can I count on you to help with the foal?"

"Of course you can."

She looked over his head. "I spoke to Pudge. He told me."

"It's been a long day," I said.

"Would you like some fry bread?" she asked Nagah. "When I got out of my Jeep I could smell it cooking. November makes the best fry bread in the whole world."

He pulled himself away. A smile widened. "I love fry bread."

"Who doesn't? Let's go."

Gemma turned him around and they walked out. Before following them, I leaned over the foal and whispered into her ear. "Don't die. A little boy is counting on you. We all are."

A HALF-MOON BATHED the yard in front of the Warbler ranch in pale light. I sat on the front porch and nursed a mug of tea. The Winchester .30-30 was leaning against the wall within easy reach. I didn't expect the fugitives to appear, but Pudge's warning about the Paiute's heightened senses kept me from reading the stories in the sky the stars told.

I knew Pudge had agreed to go along with Sheriff Burton's idea of placing emergency vehicles at the entrances to Burns because he didn't have a better plan himself. The reality was, every law enforcement officer in the state was banking on a lucky sighting. If the convicts were mobile, they were in a stolen vehicle. It may not be the same one they commandeered when they abandoned the van, but whether it was their second or third stolen car, eventually a description would be reported. A lucky sighting could also come into play if the convicts were holed up somewhere. Sooner or later, hunger, boredom, panic, or bad temper would flush one or more out. If they were hiding at someone's they knew, treachery would come into play.

A lucky sighting was no sure thing. Oregon covered nearly as much land area as Vietnam, and that country had managed to hide entire battalions of enemy soldiers and guerrillas during the three years my squad was looking for them. Oregon was mountainous and forested, and the part that was high desert was riven with gulches and gullies. There were eighty thousand miles of public roads to keep an eye on and that didn't include countless dirt roads, logging roads, and roads that were nothing more than two parallel tracks carved by a four-by-four or a horse-drawn wagon. One tenth of the state's land was in Harney County and it had more unmarked roads than people. Knowing that Loud Will had worked at Lyle Rides Alone's ranch made me think he might not be arriving on four wheels at all.

The front door creaked open and creaked back shut without slamming. Gemma took a seat on the porch bench next to me. As a lawman's daughter, she made sure to sit on the opposite side of my holster.

"Poor little guy. He's exhausted. He fell right asleep," she said.

"Do you know how old Nagah is? I figured him for about twelve or so."

"He turned thirteen this winter. He's small for his age, but I don't think he's malnourished even though that's been a problem for the Paiute. It wasn't so long ago stores wouldn't sell them food. Why do you ask?"

"Tuhudda said Loud is coming to put Nagah on the path to manhood, whatever that means."

"November's taught me a lot about *numu* customs and cere-monies, but not that one."

Gemma was holding a mug too, but since she liked a night-cap, I assumed hers wasn't tea made from wild plants November had picked.

"Have you ever met Loud?" I asked.

"Shortly after my mom died. November had moved in. Pudge was sheriff then and spending most of his time in Burns. Not that I hold it against him. I mean, it's classic textbook, isn't it? He buried the only woman he ever loved, and so he buried himself in his work."

She took a sip from her mug. "I suppose I was a classic text book case too. You know, a little girl who wouldn't allow herself to mourn, so I acted, well, to borrow an expression from Pudge, I was acting like a little shit. It was about the same time I stopped calling him Daddy. It was November's idea to take me to Lyle's."

"To learn how to ride?"

"I already knew how. My mom taught me. She was quite a horsewoman. November didn't tell me why she was taking me there, she just did. She got word to Lyle, and he showed up one morning in a pickup and off the three of us went. Of course, I was still in my little shit phase and probably sulked the whole way there. But once we got to his ranch, it didn't take long before I forgot why I was so mad. There were all these horses and foals, and it was pretty magical—cutting horses and wild horses all running together. Lyle has a real fondness for the wild ones. I suppose it's because of his Paiute half."

"And Loud was there?"

"Yes, but I didn't notice him at first. Other cowboys were working there too. Breaking horses, herding cattle, and so on. Loud was more of a stable hand. You know, mucking out stalls, shoveling manure, pitching hay, and fixing the rails in the corrals. I'd be out there a few times a week and, as time went by, I saw more and more of him because Lyle let him start working with the horses. The wild ones, mostly."

"He didn't seem strange to you?"

"Hey, I like people who are strange. It's what makes them interesting." Her eyes sparkled when she said it, and she followed up by gently elbowing me in the ribs. "Loud didn't talk much, and when he did, more often than not it was something you couldn't understand. More like yips and croaks and, well, howls. They'd just come out of him. Lyle said he was like a piano that needed tuning."

Gemma sipped some more from her mug. "When I was at Oregon State I dated a guy who was premed. He was taking a psychology class and always going on about unusual syndromes, especially the ones that were little understood and lacked treatment protocols. He told me about one called Tourette's after a French doctor who first described it a hundred years or so ago. The guy was reading the symptoms to me over dinner one night, and I immediately thought of Loud Will."

"Over dinner? Some date." I let it sit for a bit, and then said, "Do you think that's what Loud has?"

"I have no idea. I'm a horse doctor, not a head doctor. There could be any number of reasons for his condition. Life for the Paiute has never been easy. Never. And it certainly wasn't any easier when Loud was born. The country was still trying to shake off the Great Depression then, and when you think about all the people who lost their jobs on Wall Street, well, at least they had jobs to lose. The Paiute? They've always had to scratch and scramble. Proper nutrition and medical care are a luxury."

"Tuhudda told me he thinks maybe an evil spirit or trickster afflicted his son, or maybe *Mu naa'a* did it to spite Tuhudda and his wife."

"I've never been one to question Paiute ways. My point is, whatever caused Loud to act the way he does sure sounds like it got better when he was around the horses at Lyle's. From what I hear, he was worse before he got there and a lot worse after he left."

"Drinking and using drugs didn't help any," I said.

"You would know," she said.

There was no judgment in Gemma's tone. She was only stating a fact. I'd never made my heroin addiction a secret to her or anyone. Admitting to it was akin to shining a light on a demon. Gemma had told me when I first met her that, while she could never understand drug abuse, she could at least accept that it was a battle I had to fight every day.

"Was Sonny Stiles working there when you were at the ranch?"

"Toward the end."

"What did you think of him?"

"You and I've been spending more time together these past few months, but not nearly enough for you to have heard all the cuss words I know." Her ponytail swished back and forth. "Sonny deserves every single one of them and probably all the ones I don't know. I was just a little girl when I was there."

My spine stiffened against the back of the wooden bench we were sharing. "What did he do?"

"Lyle was teaching me how to barrel race. You ever seen it? It's a rodeo event where you ride your horse as fast as you can in a cloverleaf pattern around barrels. Cutting horses are naturals for it. I got pretty good at it. Even won some ribbons."

"What did Sonny do?" My voice had turned low.

"Ooh, listen to you." She gave me a look. "Anyway, Lyle was letting me ride this speedy little gray filly. I led her into her stall, put her saddle away, and finished rubbing her down and combing her mane. I was backing out of the stall to make sure the gate closed behind me when, whump, I go flying. Flat down like I'd done a belly flop into the reservoir I used to swim in. I thought I slipped on a cow pie or something. Only then I heard this squeal of laughter and realized my feet were tied together and I was being dragged across the stable floor."

"Sonny lassoed you."

"So, you do know something about working cattle. That's exactly what he did. He was always showing off with this stupid lariat. Performing rope tricks, though I don't recall ever having seen him lasso a real cow. Anyway, he's reeling me in, and I'm crying and thrashing and I manage to roll over onto my back. I was terrified. I was a little younger than Nagah, but you spend time on a ranch that breeds livestock, you learn about the birds and bees pretty darn quick. He's standing in the shadows and we're the only two in the place."

The bench was pressing hard into my spine now. "What happened?"

"I was looking for anything I could grab hold of to defend myself with. A bridle and bit that had been dropped, a hay hook. I was hoping for a pitchfork. And then suddenly there was a swish and a loud twang like a guitar being strummed. The rope went slack. Loud stepped out of one of the stables. He must've been in there mucking it out. He was holding a jackknife, but the blade looked as big as a machete to me. He brandished it at Sonny."

"Did Sonny go after him?"

"No, he didn't dare. He laughed and called Loud a retard. I loosened the noose around my ankles and ran out of there as fast as I could. I was so scared I didn't tell anybody, not even November. I knew what she would've done to Sonny if she'd found out. I didn't go back to Lyle's for a while. Not only because of that, but, well, because school was starting up and I was doing some other things too. When I did return, both Loud and Sonny were gone. Lyle told me he had to let them go for drinking."

We watched the half-moon cast shadows. The crickets were quieting down and the pair of cutting horses that Gemma had bought from Lyle were nickering in their corral.

"I hope Pudge doesn't have to kill Loud," Gemma finally said.

"He told me to tell Tuhudda he's going to do everything he can not to cause him harm, but he's got to do his job and try and take him back to prison."

We sat a little longer. My tea grew cold and I tossed out the dregs. Gemma drained her mug and then reached over and squeezed my hand. "You know what I also hope?"

"What's that?" I said.

"I hope you don't have to shoot him either. I know you don't ever want to have to kill someone again."

10

T wo days went by without a lucky sighting. The Burns city cops went back to writing parking tickets. Sheriff Burton ordered his deputies to abandon the road-blocks, but Pudge Warbler hadn't given up yet, nor had he returned home. November's cough worsened. She was still cooking meals but wouldn't eat. That morning at breakfast, Gemma announced she was returning to work.

"I'm getting emergency calls from ranchers all over the county. They have calves dropping left and right and every tenth birth is a breech or a twin. The list of first-calf heifers with prolapsed uteruses is growing longer by the minute, and so is the one for second and third timers with udder mastitis. On top of all that, an epidemic of the scours is raging in Mule Springs Valley."

Gemma gulped her coffee, wrapped a couple of pieces of fry bread in a napkin, and bolted for the door before November or I could say a word.

Keeping watch at the Warbler ranch was interfering with my job too. I needed to get down to the Hart Mountain National Antelope Wildlife Refuge and check on calving pronghorns. My spring migration bird count at Malheur Lake was long overdue. On top of all that was the upcoming performance review call with my district supervisor and the new regional director.

I asked Nagah to go check on the foal and went to Pudge's office and closed the door. Orville Nelson was still answering the phones when I called the sheriff's department. Even his usual cheery hello rang with frustration.

"It is as if the three fugitives were beamed up like they do on *Star Trek*." He groaned. "I cannot believe they have canceled my favorite TV show. It has only been on for three seasons. The last episode airs the week I leave for Quantico."

"They'll keep you so busy there you won't even have to time to miss watching summer reruns," I said. "Let me speak to Pudge."

"Sure thing, but I should warn you... he is not in an amiable mood. Have you seen the editorial in today's *Burns Herald*? Bonnie LaRue raked Sheriff Burton over the coals for failing to protect the populace by not catching a local killer. The sheriff started yelling at Deputy Warbler that it was all his fault, that it was going to cost him voters' goodwill in the next election. He even accused Deputy Warbler of doing it on purpose."

I kept my opinion of the sheriff's small-mindedness to myself until Pudge got on the line. "Sounds like Burton thinks you're giving him a taste of his own medicine."

"He's so full of himself he can't believe anyone isn't as underhanded as him. You couldn't pay me enough to take my old job back. Bust'em can have all the politics and paperwork that goes with it. Being half-retired? Well, it ain't half bad. Especially given the last couple days."

"What's the latest?"

"The prison workers union reminded the governor about their campaign contributions to him. He responded by announcing the state was offering a fifty thousand dollar reward for information leading to the arrest and capture of all three men who killed the guard and driver."

The echo of Pudge slamming his palm on his desk came through the phone line as if he were sitting right next to me.

"Every county in the state has been running a tip hotline, but once word of the reward got out, all the switchboards lighting up at once nearly blew out the hydroelectric plant at Bonneville Dam. We're gonna have bounty hunters flocking like buzzards. They're the lowest of the low."

"Still no stolen car report?"

"Nope, and you know when they grabbed one after ditching the van it meant grabbing the driver too. The way I figure it, the driver must be from out of state, maybe a traveling salesman or a long-haul trucker, because if it had been someone local, they would've been reported missing by now."

"Have other counties abandoned their road blocks too?" I asked.

"Budgets being what they are, they didn't have much choice. We did follow through with Bust'em's grand idea of calling everyone in the county and making sure they kept an eye peeled." Pudge snorted. "The college boy made most of those calls himself. He kept saying that it was only a matter of time before there'd be a system where robots did the calling for us."

"The reason I called is, I need to get back to my regular job."

"I sure thought Loud Will was coming here," the old lawman said. "I'm not afraid of admitting I'm wrong when I'm wrong, but it's that I don't think I'm wrong. I might've been wrong about Loud wanting to settle scores, but my gut is still telling me old Tuhudda is right that Loud is determined to see his son."

"I can drive over to the Will camp and check on Tuhudda. Maybe he knows something."

"Nope, too dangerous. Loud could be hiding there. I'll do it."

"If he is there, he'll bolt as soon as he sees a sheriff's rig. He doesn't know me. I'm only a Fish and Wildlife guy passing by on my way to the north shore of Malheur Lake to conduct a bird count. I'll wear my binoculars."

Pudge took some time before responding. "Okay, but be careful. Keep in radio contact the whole way. First sign of trouble, get out of there quick."

"Will do."

"And, son? Make sure you wear your gun too."

I STOPPED off at Blackpowder Smith's to buy a gift for Tuhudda. The exchange of gifts was an important Paiute tradition. The combination tavern and dry goods store was No Mountain's most thriving commercial enterprise, which really didn't mean much since there was only a handful of false front stores that made up downtown and half of those were empty. The store's proprietor was ringing up Clay Barkley in the checkout line.

"Morning Blackpowder. How are you doing, Clay?"

The BLM ranger grinned. "Hey, good to see you again."

Blackpowder eyed our khaki shirts from behind the cash register as we shook hands. "Would you looky here, twin G-men." He took his fingers off the register to stroke his billy-goat beard. "Just because there's two of you now, don't think that means I'm going start offering government employee discounts." He chuckled at the very idea.

Barkley was buying canned goods: chili, hash, vegetables, and fruit cocktail.

"If you ever get tired of eating TV dinners, let me know and I'll invite you over to my place for a real sit-down meal," I said.

"I'll have you know you're talking to the top campfire chef in the entire Bureau of Land Management. My barbecue sauce won a cash prize." He gestured at the canned goods. "These are to resupply the emergency box I keep in my pickup. I drove down to Steens Mountain on a day trip to check out that herd of mustangs you gave me the coordinates for and wound up spending three nights. Ate up all my emergency rations."

"Sounds like you were able to find the herd."

"I did. There sure are a lot of horses there. The place has all the elements to make a viable wild horse management area. It's got the size, water, and graze to sustain a healthy herd, plus it's at a high enough elevation that prevents cattle from grazing there half of the year. That eliminates a lot of conflicts with ranchers."

"It's BLM land already, isn't it?"

"Mostly," he said. "I drew up some preliminary boundaries in my notebook to go along with the sketches I made for one in the Stinkingwaters."

Blackpowder butted in. "You've been on Steens Mountain for three days? Radio reception is slim to none up there. That means you probably missed all the excitement around here. There's escaped convicts on the run and they ain't been caught."

"I heard about it as I drove into No Mountain, but the news report made it sound like they could be anywhere in the state, maybe even crossed into Canada," Barkley said.

"Maybe, but no one knows for certain." The grizzled store owner reached beneath the counter and hauled out a sawed-off shotgun. "Like I said, no one really knows."

Clay Barkley paid his bill and loaded the cans into a cardboard box. "I'm heading back to my camp to work on my notes. Tomorrow morning I'm going to take a run over to Palomino Buttes to look at the other herd you told me about. It sounds like it has the makings of a management area too. I should be finished by early afternoon. I can stop off in Burns at a butcher shop I know and pick up a couple of T-bones. What do you say? Want to test my cookout skills?"

"Deal," I said and we shook on it. "See you tomorrow."

Blackpowder kept an apiary. He charged a handsome price for the desert wildflower honey from his hives, but it was worth every penny. I grabbed a jar off the shelf along with a tin of pilot bread crackers. Tuhudda had a sweet tooth and the honey and crackers would make a fine gift.

As Blackpowder rang them up, he said, "If you don't mind me saying so, but I'm going say it regardless, you are a shining example of how living in wide open spaces can be good for whatever ails the soul. Think of it. You blew into town a raggedy-ass tumbleweed a year ago. Didn't know nobody, didn't want to know nobody, and didn't talk to nobody. Just lived in that shack by yourself, spent all your time alone on the refuges, and tore around the desert hell-bent for leather every night on that Steve McQueen motorcycle of yours."

He rapped the counter with his gnarled knuckles. "Now look at you? You're dating the prettiest gal in all of Harney County, you got people treating the refuges with respect, and you just went and made yourself a friend for life. Before you know it, thirty, forty years will pass and you and that BLM ranger will be like me and Pudge, jawing and cussing at each other over a game of chess, knowing that we can say whatever we want to each other without ruffling a feather because we've always had each other's back and we're as close as brothers."

He put the jar of honey and tin of crackers in a brown paper sack and handed it to me. "Friendships that last a lifetime are the Big Man Upstairs's reward for living true and right. You're a lucky man, Nick Drake. Real lucky."

I thought about Blackpowder's words as I drove to Tuhudda's. I never had close friends while growing up. My old man was military and we moved more times than I could count. It wasn't until I was in-country that I became as close as brothers with other men. We had to be in order to survive, though in the end, even brotherhood hadn't been enough to save us all. I often wondered if I'd met anyone from my squad in the real world, would've we become good friends. Maybe meeting Clay Barkley was a way to find that out.

I turned onto the rutted dirt road that led to the Will camp. I slowed as I approached the cluster of singlewide trailers and shanties and searched for anything out of the ordinary. A couple of pickups and livestock trailers I remembered from before were missing. So was a country station wagon—a beat up four-door sedan with the trunk lid removed. I'd seen it plenty of times in No Mountain when Tuhudda's daughters came to shop at Black-powder Smith's. The only vehicles left in the place were what Harney County folks called backyard car part stores. All was quiet. There were no yapping yellow dogs and no bleating sheep. The wild horses were grazing on the far side of the field.

I parked and gave the horn a couple of friendly taps. Then I got out and casually stood behind the opened front door to give myself a shield.

"Anybody home?" I called out.

A horse neighed in response. It was hidden behind an outbuilding. I remembered Nagah had a chestnut pony, but this was no pony's neigh. It could have been one of the mustangs, but it would've been unusual for a wild horse to wander away from the rest of the herd.

I kept a smile on my face, but gripped the butt of my pistol. "Anybody home?" I called again. "It's Nick Drake. I'm on my way to the lake for a bird count and thought I'd drop off a gift."

I flexed my knees and readied to spring, but no one answered nor took a shot.

"Okay," I said. "Maybe you're in the outhouse or taking a nap. I'll leave it on the front stoop."

I reached into the cab for the paper sack and shook out the tin of soda crackers. I twisted the neck of the sack with the honey jar still in it. Then I moved away from the safety of the door. I carried the paper sack by the neck in my left hand and walked toward Tuhudda's white single-wide trailer. As I reached it, the front door jerked open and the long barrel of a pistol jabbed out of the shadows.

I swung the paper sack upwards. The honey jar struck the gun barrel and knocked it skyward. I grabbed it with my right hand and wrenched it loose. I had it turned by the time the honey jar swung back down to my side.

"Don't shoot! I was only fooling," Sonny Stiles cried from the darkened doorway.

I jammed the gun into his chest. "I'm not laughing."

"Easy, man, easy."

"Where's Tuhudda?" I didn't let up the pressure of the gun while I drove him backward into the single wide.

"Ow, my trigger finger. I think you broke it when you sucker punched me."

"Where's the old man?" I said. "If he's hurt, you're worse."

"He's not here, I promise. Look around. No one is. They've all lit out."

I shoved Sonny toward the couch. He plopped down and nursed his reddening finger. I glanced from side to side. The door to the back bedroom was open. So was the one to the WC. Tuhudda was nowhere to be seen.

"See, I told you," Sonny said. "Now, give me back my gun. It's a Colt .45 Peacemaker commemorative model."

"What are you doing here?"

"Looking for the old Injun's son. Loud Will's worth fifty thousand bucks." Sonny squinted at me. "That's why you're here too, ain't it, zookeeper? I should've figured every jackalope in the county would be looking for that retard."

"You're breaking and entering. Where's Tuhudda?"

"I told you already. I don't know. And that's an actual, honest, true fact. There wasn't nobody around when I rode in. They took all their sheep and junk cars and left. My bet is the retard's with them. They're hiding him somewhere. Whaddaya say, zookeeper? Let's go in as partners to track him and split the reward fifty-fifty. That's a honest day's pay for a honest day's work, yes, sir."

"You rode here?"

"I sure did. That's my horse out there. Figured I could sneak up and get the jump on 'em. If I'd seen Loud Will, I'd have shot him, lassoed him, and rode off with his sorry ass dragging behind faster than you can say Geronimo." He mimed blowing smoke from the barrel of a gun. "The reward's for dead or alive, ain't it?"

"Get out of here and don't come back."

"Have it your way, zookeeper, but I was paying you a compliment there inviting you in on being partners to catch that retard redskin."

"Get out of here. Now."

"Okay, okay, but give me back my gun."

I flicked open the cylinder and emptied the bullets into my palm before handing the six-shooter over.

"What about my lead?" Sonny whined. "Give it back. That's a buck fifty's worth."

"And you don't think those horses you killed were worth two bits a piece? Go before I change my mind."

He scurried out like a rat being chased by a broom. Just before he disappeared behind the outbuilding, he called out. "My offer of going in as partners is officially off the table. It's finders keepers, and I aim to be the finder."

Sonny galloped away on a black horse with three white socks. I opened my hand and looked at the six rounds cupped in my palm. He'd cut *x*'s into the noses so the bullets would fragment upon impact and cause even greater damage. I instantly regretted giving him back his gun.

I pocketed the rounds and turned my attention to the trailer. Tuhudda wasn't hiding under any of the beds or in the closet. The only sign of him were two framed black and white photographs that hung on the wall.

One showed Tuhudda before his hair turned white. He was standing next to a woman cradling a baby. The second photo was a group shot. Tuhudda and the woman were older than in the first one. They were posing alongside three girls and a boy. I barely recognized Loud. He bore little resemblance to the mugshot I'd seen. His nose was unflattened, his face unscarred, and his throat showed no broken arrow tattoos. He was grinning from ear to ear. Wherever they were, whatever they were doing, he was having the time of his life.

11

As I drove away from the Will camp, I picked up the mike and radioed Pudge Warbler. He was still in his office in Burns.

"I looked in every building. The place was empty. I don't think Tuhudda has been there for a couple of days."

"What makes you say that?" the old lawman asked.

"The dirty dishes in the sink in his trailer. Some garbage left in the pail."

"You think he left in a hurry?"

"Looks that way. There's more. Sonny Stiles was looking for him too. Now he fancies himself a bounty hunter."

Pudge swore under his breath, but I could hear the four-letter words loud and clear. "Somebody should've run that pizzle stick out of the county a long time ago."

"What are the chances Tuhudda drove to Catlow Valley to join his daughters and their families?"

"He wouldn't want to lead Loud there. I believe he's known all along where Loud was going. Someplace that meant something to him at one time or another where he'd feel safe."

"Lyle Rides Alone's ranch?"

"Lyle's not the kind to open his door to a convict on the run no matter if he did have a soft spot for him once upon a time and even if he was the son of a good friend."

"Then where?"

"It has to be a place where something happened Loud won't ever forget. A good kind of something."

"I think I saw a picture of it," I said. "Hang on. I'll go back and get it."

I returned to the trailer and left the engine running and radio squawking while I ran inside and took the photograph off the wall.

"Got it," I said.

"Describe it," Pudge said.

"It's a black and white picture of Tuhudda, a woman who I assume is his wife, and four kids. They're standing in a row facing the camera, dad and mom in the middle. Tuhudda looks twenty years or more younger. So does Loud. I'd put him in his early teens. He's standing to the right of Tuhudda and the three daughters are standing next to their mother. You can see the silhouette of a ridge behind them."

"How do they look, the family?"

"Loud has a big grin and Tuhudda looks, well, like a proud poppa. The mother and girls look happy too, but some of their hair has come loose from their braids as if they'd been running a race."

"And their garb, what sort is it?"

"Tuhudda and Loud have on breechcloths and leggings with sashes tied around their waist. The girls' buckskin dresses have beaded designs. So do their moccasins. They're wearing lacy shawls too."

Pudge exhaled loudly. "I'll bet you dollars to donuts it was the boy's path to manhood ceremony. The girls' hair is mussed because they've been dancing."

"Where do they hold the ceremony, the same place they have round dance?"

"The Paiute have a bunch of sacred spots they've always kept secret from white folks because of the old days. There was a time when Paiute beliefs were illegal, some by law and some by preachers looking to convert them."

"Like the US Cavalry did to the Ghost Dance religion," I said.

"That's right. I might be able to ID the photo's whereabouts if I had a gander at it."

"I'm on my way to Malheur Lake. I'll stop by your ranch and fax it to you."

"That'll work."

It took half an hour to drive back to the Warbler ranch. Nagah was sitting at the dining table drawing pictures in a speckled school notebook that reminded me of the one Clay Barkley wrote his field notes in.

"Where's November?" I asked.

"In her room. She said she was going to take a nap."

The old healer falling asleep in the middle of the day was akin to a hummingbird sitting still. I passed through the kitchen and put my ear to her bedroom door. I could hear the sound of dream talking. I walked quietly to Pudge's office.

The black and white photograph slipped out of the frame easily enough. I fed it into the fax machine, dialed the sheriff's office, and hit send. The transmission clicked and trilled. No sooner had it ended than the phone rang.

"Is that you Ranger Drake?" Orville Nelson asked.

"It is. Did what I send come through?"

"Yes. What is it?"

"It's a photo Deputy Warbler needs to take a look at that might help locate a hideout. Can you take it to him?"

"Of course, but he and the sheriff are both on a call right now. Something big is happening with the manhunt."

"What?"

"I do not know all the details, but it sounds as if the convicts have been spotted. Wait, I can see the call ended. I will transfer you."

Pudge came on. I asked him what was going on.

"Word just came in the three fugitives have been seen," he said

"Near here?"

"Portland. Don't that beat all? Everyone's been thinking they went in the same direction the van was headed. No one thought they'd walk across the highway and commandeer a car going west."

"Who spotted them?"

"A professional snitch."

"Did he call it in on the hotline?"

"Nope, he met up with an undercover narcotics cop he snitches to regular. He told the narc he was standing on the street corner when George Roscoe Banks drove by in a red Cadillac Coupe deVille. There were two others with him. He knows Banks from when they shared a cell in county lockup. The cop tells him he's blowing smoke, but the snitch gives him a license plate number. It's from Idaho. The Portland Bureau—that's what the city cops call themselves—runs the plate and learns it's registered to a man out of Boise who represents a big drug company. Oregon and Idaho are his territory."

"Your traveling salesman," I said.

"Sounds like it, but he doesn't answer the phone or the door." The old deputy drew in his breath. "I'm guessing he's stuffed in the trunk of the Caddy, if not in a culvert alongside the highway somewhere."

"Have they made an arrest yet?"

"They're working up to it. The Caddy hasn't been spotted since the snitch saw it and so Portland Bureau is going back through all of George Roscoe Banks's last knowns."

"That's it? Now everyone sits and waits?"

"Most folks, yep, including me. I'll sleep in my own bed tonight and put on a fresh uniform in the morning and see what tomorrow brings."

I felt mixed emotions. On one hand, I was relieved the ordeal might soon be over. On the other, I dreaded the outcome. Someone was sure to get hurt, most likely killed. Maybe a cop, but certainly Loud Will. He told Tuhudda he wouldn't go back to prison. While he might finally get the peace and quiet he'd always been howling for, Nagah was going to lose his father, and Tuhudda, his son.

"I faxed you the photo we talked about. I'll leave the original on your desk here. It'll be waiting for you when you get home."

"Okay, but there won't be a need to identify the place if they wrap this up in Portland," he said.

"Yes, there will. There's an old man waiting out there who needs to know what happened to his son. If you can identify it, call me. I owe it to Tuhudda to tell him."

MALHEUR LAKE SPARKLED from the rays of the unobstructed sun. The ripples on the water were caused by birds not wind. Tens of thousands of ducks, geese, and swans were using it as a rest stop on their way to the nesting and feeding grounds in the far north. I set up my spotting scope and did a quick survey of waterfowl. I counted seven different species of duck, four of geese, and tundra swans. Then I swiveled to the shoreline and trained it on the wading birds. Great blue herons mixed with white-faced ibises, snowy egrets, and black-necked stilts as they all plumbed the shallows for tadpoles and fry.

The cattails that grew in the marshes and the bushy shrub willows that crowded the shoreline were a kaleidoscope of color from all the different songbirds and passerines perching in them. Splashes of red from western tanagers, yellow from warblers, and blue from lazuli buntings brightened the greenery. The air was thick with birdcall. Caws, peeps, screeches, quacks, and honks collided in an unconducted cacophony. Each sound had a different purpose—to attract a mate, warn of a predator, or defend a territory. Some were made for the sheer pleasure of it, to announce to the rest of the natural world the joy of being alive in such a beautiful spot after having endured a grueling flight thousands of miles long.

The noises made me think of Loud Will. Was that what he was doing as he barked and howled? Did he do it to defend himself in an unsympathetic world? Was he sounding an alarm that no one else could hear? Was he searching for someone who could help end his loneliness? I had an inkling of what his life must be like because I had shouted and howled in the confines of the four walls at Walter Reed and then in Harney County. I'd driven my motorcycle way out into the middle of nowhere, far from anywhere, so no one would hear my shouts of rage and anger against the madness of war and at myself for the lives I took and the lives I cost.

Even the brilliant spectrum of feathers that fluttered before me couldn't still my anticipation of waiting to hear what happened in Portland. It was akin to watching two trains speeding toward one another. I packed up my spotting scope and drove home to the lineman's shack where I ate a tasteless dinner and drank a mug of tasteless tea. I crawled into the narrow bunk without bothering to light a fire. My dread of hearing the phone ring and Pudge's voice stating what had gone down would keep me sweating no matter how cold the night might get.

I waited until after dawn broke before calling him. There was still no news. Portland police were working with the FBI to narrow down the fugitives' possible location. Pudge told me the big city cops had recently formed a special weapons and tactics team based on a concept developed by the Los Angeles Police Department following the Watts Riots.

"Those boys will be the shock force when they finally get an address," he said. "I hear a lot of them are Vietnam vets. SWAT work could always be a line of work for you if you ever get tired of rangering, son."

"Did you take a look at the photo of Tuhudda and his family yet?" I said.

"Just a glance. I need to study it closer. I'll show it to November too. Maybe she recollects it."

"I'll be around the rest of the day. Call me as soon as you know anything," I said.

It was already turning warm outside, and so I didn't bother putting anything over my T-shirt. I went to work on the outboard motor clamped on the transom of the skiff. It was 100 horsepower, twice the size of what was usually used on a sixteen-footer, but I'd found the extra speed had come in handy running down poachers and the like.

I changed the plug, adjusted the choke, and even drained the fuel line to make sure condensation hadn't gotten trapped inside. The work didn't take long enough. The phone still hadn't rung. I turned my attention to the Ford pickup next. I slid underneath, opened the oil plug, and drained four quarts of 30 weight into a rubber bucket even though I'd changed it a couple of weeks ago. It was all I could do to keep myself from taking apart the engine and cleaning the intake and valves.

By four o'clock and no phone call I was through waiting.

Whatever was going to happen in Portland was going to happen. I washed up, put on a clean shirt, grabbed a chess set, and left for Clay Barkley's camp. Spending an evening around a campfire with someone who wasn't involved with the manhunt would be a welcome relief.

12

Т he sun was arcing west as I drove north on the Stinkingwater Mountains access road. The sky was starting to pick up a little color but was still a long way from turning purple before becoming graphite and then charcoal. The ping of gravel against the wheel wells and the clang of something pinballing beneath the front seat provided counterpoint to the low hum of the scanner I kept switched on in case Pudge radioed.

I was looking forward to seeing Barkley. Sharing a meal and possibly a game of chess was only part of it. I was curious to learn more about how the Bureau of Land Management operated. It was an older sister to the Fish and Wildlife Service. BLM got its start as the General Land Office in 1812 to help organize western land settlement following the Louisiana Purchase. After World War II, it merged with the Grazing Service to become the BLM. Part of its job was to manage public lands for grazing, logging, and mining, but with one in ten acres of American soil under its jurisdiction, managing mustangs wasn't the only new duty the agency had been forced to take on as modern times tamed the wild ways of the old west.

I pulled into Barkley's camp. His pickup wasn't there. No matter, I thought. Field work ruled out adhering to a nine-to-five schedule. That wasn't a burden of the job as far as I was concerned. It was a benefit. I was certain Barkley felt the same. He'd be along eventually with a story about what kept him at Palomino Buttes. Maybe he'd run into more mustangs than he expected or perhaps he'd started sketching out a wild horse management area in his speckled black and white notebook and lost track of time. I parked and set out to make myself useful. There was firewood to be collected and the outdoor kitchen to be readied for when he arrived with those T-bones he'd promised.

The pickup door swung shut behind me. The bang spooked a pair of turkey vultures that had landed on the other side of the Army Navy surplus tent. The big birds with their six-foot wingspans had to take a running start to lift off. By the time they gained altitude, I'd already plucked the Winchester from the gun rack and was running toward the tent.

The hairs on the back of my neck stood as I swept the .30-30 in front of me. Barkley's camp table he used as a desk was tipped over. So was the folding chair. The flap of the tent was partially open. I used the tip of the rifle's barrel to part it even wider. It looked as if a dust devil had managed to get inside. Clothes and books and camping equipment were tossed about. The BLM ranger was sprawled in the middle of the clutter. Barkley's face was turned to one side, his mouth agape, his eye unseeing. The back of his head was caked with dried blood.

I let out a howl that echoed through the camp and surely rolled down the sides of the Stinkingwaters, all the way to Burns to the west, and the Seven Fans ranch to the east. Part of my howling was from sorrow at seeing my new friend dead and part of it was from rage—rage at his murder and rage at myself for allowing a thirst for revenge to surge through me. It washed away all the counseling I'd received, aimed at reining in my need for payback, a need that could only be dulled by rolling up my sleeves and jabbing a vein with a spike full of heroin cooked in a spoon.

PUDGE WARBLER RESPONDED to my radio call by speeding up to, but not into, the pullout to Barkley's camp. Orville Nelson was riding shotgun, although the young man wasn't allowed to carry an actual weapon given his official status as an intern. Two more deputy sheriff's vehicles arrived with their lights flashing. They parked outside of the pullout too.

The old lawman opened the door, but didn't get out of his rig immediately. He was on the radio.

"I just got to the scene," he said into the mike. "I left a deputy stationed at the access road's intersection with Highway 20 and sent another to block the road's south end near Crane. If anybody tries to come in or out, they'll stop them."

The sound of the voice on the other end had to compete with reverb. Pudge adjusted the squelch. "Come again," he said.

"I said, what does the crime scene look like?" It was Sheriff Burton.

"Well, Bust'em, I rightly don't know yet. Let me get out and reconnoiter. I'll put the college boy to work with that new evidence kit we got. If anybody can figure out the instructions, he can. I'll send the other two boys to take the high ground. Maybe we'll get lucky and they'll spot a dust trail on one of the other roads out this way."

"Keep me posted," the sheriff said. "This could be the break we've all been waiting for."

Pudge cradled the mike and slid out. He hitched his gun belt. The holster held a .45. He was careful not to walk through the pullout. I was standing by the campfire ring. I didn't know where else to stand.

"How you holding out, son?" he said.

"I'm holding," I said.

"You sure? I know from personal experience it's not easy seeing a fallen friend."

"I can't say for certain, but it looks like he was shot in the back of the head," I said. "I didn't see any powder burns. There's no exit wound. He's been dead since morning, maybe even last night."

Pudge winced. "I'd feel a little better if you shed a tear while you're saying all that or at least took the steel out of your voice. Then I'd know you'd already let a little out of the bottle." He squinted at me. "You got to, you know? Let a little out so you don't explode."

"What did Sheriff Burton mean when he said the break everyone's been waiting for?"

The old deputy hitched his gun belt again even though it didn't need hitching. "That thing in Portland? It was a bust. The snitch was lying about it being George Roscoe Banks."

"But the license plate," I said.

"He wasn't lying about that. The Caddy did belong to a drug company salesman from Boise. There's a gaggle of hopheads in Portland that got it into their Swiss cheese heads to steal this fella's sample case next time he came to town. One of them had been seeing a gal who worked reception at a doctor's office there and got the bright idea. The snitch was supposed to be in on the score, but then they stiffed him and so he got it into his Swiss cheese head to concoct a story thinking it'd get him the fifty thousand dollar reward."

"Is the salesman still alive?"

"He is. When the Portland Bureau finally realized it was a scam, they tracked down the Caddy. The traveling salesman was holed up in a suite at The Benson with a hooker. He'd been sampling his own wares. Seems some traveling drug salesmen have holes in their heads too."

"So, we're back to square one. The fugitives could be anywhere."

Pudge patted his paunch. "My gut telling me Loud Will would come home may not have been so wrong after all. A sheriff in Grant County took a call this afternoon from a fella who runs a mom and pop up at Summit Prairie. He says about this time yesterday a car pulls in for gas with a driver and two passengers. One of them winds up cold cocking him and leaving him for dead in the storeroom. He finally came to and found his cash register empty."

"It was them," I said.

"Sure sounds like it from the description he gave."

"Where's Summit Prairie?"

"It's about half way from here to John Day as the eagle flies. Summit Prairie is a place, not even a one horse town. Most of this fella's business is from loggers filling their rigs. His pump is near the intersection of a couple of forest service roads and a county highway, if you can call an oiled gravel road that. The thing of it is, it eventually connects to a Harney County highway that's in the same shape. That connects to Pine Creek Road that connects to Highway 20 about a mile west of Stinkingwater Pass."

I felt the hairs on the back of my neck rise again. "They took the access road because hardly anyone ever uses it and no one would see them," I said. "They saw Clay's pickup and decided to help themselves to another vehicle. He tried to stop them."

Pudge nodded. "Makes sense. State troopers are on their way to the Will camp now, if they're not there already. I told them Loud wouldn't be there, but no one wanted to listen, especially when I couldn't tell them where he might be. I couldn't identify that photo you left."

"We need to get to your ranch fast," I said. "If Loud meets up with Tuhudda, he'll find out Nagah is there."

"I got ahold of Gemma on the radio. She was on the Double O Ranch Road heading home. I told her to lead foot it." He eyed me. "You know she can handle a gun better than most. I taught her when she was five. She knows where the key to the gun cabinet in my office is."

"She's only one person," I said.

"That's why I also radioed Blackpowder. Between them and November, sick or not, no one's gonna come through a door or window, and if they try, well, that'll be the last thing they ever try."

"I need to get there."

"Hold on, son. We need to look for answers here. Let's take a minute and see what we can find."

I led the way to the tent. Orville followed us with a black aluminum suitcase hanging from a strap over his shoulder. We stopped at the tent flap and I ran them through what had happened from the moment I parked.

"So you went inside and did what again?" the lawman asked.

"I checked Clay's pulse to make sure."

"Natural response. I'd've done the same. What else did you touch besides his neck?"

"Nothing. I was holding my rifle. I went right back out and radioed you."

"You didn't do nothing else?"

I didn't tell him about howling. "That was it. Then I went over to stand by the fire ring. I didn't want to track up the camp in case anyone left shoe prints." I turned to Orville. "Does your kit let you take impressions? I also noticed a lot of different tire tracks in the pullout. The dirt there is a lot softer than the hard-packed road."

"It does." The FBI hopeful looked expectantly at Pudge.

"It's why we didn't park in it, but let's do the tent first," the deputy said. He jabbed a finger at me. "Stay right there."

The first thing Orville did was put on a pair of surgical gloves. Then he took Barkley's fingerprints. Once he had them, he grabbed a magnifying glass and a pair of tweezers from the black case and began examining the back of the ranger's head as well as the tent floor around the body.

"There appears to be a significant amount of damage to the skull, but a bullet is not readily apparent. It will take surgical tools to locate and extract it," he said.

"What happened to Doc?" I said, meaning Harney County's longtime coroner.

"He's on his way," Pudge said. "But, well, fact of the matter is, when he took a look at this newfangled evidence kit Orville's lugging, he said he was an old dog and would leave the new tricks to the pups. Doc will take over when he gets the body, er, I mean, Barkley here, back to the morgue to do the postmortem."

Orville finished tweezering things and sealing them in plastic bags and tubes. He took a camera from the case and began photographing.

"I can dust all the ranger's belongings for fingerprints, but that is going to take some time," he said.

"Why don't you bag it all up for cataloguing and printing back at the station house once you're finished taking pictures," Pudge said.

"I agree that will be a more efficient use of time," Orville said. "Locating and identifying the murder weapon is the top priority."

"I haven't forgotten that," the old deputy said. He turned to me. "His rig is missing and I'm assuming any long guns he had in the rack are gone with it. He carry a sidearm?"

"A standard issue .357 magnum like mine."

"We'll search for his wallet, but I'm banking they took that too. Anything else valuable you can think of they might have swiped?"

"Clay struck me as living pretty lean. I'm sure he had a pair of binoculars and probably a spotting scope. They could be somewhere in this mess or still in his pickup. The thing he would have valued most was his notebook. It held all his field notes. But that wouldn't be worth anything to anybody else."

Pudge nodded. "The way I see it, he was outside when they showed up. The table and chair got knocked down, probably in a struggle. Maybe he told them his wallet and keys were inside the tent. They must've marched him inside, got what they wanted, and shot him."

I could see it all play out as the deputy described it, right down to the faces of the three convicts whose mug shots I couldn't forget.

"You got the eagle eye," Pudge said. "How about me and you walk the site together and see what we can turn up. Maybe we'll get lucky and find they left some brass or dropped the gun on their way out."

"I'd rather look for the fugitives. Banks needs to be stopped. He's the one who killed Clay."

"You don't know that."

"He's the most likely of the three," I said. "He's the one with the history of killing and, more importantly, a history of liking it."

"You may be right," the old lawman said, "but we got to take care of business right here and now so if and when we do catch him, we'll have the evidence that can send the Grin Raper to meet the Grim Reaper."

13

W e didn't find a shell casing or a gun. Orville took plaster casts of shoe prints before moving on to the pullout in front of the campsite. He pointed out tire tracks and tread marks in the soft dirt that had to have belonged to Barkley's pickup given their frequency. The FBI hopeful identified the newest set and photographed it. He also photographed my tire tracks coming into the pullout and took a plaster cast of the tread pattern as well as one of Barkley's tires too.

"Here is another set that looks pretty fresh," Orville said as he continued examining the pullout. He took more photographs and then measured the distance between the two parallel tracks. "Did the gas station owner in Summit Prairie provide a description of the assailants' car?"

"All he remembers is a newish sedan that was either white or tan," Pudge said. "No make or model. No license plate either."

"This set could be from a sedan. The wheelbase is closer together than a pickup's. The tire size is smaller and the tread pattern unlike a pickup's too. I will need to compare it to a tread pattern book to confirm." Orville frowned. "Of course, the FBI conducts its tread matches on a computer database management system now."

"You'll have to make do with the old fashioned way until you get to summer camp," Pudge said. "Go ahead and take a plaster of it. If we can match it to whatever car they stole, it won't only be Barkley's murder we can tie them to. I reckon the owner of that sedan is dead too."

Orville found a fourth set of tracks. "These are wider apart like a pickup's and the grooves and lugs in the tread pattern are knobby. It could be a four-wheel drive."

"Then make a plaster of it too," Pudge said.

Orville made wheel base measurements and took more photographs of the two sets of tracks before making the casts. We returned to the tent to help put Barkley's possessions into plastic garbage bags. The intern picked up a scrap of paper from the tent floor and unfolded it.

"Who is Lily?" he asked.

"Why, what did you find?" I said.

"It is a note signed *Lily*."

"That would be Lily Calla."

Pudge cocked his head. "Where have I heard that name before?"

"She's the wild horse advocate I asked you if you knew," I said. "I met her here the other day."

Pudge took the note from Orville and read it aloud. "I stopped by to tell you I saw another herd near here. They're in danger too. Is anybody doing something about the Fannings? I hope so. And I hope to see you soon too. XO Lily."

He looked up. "Were they, you know, chummy?"

"Maybe, but I don't know for sure. Lily's pretty passionate—"

The deputy cut me off with a wave of the note. "About Barkley or men in general?"

"I was going to say pretty passionate about saving wild horses. It's her thing."

"Her *thing*? Now, what's that supposed to mean?"

"It's what she's into. You know, her cause. Her thing."

Pudge glanced at the note again. "Doesn't have a date on it, but she had to have written and left it sometime after you found the foal."

"Clay spent three days down at Steens Mountain before coming back here yesterday. Lily must have stopped by while he was gone."

"This note reads like she's sweet on him. She needs to hear what happened before she reads about it in the *Burns Herald*. That's the right thing to do."

"Don't look at me," I said. "I need to get to your place and ask November if she knows the location of that photograph of Tuhudda and his family."

"It won't take both of us to ask her because I'm going straight home myself. You go break the news to Miss Calla, seeing you're the one who met her. A familiar face delivering bad news makes it a whole lot easier to swallow."

"I don't know where she lives," I said.

Pudge hooked a thumb at Orville. "The college boy will find Miss Calla's address for you. He probably already talked to her from when he called everyone in the county about Loud Will and the other two being on the loose, thanks to Bust'em's dumb idea."

"I made a spreadsheet of all my calls," Orville said. "I had a better than 90 percent connection and completion rate. If she is on it, it will include her address."

"There you go," Pudge said. "You two go straight to the office and find it. Orville, while Drake's breaking the news to Miss Calla, start going through all the stuff from the tent we collected.

Get the prison bureau to send over the fugitives' fingerprints and see if you can match them."

"What about Ranger Barkley's body?"

"I'll wait until Doc gets here. He should be along any minute. Pack up and go with Drake."

Orville closed the latches on the black suitcase holding the evidence kit, grabbed a couple of the full plastic garbage bags, and headed outside.

"If you find out where Loud and the others are, call me before going in," I said. "I want to be there when you do."

"Want or need?" Pudge asked.

"Is there a difference?"

WHEN I TOOK the Freedom Bird home from Saigon, I set out to visit every address on a list I'd scrawled on the back of my DD 214. I had to steel myself to push each doorbell and knock on every door. Among them was a bleak farmhouse in the middle of a wheat field in North Dakota, a one-bedroom apartment in a building in dire need of paint outside of Dallas, and a tract home in a cookie-cutter subdivision in Southern California.

Behind each door was the loved one of each man in my squad who would never walk through that door himself. The family had already received official notice of the death of their son, their brother, their husband or their boyfriend, but they hadn't spoken to anyone who'd been with him when he died, someone who could answer their questions, someone who could tell them what his last words were. I owed it to my men to meet with their families and speak for them. I also hoped it would erase my guilt, but it turned out not to be enough.

I couldn't shake the memory of those hard, sad visits as I stood on a sagging front porch of a bungalow whose vinyl siding was coming apart at the seams. The doorbell was a chime, not a buzzer, and a screen door stood between Lily Calla and me when she answered.

"You don't look like the Avon lady," she said with a smile. "How can I help you?"

"It's Nick Drake with Fish and Wildlife. We met the other day."

"Oh, I didn't recognize you. Has your department finally decided to do something about those horse killers? I hope so."

"May I come in?"

"Of course, where are my manners?" She opened the screen door. "Excuse the mess, but I'm so busy I don't have time to straighten up. Would you like a Coke or something?"

"Water is fine," I said.

On those visits to my squad's families, I always accepted whatever was offered. I'd learned that giving me a drink or a meal was a substitute for them being able to soothe their loved one's brow, to be there to hold his hand and tell him they loved him as the light faded in his eyes.

I'd been served water, coffee, and soft drinks. Cookies, cakes, and entire meals too. Though I had no thirst or appetite on those visits, I drained every glass, cleaned every plate. I turned every page of every photo album I was handed and complimented baby pictures and prom pictures alike. I admired baseball mitts and football trophies and prized hockey sticks too. I made a point of reading out loud each word in the framed letter from the Department of Defense that commended the family for having made the ultimate sacrifice as if it were the first time I'd ever seen one.

The only thing I wouldn't accept was the offer to spend the night no matter how far the walk back to the bus station or how cold and rainy the night was to stand on the side of the road thumbing a ride. I wouldn't stay out of fear that I would fall asleep and then have a flashback and prowl through the house searching for enemies to kill. The families had suffered enough already. The last thing they needed was a living, breathing casualty of war under their roof.

Lily brought out two glasses of water and put them on the coffee table. She sat down on the faded flower print couch. I sat on a stuffed chair with dish towels covering the threadbare arms. I picked up the glass and drank. As I did, I looked around. Posters of horses with inspirational quotes were thumbtacked to the walls. A potted philodendron with leaves covered in liver spots drooped thirstily from a macramé hanger. The smell of a cat litter box drifted from the kitchen.

I put the glass down next to a heap of magazines with dates as old as those found in a doctor's waiting room. "I'm afraid I have bad news."

Lily clasped her hand to the base of her throat. "Oh no! Don't tell me more horses have been poisoned."

"It's about Clay Barkley. He was assaulted. I'm sorry, but he's dead."

Her face drained of color. "What? What are you saying?"

"I just left his camp. I was there with the sheriff's deputies. Clay was murdered."

"Murdered? Why? By who?"

"It appears they were after his pickup."

"They? Why do you say they?"

"We think it might be the men who escaped from prison. Orville Nelson from the sheriff's office spoke to you about them when he was making calls as part of a countywide alert. It's how I got your address."

When Lily shook her head, her short hair whipped across her temples. "Is the sheriff sure it was the escaped convicts? What about the Fannings? They already threatened him once. Well, their foreman did. His name is Sonny."

I didn't respond. When I first discovered Barkley's body, I immediately thought of Sonny Stiles too. After I chased him away from the Will camp, he could've easily ridden his horse straight to Barkley's, killed him, and stolen his pickup. But I ruled him out just as fast. There were no horseshoe prints around the camp. The tread impressions Orville had taken might prove Sonny had driven there before or after, but there was still the matter of Clay's missing rig. It hadn't driven away on its own and there were no tire tracks showing it had been roped to another vehicle and towed.

"I know you're from the East, but do you have any family nearby? Or a close friend or someone?" I said.

"Why?"

"I'm sure this comes as a shock. It might help if someone can come over to be with you."

"I haven't lived here that long and I've been too busy with the horses to meet many people." Her bottom lip quivered. "How was he killed? Did he suffer?"

I fumbled for the same words I'd used on those hard, sad visits. "It was quick. Clay never felt a thing."

Lily gasped and then sighed.

"Are you sure you don't want me to call someone? You and Clay were, well, close, right? We found a note from you in his tent."

"A note?"

"It said you hoped to see him soon."

Lily shook her head. "Oh no, you have the wrong idea. We both liked wild horses, but that was it."

"You signed it with an *x* and *o*."

"I sign everything that way. It takes love to save wild horses, and the world could use a lot more of it."

I let it go and took another sip of water to buy time. Shock came in many forms and wasn't always immediate. I'd met family members who told me they hadn't cried when they first heard about their loved one's death, but when I showed up, they broke down. Mothers would cling to me when I said goodbye and beg me not to leave. Fathers would shake my hand and hold on for way too long.

"Did Clay tell you anything about his family?" I asked. "I know he worked in Nevada before coming to Oregon, but I don't know if that was his home."

"I wouldn't know either. We only talked about wild horses."

"His family needs to be notified."

"The only thing I know is he was conducting a study for a management plan, but whatever the BLM does, it won't be enough. Not as long as the law allows people like the Fannings to kill horses."

I put the water glass down. "Are you sure there's no one I can call? A priest? A neighbor?"

A tricolored cat slipped into the room and jumped on Lily's lap. She began patting it. The cat purred.

"I'm fine," Lily said. "I mean, I'm sad about Clay, but I'll be okay."

"If you change your mind, call me." I placed my card next to the empty glass. "If you need anything at all, okay?"

"The only thing I need is help saving the wild horses. I can't do it all myself."

She picked up the purring cat and hugged it to her chest.

14

Dusk had come and gone as I pulled away from Lily Calla's bungalow. Pudge and I never discussed notifying anybody else, but since Lily didn't seem particularly close to Barkley, I owed it to him to find someone who was and deliver the bad news myself.

I drove west from Burns. The BLM's district office was a couple of miles past the neighboring mill town of Hines. While it was unlikely it would still be open, I had to give it a shot. I was in luck. A light shined from inside the brown building with a green shingled peaked roof. The front door was unlocked. No receptionist was on duty and the front cubicles were unlit. I followed the light to a corner office. A balding man in a short sleeve khaki shirt with epaulettes was sitting behind a desk reading a sheaf of papers. I knocked on the door frame. He looked up with a start.

"We're closed." He eyed my uniform. "Who are you?"

I told him. "I'm here about Clay Barkley, the ranger from the Carson City office."

"If you have a compliment, I'm all ears. If it's a complaint, file it with Carson City." He didn't let go of the stapled papers.

"Clay's dead. He was killed in a robbery, and I'm trying to track down his next of kin."

"Oh my goodness." The BLM man jerked backward and sent his desk chair rolling. "Where did it happen, in a bank or something?"

"No, Clay was at his camp in the Stinkingwater Mountains."

"Wait a minute. What are you doing here and not Burns City Police or Harney County Sheriff's?"

I explained how I discovered the body and was working with Pudge Warbler. "About contacting his family..."

"Sorry, can't help you."

I pointed at the gold desk plate that spelled out his name and title. "You're the district supervisor."

"I am, but Barkley wasn't my direct report. The Carson City office should have that information. If they don't, BLM's main office in Reno will. Neither one is going to be open this time of night, though."

"Then I'll give them a call in the morning."

"No you won't. I will. That's protocol. Have to stick to it. Barkley's supervisor will want to make the notification himself. Killed as in murdered, you say? And robbed? Was he shot?"

"It looks that way, but they won't know for sure until they perform the autopsy."

"What was stolen?"

"Clay's pickup and service weapons. Were you familiar with the work he was doing?"

"Barkley checked in when he got to town, but that was the only time I saw him. Some of my rangers shared information with him. Plenty of mustang herds roam this district. I can't say I envied his job any. When it comes to wild horses, BLM gets criticized for doing too little or doing too much. For every person who wants us to leave the mustangs alone, there's someone else who'd just as soon we round them up and sell them to dog food companies."

"Where do you stand?"

"Me? I'm of the mind that BLM has been in the business of managing public lands for more than one hundred fifty years, so adding a few wild horses to the honey do list is no big deal."

"I'd appreciate it if you gave me a call after Clay's family has been told. I'd like to express my condolences."

He read my card. "No Mountain, that's where the Fish and Wildlife local office is now? It used to be in Burns."

"I spend most of my time in the field. It's more central to the refuges."

"You know, there's a shortcut you can take from here if you're heading home. It'll spare you from having to backtrack to Burns." He told me how to find it. "It's a gravel road, but it's in fair shape considering the hard winter we had."

I told him thanks and got on my way. I was glad for the shortcut. It would save time getting to the Warbler ranch. If Pudge had succeeded in learning anything from November about the location of Loud Will's path to manhood ceremony, he'd be planning a raid and I didn't want to miss out.

The road cut across a valley that was mostly desert scrub and alfalfa fields. Shallow lakes that would turn dry by summer were ringed with wildflowers whose petals were already closed for the night. The lights from distant ranch houses twinkled on the horizon. I passed the turnoffs to a dozen dirt roads. None had signposts or mailboxes. I braked when my headlights shined on something other than gravel. It was a bridge that had been made by placing the bed of a freight train flatcar over a gully. I guessed it had come from the abandoned railroad the same as my lineman's shack.

The ersatz bridge was a little wider than my pickup. It had

no guardrails either. I crossed over slowly. A creek burbled in the darkness below. My tires drumming on the bridge spooked swallows living on the underside. They swarmed out of their mud nests, chittering their annoyance. Once I reached the other side, the road straightened.

Antsy to get to Pudge's before he grew antsy himself, I sped up. As soon as I did, something darted into the road. I slammed on the brakes. It was too late. Whomp! The bumper struck and sent it flying into the ditch on the opposite side. I fishtailed to a stop, turned on the side mounted spot light, and began searching for whatever I hit, hoping it wasn't a wild foal like the one in Gemma's stable.

I swept the light back and forth, up and down, and then zigzagged the beam. There! I reversed and trained the light. It was no mustang foal. No coyote or deer either. A man was squirming toward a thicket of brittlebush by pulling himself by his elbows, dragging his lifeless legs behind. I jumped out and scrambled down the ditch and up the other side. His feet were still in the spotlight's beam. I stepped on his heel and cocked the hammer of my .357 so he'd hear it.

"You're done running, Donny Gray," I said to the slight young man with a mop of blond hair.

"Thank God," he groaned before hacking a gout of blood and losing consciousness.

GEMMA ANSWERED the police radio at the Warbler ranch. "You missed dinner," she said. "November and Nagah whipped up a feast. Pudge and Blackpowder are so full they can't push away from the table."

"I need to speak to your father right away. I found one of the fugitives."

"Loud Will?" she said.

"The young one. Get Pudge."

She shouted for him. The sound of his bootheels clomping down the hall came across the radio.

"It's Nick," Gemma told her father. "He caught one."

"What the Sam Hill?" the old lawman thundered. The radio clicked and hummed as the microphone exchanged hands. "Who is it?"

"Donny Gray."

"Where?"

"I'm on a gravel road between the BLM office and No Mountain, just past a bridge made out of a flatcar."

"I know the place. That bridge is over Sage Hen Creek. How did you catch him?"

"He ran in front of me and I hit him. He's barely alive. It looks like he has internal bleeding, maybe a collapsed lung. One of his legs is broken. Maybe both."

"Oh Lord." Pudge sucked in air.

"He also has a bullet wound in the back of his shoulder."

"Running him over wasn't enough, you had to shoot him too?"

"He was already shot."

"By who?"

"I don't know. He stopped talking. It's all he can do to breathe."

"Any sign of the other two?"

"Not yet."

"They could be on you any second. Watch yourself."

"I am."

I had moved Donny in a fireman's carry and placed him in the front seat. I was standing beside my pickup with the lights off and using the open front door as a shield again. I had the radio mike in one hand and my Smith & Wesson in the other.

The Winchester already had a round levered into the chamber.

"Is it safe to stay put til I get there?"

"Not for Donny. He won't last long without a doctor. It's why I put him in my rig. An ambulance will take too long to get here."

"Okay, get him to the hospital pronto, but don't kill him doing it. We need him alive. He can tell us who did what, where they're hiding, and where they might go next. I'll alert Bust'em you're on your way."

"You know if you do that, the first thing he'll do is call a press conference."

"Nothing I can do to stop him. It might even work in our favor."

"How so?"

"Flush the other two."

"Are you coming to Burns?"

"Nope. Best to start tracking them now while the trail's still fresh."

"It's dark out here. The moon's not up."

"I'll bring a flashlight."

"I'll drop Donny off at the ER and meet you back here."

"Uh-uh. Stay at the hospital and stand guard until Bust'em or one of the other deputies get there. It might take a while. They're scattered all over the county looking for the jailbirds."

"Donny is in no shape to run. He won't leave the hospital."

"Probably not, but maybe he already tried to make a run for it and that's why he got a bullet in the back. His fellow outlaws didn't want him getting caught or turning himself in and spilling the beans. If they see you carting him away, they'll want to finish him off. The hospital will be the first place they look if they don't get you before you reach it."

"And Sheriff Burton telling the press that's where he's at will all but guarantee it," I said. "You're baiting a trap."

"Insurance in case I don't catch them tonight."

"You can't take Banks and Loud on your own, Pudge. They're armed and dangerous."

"So am I, son. So am I."

15

Donny Gray stopped breathing five minutes after I turned my pickup around. He'd been wheezing, gasping, and sputtering before then. I flicked on the dome light. His face was blue. I stopped in the middle of the gravel road, unbuckled his seatbelt, grabbed the front of his shirt, and pulled him toward me, wrenching him around so he'd be on his back. I tilted his head, pinched his nose, and gave him a few breaths. Blowing air into a paper bag with no bottom had the same effect.

On the first day leading a patrol, my squad came under heavy fire. A private took a round in the chest. His struggle to breathe made a sucking sound that was louder than trying to wrench a combat boot out of deep, sticky mud. Donny Gray was making that same sound. I didn't miss being in Vietnam, but I sure wished I had the squad's corpsman with me now. When that private got hit, the medic pushed me out of the way as I started mouth-to-mouth.

"Won't do no good, Sarge," he said. "His lung's collapsed. I got to do a thoracotomy to pump it back up."

The corpsman was nineteen years old and had a peach-fuzz

moustache and a pack of Winstons strapped around his helmet with a gray elastic band that he sometimes used as a tourniquet. He grabbed a scalpel from his kit and gripped it between his teeth as he ripped the private's shirt open and splashed his chest with water from a canteen. Mumbling around the scalpel, he kept count as his fingers moved down the wounded man's ribcage like a pianist going from *A* to *D* on the ivories.

He stopped when he reached *D*, took the scalpel from between his teeth, and made an incision between the fourth and fifth rib. He spread apart the flesh and bones with his fingers and inserted a plastic tube into the incision. The trapped air inside the private's chest hissed like a snake as it escaped.

"Can I help?" I asked him as he held the tube in place.

"Maybe lay down some cover fire while I bandage him up, Sarge. Charlie's getting awful close."

I didn't have a medic with ice in his veins or a scalpel, but I did have a pocketknife. I pulled up Donny's shirt and ran my palms down his chest. The broken ends of three ribs on his left side bobbed beneath his skin as if they were the tips of low branches on a tree growing alongside a river swollen with snowmelt. I figured his left lung was the one that had collapsed. I glanced up at the driver's side visor. I kept my ticket book for writing up violators wedged there. A thick rubber band held a ballpoint pen against its leather cover.

I went over what I was about to do. Take the ballpoint and twist it open and shake out the ink cartridge. Take my pocketknife, stab Donny Gray in the left side of his chest without hitting his heart, and then jam the hollow half of the ballpoint pen into the hole and let out the air.

Pudge's voice echoed in my ears as I reached for the visor. "Oh Lord, I told you not to kill him."

As I grabbed the pen, Donny Gray coughed and sputtered. He sucked in air and blew it out. He did it a couple of more times. His breathing grew less noisy. His chest rose and fell like bellows. His eyes fluttered open.

"Wha, wha, where am I?"

"Back among the living."

Slumping against the door with the seat belt buckled around him must have prevented Donny's damaged lung from inflating. Laying him flat on his back had saved him from suffocating and spared me from possibly killing him.

I switched off the dome light, knowing it made us sitting ducks should Banks and Loud Will be hunting for us. I shifted into first and started rolling again with the young fugitive's head snuggled against the empty gun holster on my hip. I'd already slipped my revolver into my waistband on the left side for a quick cross draw if need be.

"Are, are, are you a cop?" Donny stuttered between wheezes.

"I'm the man taking you to the hospital."

"You, you, you hit me."

"You ran in front of me."

"I di-di-didn't see you. Ha-ha-had my head down to keep from getting shot again."

"Who shot you?"

"George. He's cra-cra-crazy."

Donny sucked in air and it whistled coming out. He coughed and blood bubbled between his lips.

"Don't talk," I said. "Save your breath."

"I di-di-didn't kill anybody. George did. I di-di-didn't plan the escape. George did."

"Save it."

"George, he-he-he—"

"I get it. He's crazy."

"He-he-he did things to me." Donny struggled for air again. "I ran away last night. He cha-cha-chased me. I hid during the day."

Something flashed in the rearview mirror. It wasn't lightning. Another vehicle was on the road. I increased speed and did some math, calculating how soon we'd reach the blacktop by the BLM office.

"I want to go back to prison," Donny gasped. "It's sa-sa-safer. I never want to see George again."

I kept one eye on the mirror. The vehicle was closing the gap. I'd never been one for retreating. I'd been trained that to turn your back on the enemy only gave them a bigger target. Now instead of going through the steps to treat a collapsed lung, I plotted moves on how to confront the driver. I'd floor it to increase the distance, slam on the brakes, and swing broadside to block the road. I'd hop out and fire a few warning shots. If that didn't scare the driver into turning around, I'd run into the desert so I could shoot from the side without their headlights in my eyes. We'd see who the sitting duck was then.

Pudge's voice echoed again about keeping Donny alive so he could tell them who did what. I believed the young fugitive when he said he hadn't killed anyone. I also believed him when he said Banks had initiated the escape. By keeping Donny alive, I'd be able to learn how Clay Barkley died. I needed that information for when I paid the hard, sad visit to the BLM ranger's next of kin.

I stepped on the gas and pushed the Ford even faster.

The vehicle behind kept pace and then some. The headlights grew closer. I could tell by their height it was a pickup, but I couldn't make out the make or color to know if it was Barkley's. The road washboarded. Donny Gray's head jostled. His body started to bounce off the seat. He moaned and wheezed and sputtered. I was killing him as surely as if I had plunged my pocketknife into his heart.

I let off the gas, picked my spot, turned off the headlights, and steered off the road. The pickup bucked when it hit the desert floor. I held on to the steering wheel with one hand and pinned Donny to the seat with the other as we tore through sagebrush and bumped over ground squirrel burrows.

He screamed and then grew silent. I couldn't hear him breathing any longer because my adrenaline had kicked in and the beat of my heart was pounding in my ears. We came to a stop. I hopped out. My pulse slowed. My hands grew steady as I sighted the Winchester on the oncoming pickup. Brake lights flashed as it neared where we'd left the gravel road. The headlights switched off. The idling engine clicked and hummed. I still couldn't see the color of the paint.

The dome light didn't turn on. Maybe it was broken. Maybe nobody opened the door and got out. I counted to ten. The engine continued to idle. I had no proof it was the stolen BLM rig. Pouring rounds into the cab could result in the death of an innocent rancher on his way to Burns. I counted to ten again. Still no dome light came on. Still no door opened and shut. Maybe Banks and Loud had already rolled down their windows and slithered out. Maybe they were snaking through the desert to catch me in a crossfire.

I raised the .30-30's barrel a couple of inches and pulled the trigger. Once, twice, three times I levered and fired. The pickup's engine roared to life and metal on metal whined as the transmission engaged prematurely. The vehicle backed up at high speed and then whipped around.

I watched until the red eyes of the retreating pickup's taillights were swallowed by darkness.

16

The ER's ambulance bay was empty when I slammed to a stop. An orderly was smoking a cigarette near the swinging entrance doors. "Where's the fire, buddy?"

"I got a guy who's badly injured," I shouted from behind the wheel. "He's barely breathing."

He flicked the cigarette and hollered, "Got us a Code Blue out here."

By the time he reached me, the doors to the ER had swung open and a gurney came wheeling out, steered by another uniformed orderly with a redheaded nurse trotting right alongside.

"Get out," she barked at me.

I did. She leaned into the cab and began palpating Donny with both hands. "Pneumothorax. Dyspnea. GSW upper quadrant," she called out. "Multiple fractures to the lower extremities. Patient is V-fib. Move people. Move."

She stood to the side as the two orderlies slid Donny onto the gurney. They started wheeling him.

"It's not a cakewalk, people," the nurse urged as she cradled Donny's head to prevent it from lolling from side to side.

The orderlies picked up the pace and used the gurney as a battering ram to bang open the swinging doors. A blur of white uniforms disappeared inside. I grabbed my 12-gauge pump from the gun rack in case of a close-in attack from Banks and Loud Will before following. I had gotten Donny Gray this far and I wasn't about to lose him now.

Another nurse who was working at the intake desk put her hand up like a crossing guard as I strode into the ER. "Whoa, big fella. Where do you think you're going armed to the teeth?"

"That man's my prisoner. Where he goes, I go."

She kept her eyes on the shotgun and didn't bother to study my badge. "They're taking him straight to the OR, deputy. You can't go in there."

"Then I'll stand outside the door."

"He could be in there for hours."

I brushed past her and quick marched down the hall. The linoleum floor gleamed from a recent buffing, but the stench of vomit and worse overpowered the scent of wax. I passed curtained cubicles. Moans came from one. Sobs from another.

The redheaded nurse was talking with a man in surgical scrubs. She shot me an annoyed look. "You can't be here. You have to stay in the waiting room."

"He's my prisoner." I turned to the man in scrubs. He was soap opera handsome. "Are you the surgeon?"

"Dr. Goldman," he said. "What do you mean your prisoner?"

"He's one of the escaped cons. Sheriff Burton and his deputies are on their way. I need to stand guard until they get here."

"There's no need. This man isn't going anywhere. He'll be lucky if he's walking in two months. The only thing he's lucky about is the bullet lodged in his upper trapezius and didn't fracture his scapula on the way out. Is it yours?"

"Someone else's. You already X-rayed him?"

"I don't need to. I've seen plenty of GSWs."

"Here or in-country?"

The surgeon looked at me more closely. "Two tours at a MASH. And you?"

"Three years forward operating. First Cavalry scouts, but I did spend some time in a MASH courtesy of the home team." I refrained from patting the scar on my thigh.

"Glad one of my colleagues could be of service. Now, if you don't mind?"

"Is that the operating room?"

"It is."

"Then I'll be right out here."

"If that's your job." Dr. Goldman turned back to the nurse with red hair. "And to think I only had thirty minutes to go before my thirty-six hours was up."

"Oh, Golden Boy, what would we do without you?" she said.

The surgeon puffed his chest, her sarcasm lost on him. "Pine and cry, I imagine."

AN HOUR WENT by and still no sheriff or deputy arrived. Neither did George Roscoe Banks and Loud Will. I had radioed Pudge shortly after I'd fired shots at the pickup to warn him it was now barreling his way, but he never radioed back to tell me if he intercepted it. He didn't try to reach me at the hospital either.

Despite her no-nonsense demeanor, the nurse brought me a chair. "Don't fall asleep and trip somebody," she said.

I had the hall to myself until a woman stepped out from one of the curtained cubicles. Her wavy hair was gray and styled in a permanent. She wore a flower print blouse and glass beaded bracelets with Paiute designs encircled both wrists.

"I recognize you," she said. "You are the one they call the bird man."

"I haven't heard that one, but I've been called worse. I'm sorry, I don't recall meeting you."

"I am Wyanet Lulu."

"Beautiful Rabbit," I said.

"You speak *numu*?"

"Some."

"You are a friend of Sheriff Warbler and his daughter, the horse doctor. Girl Born in Snow must have taught you *numu*."

"She did. You know her?"

"Of course. We *Wadadökadö* are fewer than three hundred now." The name of her band in English was the Wada Root and Grass-Seed Eaters.

"Are you visiting someone or do you work here?" I asked.

"I am here with my husband. He has the cancer. He will soon pass into the spirit world. Maybe tonight."

"I'm sorry," I said automatically.

"Don't be. His pain will be over and my suffering from worrying about him also." She paused. "I worry about Girl Born in Snow also. She is not well."

"Gemma has tried to talk her into coming here for treatment, but..."

"She will never. It is not her way." Wyanet Lulu pointed at the door to the operating room. "You look after the first people, the *nuwuddu*, not the second people. How come you are here and not the sheriff?"

"He's down two deputies and needed some help. As soon as one gets here, I'll leave."

"And the man they are trying to heal in there, I heard you tell the doctor he escaped from prison."

"He did."

"Is it Louder Than Wolf Will?"

"No."

"I do not know how I feel about that, if that is a good thing or a bad thing for him," she said.

"How is that?"

"If it was him in there, then he is done running. If it is not, then he is still running and it will end badly for him."

"Let's hope it doesn't come to that."

"Louder Than Wolf has always been unlucky. The trickster greeted him the moment he came into this world. Tuhudda could do nothing to stop it, and he blames himself. His wife did also. She was my friend. She, Girl Born in Snow, and I were dancers. Have you met him?"

I shook my head. "I've only heard about him."

"He is not easy to get to know because he does not let people get too close. I think it is because he is afraid he will bite them. The picture they ran in the paper is not the way he once was. He and my son are of the same age. When they were children, they were playmates. One summer they found a big box and it became their favorite toy."

"What kind of box?"

"It once held a washing machine. They found it behind Beverly Sweetgrass's trailer house when she replaced her clothes wringer. That Beverly, she was always showing off. The boys carried it to my house like it was made of glass." Her eyes lit up. "That summer, my son and Louder Than Wolf played in it every day. They loved that box. No toy in a toy store was as good. It was an airplane, a rocket ship, a pirate boat."

"Whatever they imagined it to be," I said, remembering a couple of planks my old man nailed across the limbs of a tree.

"This is true. It was a new game every day. Ah, how they loved that box, but then the winter rain came early and the box was left outside and was ruined." Wyanet Lulu looked down at her feet. "My son was sad, but Louder Than Wolf could not be consoled. He howled in anger and sadness for days. Poor Tuhudda and his wife. I told them all they needed to do was get another box, and they did. But it was not the same."

"Does your son live here?"

"No, he has a good job in Nyssa. He works at a tire store. Have you been there?"

"To his store? No."

"I mean the town. It is on the Snake River."

It felt like weeks, not days, since I'd patrolled the riverine islands at the Deer Flat Refuge. "I have. Your son lives in a beautiful part of the country. The Snake River provides the blood of life for this part of the world."

"You speak with the heart of a *numu*. I can see why Girl Born in Snow likes you."

"I wouldn't go so far as to say that about her."

"The piñon pine has the toughest cone because the seed inside is sweet and tender."

"I'll remember that next times she upbraids me."

The slightest of smiles brushed the old woman's lips.

"Is your son coming here to be with you and your husband?" I asked.

"Yes. He is on his way. Even though he lives in Nyssa, this is still home. It is where he grew up and became a man."

I tried to maintain a poker face. "Did he take part in the path ceremony with Loud Will?"

"Yes, they are the same age."

"Down by Sage Hen Creek," I said casually.

"No, that is a woman's place. They took the path at Little Battle Gulch below Lookout Ridge. It was a good day. During the ceremony wild horses came to watch. That is always a good sign. Horses saved the *numu* from our enemies long ago. Maybe they will again one day."

"Maybe I'll be able to meet your son if he arrives before I leave."

"Maybe," she said. And then Beautiful Rabbit ducked back into the curtained cubicle to be with her husband as he prepared to journey to the spirit world.

17

The deputy who came to relieve me was one of the pair who took the high ground at Clay Barkley's camp. He pointed at the operating room. "How much longer?"

"It's anybody's guess." I said. "Has anyone heard from Pudge?"

"Not for the past couple of hours or so. He's radio silent. The last time I talked to him was at the murder scene. He asked me to go to the Will camp and tell the state troopers they were wasting their time."

"Did they listen?"

"The boys in pressed blue?" He rolled his eyes. "They wear chin straps to keep their hats on even when they're driving. Okay if I sit in the chair you've been warming? I've been on duty since sunup yesterday."

"Help yourself."

"Have you tried the cafeteria?"

"You don't want to leave your post. Banks and Loud Will could still show."

"Maybe I can sweet-talk that red-haired nurse into bringing me some Jell-O."

I didn't warn him how that would go over.

My route out of the hospital took me through the ER's waiting room. The only people in it were Sheriff Burton, a man with two cameras dangling from straps around his neck, and a tall middle-aged woman dressed in a stylish gray suit who I recognized as Bonnie LaRue. The editor and publisher of the *Burns Herald* was peppering the sheriff with questions.

Burton didn't have a five-o'clock shadow even though it was close to midnight. He'd taken the time to shave before coming to the hospital. His camera-ready appearance told me he'd called the newspaper people to meet him there. When he spotted me, he signaled no acknowledgment, but the momentary shift in his gaze didn't get past Bonnie LaRue's sharp eyes.

"Why, if it isn't the elusive Nick Drake," she said. "Don't tell me you being here is a coincidence?"

"Evening," I said without breaking stride.

Her high heels tapping across the freshly waxed linoleum were as relentless as a telegraph operator's fingertips. The photographer scurried behind her and nearly tripped over a chair as he screwed a 35mm camera to his eye.

"Don't try and dodge me again," she said. "I haven't forgotten last time."

"Neither have I."

Her smile was wry. "Whatever you may think of me, it's my job to keep the public informed. The sheriff told me a BLM ranger was murdered and now one of the convicts has been captured and requires surgery. He didn't say anything about who did the capturing. It was you, wasn't it?"

The photographer began snapping pictures with a flash. I threw up my hand to shield my eyes. The bright, strobing light was too much like the bursts from the white phosphorous grenades I'd lobbed into Viet Cong tunnels.

Bonnie LaRue continued to press. "An orderly told me the

fugitive's injuries were the result of being shot and run over. Did you shoot him with your handgun or your rifle?"

"Nice try," I said.

"But you did bring him here. I saw a Fish and Wildlife Service pickup in the ambulance bay. Why did you shoot and run him over? Was it the only way to stop him or was it retribution for him killing a fellow ranger." She mimed fanning herself. "My, this is turning into a big news day."

"Don't answer that," Sheriff Burton said. "Come on, Bonnie, you know our agreement. I'm the only one who speaks for the department."

"But Nick isn't with your department. I'm sure his supervisors will be proud of the role he played in apprehending a dangerous fugitive." She turned back to me. "It's Loud Will in there, isn't it?"

"Don't answer that," Burton warned again.

She stepped so close her perfume overwhelmed the sickly smell of the hospital. "What did he tell you? Did he confess to shooting Ranger Barkley? Did he tell you where the other two are?"

"Loud Will didn't say a word to me," I said.

"I don't believe you, but I'll find out one way or the other. I notice Pudge Warbler isn't here. That can only mean one thing. He's busy chasing the other two. I'm right, aren't I?" I didn't answer. "I'll take that for a *yes*." An eyebrow arched. "That wily old lawman, he'll talk to me, you'll see."

"Don't count on it."

"And don't you underestimate me," she huffed. Her expression quickly switched to a wink and a smile as if sharing a confidence. "You know, I've always regretted Pudge and my romance didn't fully blossom. I was willing to put an end to my widowhood, but Pudge? Well, he couldn't do the same even though his wife has been gone for years. And they say women are the weaker sex when it comes to matters of the heart."

"Good night, Mrs. LaRue," I said and stepped around her.

She countered as if we were dancing a waltz. "I heard you became friendly with Tuhudda Will and his grandson last fall. How are they taking it, Tuhudda knowing his son is killing people again, and the boy learning more about his father's criminality?"

"Leave them out of this."

A look of triumph crossed her face. "Now why is that? The public has a right to know."

"Not about innocent bystanders, they don't."

"Innocent? I'd hardly call Tuhudda innocent. My sources at the Oregon State Police tell me his camp is empty. No one knows where he and his grandson are." She glanced at Burton. "Aiding and abetting, isn't that what the charge against Tuhudda will be, Sheriff?"

"You don't even think about who gets hurt when you jump to conclusions," I said.

She tilted her head against the tip of her index finger. "Now let's see, you're here, but Pudge isn't. Hm. Where could Tuhudda and Nagah possibly be and who's looking after them? Is it November? Or maybe it's Gemma."

"It's not Loud Will in there," I said. "It's Donny Gray. He told me he was running away from George Roscoe Banks and Banks shot him. He said Banks killed the driver and guard."

Another look of triumph flashed. "I'm going to quote you on that, Nick Drake."

"But I was just about to tell you all that, Bonnie," Burton sputtered. "I was."

I quick marched to the swinging doors that lead to the ambulance bay. The last thing I heard as the doors swished shut was the newspaperwoman warning the sheriff that he'd better speak up a lot faster if he wanted her help winning the next election.

∼

PUDGE DIDN'T ANSWER when I tried radioing him. I didn't try twice in case he was within earshot of Banks and Loud Will. I pulled out a stack of folded topographical maps from the glove box and thumbed through them, searching their titles for Little Battle Gulch or Lookout Ridge. Neither name showed up. Either the places were located in a quadrant with a more recognizable landmark for the map's title or Wyanet Lulu had called them by a local name and not one formally recognized by the US Geological Survey.

I slapped the steering wheel. Clay Barkley's killer was out there driving around in the murdered man's stolen rig, I was sure of it. I wanted to find him and I wanted to make him pay. The engine revved when I turned the key and the tires left scratch as I popped the clutch and sped off. I blew through stoplights while racing toward Hines and the gravel shortcut. This time if I got chased, I'd turn around so my headlights were shining in their eyes. I'd start by shooting out their tires and work my way up to the top of the cab without blinking.

I cooled off by the time I reached the flatcar bridge. The only signs of life were the easily startled swallows nesting beneath it. I reached the spot where I'd hit Donny Gray and parked on the shoulder. I got out and looked for where he'd darted into the road. My flashlight picked up a couple of footprints. I swept the desert floor in the direction they came from. A faint deer trail appeared in the beam.

Donny hadn't bothered to hide his tracks. I followed them to a dry wash where the trail forked in many directions. I stayed straight and picked up his footprints again. After a quarter mile

I came across a jumble of boulders. A gap between the two biggest rocks looked like a good place to lay low during the day. I examined the walls and found a blood smear shoulder high. The young fugitive had been hiding there. When it grew dark, he resumed his dash to the safety of four walls of a prison cell.

I followed the deer trail to the other side of the boulders and picked up his sign again, but the tracks disappeared in a rocky field that covered an acre or more. It would take hours to search it in the dark. Even if I did find Donny's trail, there was little chance it would lead me to the other men. Once he'd gotten away, they were sure to have abandoned wherever they'd been hiding.

I turned around and followed my own tracks back. I stopped a football field length away from the road. A pickup with its lights off and front bumper nosed against mine was silhouetted in the light of the half-moon. Good, I thought, they're back.

I started walking heel to toe, keeping my knees bent, my center of gravity balanced, and rolling on the balls of my feet. Walking without making a sound, even in a barren desert, wasn't easy. Sand crunched. Rocks rattled. Sagebrush whispered. I kept my eyes forward and not on the ground. It was a key to walking silently. It also allowed me to look for Banks and Loud should they be lying in wait in the darkness. I hoped they were. I led with my rifle, occasionally taking a moment to use the scope to sight on the pickup silhouetted on the gravel road, willing myself to see a BLM sticker on its door.

When I was thirty yards out, my shoulders sagged. The outline of the bar of emergency lights on the cab became visible. So did the short-brimmed Stetson perched on the head of the driver.

"I figured on you coming back here," Pudge said as I drew close. The old deputy had the driver side window down and his .45 resting on the top of the dashboard.

"I take it you didn't run into Banks and Loud tearing along in Clay's rig."

"Nope, but I did run into another no count. Your friend Sonny Stiles. He was heading straight at me, but I didn't know who it was, so I hit the high beams and siren and kept on keeping on. I figured we'd see who cried chicken first."

"He's still playing bounty hunter."

"Yep, but I doubt he will any longer. According to him, he caught sight of the fugitives and chased after them. They drove off the road and then started shooting at him. He said he would've kept chasing after them but his rig's four wheel drive wouldn't engage." Pudge scoffed. "It was you, not them, right?"

I nodded. "As much as I dislike the little horse killer, I'm glad I aimed high."

"Me too," Pudge said. "Horse killing ain't illegal, but killing a man is, even if you mistook him for a murdering escaped con. I wouldn't want to be the one to arrest you. No telling what Gemma would do to me."

Pudge and I hadn't spoken much about Gemma and me. After our first night together, I sought the old lawman out the next day and told him I'd grown fond of his daughter. He put an end to the conversation right then and there by saying, "Gemma's a grown woman and her business is her business, but I do appreciate you telling me straight to my face. Of course, I expect nothing less in a man."

"What are you going to do about Sonny?" I asked.

"I'll drive out to the Seven Fans when I have a spare moment and tell Lester and Darlene about the facts of life. Maybe they'll send Sonny to his room without any supper."

"I don't suppose you spotted Tuhudda Will?"

"Nope. I didn't see hide nor hair of the old brave even though I must've driven every dirt road connecting to this one. Some of them looked to be left by wagon trains that took a wrong turn off the Oregon Trail."

"Did you speak to Burton?"

"I did a little bit ago. He filled me in. Bust'em's none too happy about you and Bonnie LaRue chatting it up."

"I had to tell her about Donny Gray because she threatened to use Tuhudda and Nagah as leverage to get her story."

"She did, did she? Well, that woman's pretty darn good at her job. Doesn't always make people like her, but it does make them take her serious. It's how she's been able to keep a hold on that paper after her husband died. Lot of people thought a woman couldn't run it and tried to buy her out for pennies on the dollars. Bonnie's proved them wrong time and time again."

"She called you 'wily,' by the way."

"Well, she is in the truth business."

"I followed Donny's trail from here," I said. "He was holed up in some rocks. He told me it was Banks who shot him. He's the reason Donny ran away. He says Banks initiated the escape and did all the killing."

"That include Barkley?"

"Donny passed out before I had a chance to ask him. I told Lily Calla about Clay. She said they weren't anything more than fellow wild horse fans."

"Do you believe her?"

"I don't have a reason not to."

"Donny wasn't able to tell you where they've been hiding?"

"I doubt he knows. He started running the first chance he got. He didn't pick a direction, he only ran. It was lucky he chose the trail he did. He could've as easily run into a part of the desert without a water hole for a hundred miles."

Pudge rubbed his jaw. "I've been cogitating on why a man like Banks is still running with Loud Will. Loud's got a reason to come to Harney County, but Banks? He's not from here. He's got no allegiance to Loud. They weren't cellies in the pen. Heck, Loud spent most of his time in the hole."

"I thought about it too," I said. "From what I read in Banks's rap sheet, he was born and raised in Portland. Never left the city. The same is true with Donny Gray. Maybe Banks was going to leave Loud shackled in the prison van and Loud convinced Banks to take him with him in exchange for being his guide. He told him he knew all the back roads and places they could hide. Banks realized it was his best option for avoiding getting caught."

"That's a scorpion and frog bargain if I ever heard one. Banks will kill Loud once he doesn't need him. Either because he likes killing or because he doesn't want to leave any loose ends."

"Loud has got to be thinking that too. He saw Banks try and stop Donny."

"It's hard to know what a man like Loud thinks. But as long as they're running together, we got two scorpions to deal with. As soon as it's daylight, Gemma and some of the ranchers who agreed to look for rustlers are gonna take to the air and look for the fugitives instead. Though being ten thousand square miles, Harney County is a pretty big place to play hide and seek, even from the air."

"Maybe I can narrow it down. I met a woman at the hospital. She's a Paiute whose son grew up with Loud. She told me they both took the path ceremony together at a place called Little Battle Gulch below Lookout Ridge."

"What's her name?"

"Wyanet Lulu. Her husband is in the ER dying of cancer."

"She have a beauty shop hairdo, pretty for her age?" When I nodded, Pudge said, "I don't know her personally, but I know of her. She, November, and Tuhudda's wife were big time dancers back in the day. They traveled to all the different Paiute communities for weddings and ceremonies, from here to the reservation at Fort McDermitt and all the way down to the one at Pyramid Lake."

"Do you know where Little Battle Gulch is?"

Pudge rubbed his chin. He squinted while he did. "Oregon's filled with names like that. Battleground Buttes, Battle Creek, Battle Ax Mountain, Cape Lookout, Lookout Point, Lookout Mountain. It goes on and on. I'd have to look at a map. Did she say it's in Harney County?"

"She didn't. I'm only assuming it's near the reservation."

"The Paiute have always been big wanderers. It could be anywhere in the entire Great Basin. Those names are probably also an English translation of a place that means something entirely different in *numu*. You speak some now. You know how it is. We say pronghorn, and they use four words to say the same thing. Whether it's a buck pronghorn with a dirty tail or a pregnant pronghorn or a pronghorn that ran up a mountain and leapt across a creek and ran down the other side. Every name has a story and all the words to tell it. When they translate it for us, they dumb it down considerable."

"I'll ask November when I see her. I'm going to your place now. What about you?"

"I'm on my way to the hospital to fill in Bust'em and keep an eye on things."

"Do you still think Banks and Loud might take a run at Donny Gray?"

"I haven't ruled it out, but we won't have to guard him much longer. Bust'em said as soon as the doc who patched him up says it okay, Oregon State troopers will transport him to the prison hospital. The governor wants this mess cleaned up lickety-split. Escaped prisoners are bad PR when he's busy asking taxpayers to foot the bill for building all the new prisons he wants."

The old lawman gave a loud sigh. "The governor's also ordered an army of deputies from surrounding counties and state troopers here. As if I don't got enough to deal with, now I'm gonna have to babysit those fellas."

"We should move Nagah to a new location," I said. "It's not safe keeping him at your ranch any longer. It should be a place Tuhudda doesn't know about so if he and Loud find each other, he won't be able to tell him even if he doesn't mean to."

"I'm one step ahead of you, son. Blackpowder's got a fishing cabin on the Owyhee River."

"The Owyhee? I was just at its confluence with the Snake River when I was patrolling the Deer Flat Refuge islands."

"Blackpowder's cabin is about twenty-five, thirty miles upriver from the mouth. I've gone on a couple of fishing trips there with him. The big browns make the drive worth it. Boy, do they put up a fight."

"When do you plan on moving him?"

"As soon as you can get yourself packed."

"Me?"

"That's right. You're the best person to take him. I don't get paid to babysit. I get paid to catch convicts and stop killers. The sheriff's department is still two cards shy of a full deck. We need your help more than ever."

18

Blackpowder Smith was sitting on the front porch bench with one of November's striped wool blankets draped over his shoulders to ward off the predawn cold. His sawed-off shotgun was cradled on his lap. A four-foot-long rifle was leaning against the wall.

"All quiet on the Western Front?" I said as I walked up the steps.

"You're lucky Pudge radioed ahead to tell me you were coming. I'd've blown a hole clear through your engine block."

I nodded at the long rifle. "With that antique? It looks like a flintlock."

"That there is a Sharps buffalo rifle and fires as good as the day it was made in 1872," he said. "Pudge told me you nailed a convict. One down, two to go. Catch the others and you're going collect a big payday, bounty wise." He paused. "By the way, I'm sorry about your friend. He seemed a straight shooter."

"He was."

The old codger cocked his head at the front door. "They're all tucked in, the boy, Gemma, and November."

"How's November doing?"

"Showing her age, but don't we all when we got more calen-
dars behind us than ahead. I'd get up from this bench to shake
your hand, but if I did, my knees would pop so loud, Gemma
would wake up thinking it was gunshots and come running out
here with her LadySmith blazing. That girl's a pistol, has been
since the day she was born."

"Why don't you turn in? I'll take up watch out here."

"No need. I don't sleep much anymore anyway. If I'm not
getting up every hour to use the john, I'm lying there counting
sheep, and I don't even like the taste of lamb. You go on ahead."

I wasn't tired either. The roller coaster of a day had left me
too keyed up to fall asleep. It wasn't that long ago I'd need a fix to
nod off. "I don't want to wake anybody. I'll go check on the foal."

"She's a cutie. I hope she makes it," Blackpowder said.

The foal was lying in her stall, but no longer had an IV tube
poked into her neck. The bed of straw was thick and fresh and a
saddle blanket covered her from withers to tail. She lifted her
head when I approached, but didn't try to scramble up.

"Good girl," I whispered as I sat beside her. "Go back to
sleep."

She put her head down, but didn't close her eyes. I stroked
her muzzle. It was downy soft. "Everything's going to be okay.
You're going to be all right."

I sat there stroking the foal and started thinking about the
little girl I'd spirited from the burning hooch. They loaded her
into the bay of an EVAC chopper that was full of bloodied GIs.
The engine whined and the blades spun. A door gunner
clutching an M60 secured to the doorway by a bungee cord and
I exchanged seen-it-all, done-it-all looks. The Jolly Green Giant
lurched awkwardly and finally got airborne. No AA chased it as
it cleared the surrounding green hills. By the time it did, I was
already back in the fight, firing my M16 while running.

I never saw the little girl again. I never knew if she made it, whether her burns were treatable, whether they transferred her to the orphanage, whether the Buddhist monks were able to feed and care for her. But there were many nights in-country when I'd picture her smiling, laughing, and playing like a child would in a world without war as a way to try to fall asleep. Sometimes it even worked.

Gemma walked in wearing a sheepskin coat. She sat down, yawned, and put her head on my shoulder.

"The foal looks better," I said.

"She's getting there. How about you? How are you doing?"

"Okay, I guess."

"You guess?"

"What do you want me to say, that I'm pissed off my friend was shot in the back of the head, that I had to suck it up and tell people who knew him he'd been murdered and his killer is still free?" I blew out air.

Gemma winced. "Ouch. I asked for that one, didn't I? I'm sorry."

I took a deep breath and patted her knee. "I'm the one who should be apologizing. It's not your fault. I'm just—"

"Pissed off, I know. You have every right to be."

We sat in silence for a bit. Then, she said, "Was one of them a woman named Lily?"

"Lily Calla, yes. Why?"

"I met her."

"When?"

"The other day. She showed up here asking about the foal." Gemma stroked the baby horse's neck. "She told me she had come straight from Clay Barkley's camp where she met you, that you told her I was taking care of this one."

"That's right, but I told Lily to call you first."

"I didn't mind. In fact, I was glad I was here to show her. It seemed to help her, I think. Help Lily, I mean, not the foal."

"She's a wild horse advocate. Moved out here from Vermont."

"So she said. She's, well, very devoted to them."

"Lily wears her heart on her sleeve about the wild ones, for sure. Clay said it all started when she read a story about mustangs in college."

"I can relate to that. Soon after my mom died, this children's book came out about these two orphans and a pair of wild ponies that live on an island off the coast of Virginia. A mare and her foal. The brother and sister find them and work to get them and then lose them and then get them back only to wind up letting the mare go. I must have read that book a hundred times."

"Is it what made you want to become a horse doctor?"

"I'm sure it had something to do with it, but, looking back on it, I realize the book helped me come to grips with losing my mom. I think maybe Lily is going through something similar."

"What makes you say that?"

"When I brought her into the stall to see the foal, she broke down. At first I thought it was because she was so upset by seeing the foal in such a weakened condition, but then I started to think it wasn't the foal at all, but someone close to her she'd recently lost." Gemma shrugged. "I don't know. It was a feeling I got, is all."

She snuggled closer. The top of her head rubbed against my cheek. "I'm glad you're safe. I was worried about you. Pudge told me you're going to take Nagah to Blackpowder's cabin, but I know you won't rest until you catch Clay's killer."

"Don't worry about me. It's nothing I can't handle."

"But I don't like worrying about people. Not Pudge, not November, and now, not you. I watched cancer eat my mom alive, and after she died, I promised myself I'd never worry about anybody again."

"Worrying, one of those corrals you don't like being put in," I said, remembering her explanation of why she divorced her husband after six months. Her ex didn't want her to leave his ranch to tend to other ranchers' livestock.

"See, that's just it. You're starting to know me too well." Gemma sighed. "That's the trouble with falling for someone, all the complications that go with it. Like, wondering how he's feeling after his friend got killed. What happens if he kills somebody and it turns out to be the wrong somebody? What happens if somebody kills him? Those sort of things."

"Then don't think about the someone so much."

"How am I supposed to do that? You're the someone."

"When I was in basic at Fort Hood, my DI had all these sayings. One was, 'Don't borrow trouble, make some.' "

"Maybe I should've enlisted like you."

"I'm kind of glad you didn't."

"Kind of?" Gemma paused. "You don't worry about me?"

"Sure, I do. Every time I think about you getting in that old airplane that you only learned how to pilot a few months ago, flying off into a storm, and landing on some dirt strip that a cow could easily wander onto just as you're setting down. It wouldn't end well for you or the cow."

Gemma elbowed me. "Ah, that's the sweetest thing I've ever heard, mentioned in the same breath as a cow."

The truth was, I was worried about her taking to the air and looking for George Roscoe Banks and Loud Will. Like her dad, Gemma didn't have quit in her. If she spotted them, she would radio in their whereabouts and then stay on them even if they started shooting at her plane. I wouldn't put it past her to land and try to arrest them all on her own.

The foal's breath grew heavy. "Listen, she's dream talking," I said.

"You're trying to change the subject," Gemma said.

"What subject?"

"You know what I'm talking about. The falling for someone subject. Falling deeper and deeper until there's no way out, not that you want there to be one, but it's still falling and you're always going to wonder how do you stop yourself if you have to."

"What happened to taking it slow, keeping it simple, letting what happens happen?" I said.

"I'm still all for it, but we have to face facts. The more time we spend together, the more we see into each other, and the deeper we fall."

"Sounds like what November warned me about. People will see my *puha* and steal it if I shed my antlers, so I'd better not."

"I'm being serious," Gemma said.

"I know you are. Do you want to slow things down?"

She paused. "Maybe we should."

"If that's what you want, then let's slow it down." I pictured the Snake River and the drops of water endlessly flowing past. "We have plenty of time."

We huddled close listening to the foal's breath some more. I didn't take my arm from around Gemma and she didn't take her head off my shoulder.

"Slow is good," she finally said.

"Slow is good," I said.

"But so is fast. You know what I mean? Like the first time. *That* night."

"At the lineman's shack, when I cooked you chili."

"That was the longest meal of my life," she said. "I was waiting for you to make a move. You sure took your sweet time about it."

"What are you talking about? We didn't get close to halfway through finishing dinner."

"We didn't?"

"The next morning, I had to clean up all the plates and food-stuff that got swept off the table."

I could sense her smiling even though I couldn't see it. "That rickety wooden kitchen table of yours. It sure is a lot stronger than it looks," she said.

"It sure is."

I leaned backward onto the fresh bed of straw, pulling Gemma with me. As she slipped out of her sheepskin coat, she whispered, "Let's make it count for two."

19

Blackpowder Smith drew a map to his cabin while we ate breakfast. "It's been in my family a long time, long before they built the dam behind it in '32," he said. "The Owyhee is named for two Kanakas. That's what native Hawaiians called themselves when white folks were still calling Hawaii the Sandwich Islands. They worked for a fur trader. He sent them to explore the river but they never came back."

"I thought it was an American Indian name," I said.

"Nope, it's the old-timey spelling of Hawaii, but it do run through Shoshone and Bannock country. The fur trader believed his people were killed by Bannocks led by a chief named The Horse, but they never found any bodies. The river's had its share of tragedy, that's for sure. The son of Sacajawea, the Shoshone woman who guided Lewis and Clark, died of a chill he caught crossing it. He's in boot hill in Jordan Valley."

"A topo map shows the river originates in Nevada."

"It does, down around Elko. It flows north into Idaho and then winds back and forth through Oregon, picking up forks and creeks before joining the Snake. Cuts a deep canyon doing it. The Grand Canyon of Oregon. The dam made a fifty-mile-long lake. It's the longest in the state."

Blackpowder poured more coffee. "My cabin is a couple miles below the dam. It sits alongside an underground spring-fed creek that runs through a narrow box canyon that's got two formations in it you'd swear were gigantic heads with faces and everything." He chuckled. "Maybe that's what happened to the Kanakas. Some evil spirt turned them into stone, though the Paiute have a different interpretation."

Nagah came in from the kitchen where he'd been helping November make breakfast. The boy carried a woven basket.

"How ya doing, little fella?" the old codger asked him.

"I am fine, Mr. Blackpowder. Would you like some fry bread?"

"If November made it, you betcha. None beats hers for taste. She teaching you?"

Nagah nodded. "Dr. Gemma already left to go fly her airplane. She told me she will give me a ride someday. She wants to teach me how to take care of livestock. Maybe she will teach me how to fly too."

"You're a brave boy. Now me, if I was meant to fly, I'd've grown wings." The store owner-barkeep flapped his arms and squawked before turning to me. "Who knows, maybe Pudge's air posse will do the trick."

"It's a lot of country to cover," I said.

Blackpowder turned back to Nagah. "You like to fish? Good, because my cabin happens to sit on the best fishing hole on the entire river. These big old brown trout lay in there day and night eating the bugs that come washing down this little feeder creek. When you get there, take one of the rods hanging on the wall and walk down to that hole and cast any bait you want. I guarantee you'll catch a whopper."

Nagah smiled shyly. "I'd like that."

"Well, I gotta shove off. My business won't run itself. You boys have a good time up there and catch lots of fish."

After he left, November came in. "I am ready to leave now."

"Where are you going?" I said.

"I am going with you."

"Pudge didn't say anything about that."

"He does not tell me where I can and cannot go. We should get going. It is a long drive."

"And very rough once we leave the paved highway. Are you sure you're up to it?"

She tsked. "I am Girl Born in Snow. I came into this world during a blizzard. I have walked this land for many years. If you will not drive me, my two feet will carry me."

I gritted my teeth. I knew how stubborn November could be, but this was foolhardy. Her cough had the same sound as rattling one of the cans I filled with a new pebble each morning and each night to mark how long it had been since I'd taken a shot of heroin. The rheum in her eyes had turned a ghastly yellow.

"You don't need to come," I said. "I'll look after Nagah."

"I am going because Shoots While Running calls to me. He told me the answer to what he whispers is there."

"But Blackpowder's cabin is on the Owyhee River, not the Snake." I stopped myself before adding, "where your husband and daughter died when their bus went off the bridge."

The old woman tsked again. "All the rivers in this land are one. Is it not the same sky above them? Does not the rain and snow that feed the rivers come from the same sky?"

I couldn't argue with her there.

November started coughing. When she caught her breath, she said to Nagah, "Come help pack food for the journey. Hurry now, did Tuhudda teach you nothing? When you journey, you always keep your shadow behind you and not in front."

I swallowed the rest of my coffee and then went to Pudge's office to call and let him know about November. The hum of the facsimile machine spitting out paper greeted me. It was a new report from the prison bureau listing George Roscoe Banks's murder victims in Portland.

Gina Pinelli had been widowed for six years. Her husband had fought at the Battle of the Bulge and liberated death camps in Poland. During their marriage he worked the graveyard shift at an Italian bakery and she worked part time as a bookkeeper to help pay the bills. After retiring, she looked after her seven grandchildren and knitted them sweaters and scarves for Christmas. In her spare time, she crocheted baby booties that she donated to the Catholic hospital gift shop. The proceeds helped the maternity ward purchase an incubator for preemies.

Ettie May Jefferson lost her husband of 42 years to a stroke two years prior. They'd been married since high school. She lived off his pension as a bus driver and social security. Her only son had moved his wife and three kids to Chicago for work. Arthritis made it difficult for her to walk. She rarely left the house, and when she did, it was to attend choir practice and services at New Hope Baptist.

Millicent "Millie" Lundgren had won the Miss Multnomah County Beauty Pageant when she was seventeen. Forty years later she could still fit into the gown she'd worn the day she was crowned. She worked as a legal secretary. Millie was the only one of Banks's victims who was still married; her husband was away on business the night she answered a knock on the door. Banks confessed he killed her, not because she was ashamed and begged him to, but because he wanted to torment her husband as the Grin Raper.

I finished reading the report and tossed it on Pudge's desk. Then I went to the bathroom to scrub my hands. It was not to clean the smudges of ink left by handling the fax pages, but to try to wash away the stench of George Roscoe Banks. As I did, I glanced into the mirror and saw the look that I'd seen on Clay Barkley's face as he'd worked himself up to put the wild horses down. The sorrow in my expression was for the women. The savagery was for their killer when I finally got hold of him.

I turned away and knew there was no way I could leave November home alone as long as Banks was loose.

OUR FIRST STOP after leaving the Warbler ranch was the lineman's shack. I hooked the boat trailer up and loaded gear into the bed of the pickup. I was taking a last look around to make sure I hadn't forgotten anything, when the phone rang.

"Where have you been?" my district supervisor bellowed when I answered. "You hung me out to dry and left me flapping in the breeze in front of the new regional director."

The performance review call. It had completely slipped my mind. "I apologize," I said. "There's been a situation down here. The escaped convicts? Well, the local authorities believed they were coming here. The sheriff's department is down two deputies and—"

He cut me off with another bellow. "You're not a deputy. You're a wildlife ranger. You don't work for the sheriff. You work for me."

"They killed a BLM ranger here. I discovered his body."

The sound of the district supervisor gulping came across the telephone line loud and clear. "A fellow ranger, you say?"

"His name was Clay Barkley. He was working on the wild horse study I told you about."

I could see him cringing at his desk. Silence filled the line. After a minute or more, he came back on.

"Look, that's a tragedy, but it doesn't change a thing. You're an employee of the US Fish and Wildlife Service. The agency has to be your top priority. Not wild horses. Not escaped convicts. Not catching murderers. I'll explain what happened to the regional director. He's a by the numbers kind of guy, but maybe, and just maybe, he'll cut you some slack. We'll have to see. In the meantime, I'm going to give you one more chance. You call me tomorrow morning at 10:00 a.m. sharp for the performance review. Maybe the regional director will be on the call, maybe he won't. That doesn't matter. What does is, you make the call. I can't put it any plainer. Keeping your job depends on it."

20

Nagah sat in the middle as we drove east across Harney Valley, over the Stinkingwater Mountains, and crossed into Malheur County. I kept an eye on the rearview mirror even though it was unlikely Banks and Loud Will could be tailing us. It was also a long shot that Sonny Stiles still had an appetite for bounty hunting after I'd shot at him, but I'd learned the hard way never to rule anything out.

November appeared to be asleep as we crossed a sun-kissed landscape of nameless ridges, sandy hollows, and sagebrush covered flats. The boy was silent, but his eyes were wide as he drank in the scenery.

"Have you ever been on this side of the Stinkingwaters?" I asked.

"No, Mr. Nick. Never. The only place I ever went is Catlow Valley when I tend our sheep."

"We're about to see the Snake River. We'll follow it up to the confluence where the Owyhee River flows in from the west and the Boise River flows in from the east."

"That sounds like a lot of water," he said.

"Three mighty rivers joining together is a sight to behold."

Our route took us through the town of Nyssa. November finally opened her eyes as I slowed down.

"I met Wyanet Lulu," I said. "She told me her son lives here."

"Where did you speak with her?" she asked.

"At the hospital in Burns. She was there with her husband."

November nodded. "He had the cancer, but no longer. He passed into the spirit world."

"How do you know that?"

"My husband told me in a dream. Shoots While Running was pleased to welcome his old friend."

I let that thought sit for a moment. "I understand you danced with Wyanet Lulu and Tuhudda's wife at ceremonies."

"For many years, yes."

"She also said her son and Loud Will took part in the path to manhood ceremony together." When the old woman didn't reply, I said, "She said the ceremony was in Little Battle Gulch."

"It is possible. I do not know for I did not have a son and so I did not go to dance for the boys when they started the path."

"But you do know where the place is."

"I already told Pudge my answer."

"Which is?"

"There are as many places in this land as there are rocks and just as many names for them."

I tightened my grip on the steering wheel and bit my tongue. Pushing November to where she didn't want to go was pointless.

A view of the Snake River filled the windshield. Nagah's eyes grew even bigger. "It is so wide."

"It's swollen with spring runoff," I explained. "We'll reach the confluence in a couple of miles."

"Can we stop and put our hands in? Mr. Blackpowder told me if I did that, I would be touching ten thousand creeks and rivers all at once and could drink the melted snow from the tallest mountains."

"The Rocky Mountains," I said. "The Continental Divide."

"I would like to climb to the top of them like Mountain Sheep did. He touched the stars and became one."

November tsked. "That is because he was very brave. Do not forget always to be brave also. You must never run away. You cannot run from shame."

"You already told me that," he said quietly. "I won't."

"We need to go straight to Blackpowder's cabin," I said. "We can come back to the Snake another time."

"I would like that very much," Nagah said.

"I want to go now," November said. "I need to touch the river."

"I'll take you, but not today."

We followed a narrow, winding road up the Owyhee. Like the coils of a gigantic spring, each bend of the river was a mile long and a mile apart from the next. The waters of the sinuous river were brown from all the sediment it carried as it cut a deep course through old lava flows that had been spewed by now extinct volcanoes. The canyon carved by the river was the geological equivalent of a time machine. Each mile exposed a layer of Earth one hundred thousand years older than the next.

The cut formed towering canyon walls of rhyolite as red as bricks. Ospreys perched on ledges surveying the river below. When they spotted a trout, they catapulted themselves and unsheathed their talons. Chunks of basalt had slid down the cliffs and pinched the river in places. The roar of the river's rapids trying to squeeze through them was as noisy as cannon fire. Clumps of sagebrush and shrub willows clung stubbornly along the banks. The sound of water lapping the gravel bars was the same as a washboard being scrubbed.

I counted the side canyons formed by creeks. Blackpowder told me his cabin was near the mouth of the fifth, a narrow box canyon. When we reached it, I turned down a narrow single track. It led to a bench overlooking the river. Standing alone on the bench was a single-story cabin constructed of rough-hewn planks set on a foundation made of river rock. Hand-split shakes shingled the roof. The stovepipe wore a conical metal hat to keep the snow and rain out. The spring-fed creek burbling down the box canyon ran right alongside the cabin.

"We're here," I announced as I pulled to a stop.

"It took long enough," November groused. She opened her door. When her moccasins touched the ground, she started to sway. I thought she would tip over, but she righted herself and tottered to the cabin. The door was unlocked and she disappeared inside.

"Help me unload our gear," I said to Nagah.

The boy was eager to help. He skittered around the pickup and used a rear wheel as a step ladder to reach inside the bed. Despite his slight build, he was strong and able to carry a box of food, a bag holding his clothes, and a Pendleton blanket rolled into a bundle that contained whatever mysteries November had brought.

As Nagah followed the old woman into the cabin, I scouted the terrain for defensive positions and retreat routes. When I'd marked them, I went to the cabin's front door, closed my eyes, and then walked what I'd mentally mapped so I would be able to find them in the dark.

Blackpowder's cabin was larger than my old lineman's shack. A wood stove dominated its main room, but in addition to a bathroom, it had a separate bedroom with twin bunks. November had already claimed one for herself and the other for Nagah.

"You sleep on the porch," she told me when I came in. "And do not close both eyes when you do."

Nagah was examining a pair of fishing rods that hung on the wall. They were bamboo flyrods and their tips were as supple as cat whiskers. A couple of glass spinning rods stood in the corner next to a tackle box.

"Can we go fishing now? I want to catch our supper," he said.

Before I could answer, November said, "It is time for lunch. You can go after you eat."

She had packed sandwiches and Nagah took his outside to eat. I helped myself to one but November wrinkled her nose when I tried to hand her one.

"Have you ever been to the Owyhee River before?" I asked in between bites.

"A long time ago. It was when I first met my husband, before the white man built all the dams on the Columbia and Snake Rivers. Before they built the dam behind us."

"When the salmon could swim freely between the Pacific and Rockies," I said.

She nodded. "When Shoots While Running was a boy, his family fished the great river his people call the *Yampahpa*. They would make basket weirs to trap the fish or stand on rocks and spear them. The banks would be lined with racks strung with the red meat of the salmon being dried or smoked and the Shoshone would have plenty to eat during the winter. My husband wanted to show me that life and so I could eat the fish too, for he told me I would taste the ocean that I have never seen in each bite."

I thought I saw a smile on the old woman's lips as she became lost in reverie, but it was hard to tell for sure because she looked so tired and weak. I finished my sandwich and licked my fingers.

"How far up the Owyhee did you come?"

"A few days walk from where it joins the Snake. We'd walk and fish and make camp."

"Sounds like that would've brought you right around here," I said.

"Perhaps," she said in her vague way.

"Blackpowder told me the canyon where the creek comes out of has interesting rock formations. He said they look like giant human heads, faces and all."

"There are many rocks with faces of our ancestors throughout this land. They are sacred. You will take the boy fishing now. I am tired. I will lie down. When you come back, I will cook the fish he catches."

"What about the fish I catch?"

"We will have to see if you can catch anything. Go now. Take the boy with you."

21

Nagah and I caught several brown trout, but we released all but two to fight another day. November cleaned the pair with a knife with a deer antler handle that looked identical to the one Tuhudda had flashed at his camp. She inserted the tip of the shiny blade into the first trout's anal opening, slit the plump belly up to the tongue, and pulled out the gills and guts in one quick yank, leaving the head on. She ran her thumbnail up the blood line to remove it and gutted the second trout the same way. When she was satisfied both were clean, she rubbed them with herbs she'd gathered from around the river bench and threaded a green willow stick lengthwise through each fish to make spits.

The wood I'd gathered and lit in a ring of river rocks created a bed of coals. The old woman bridged the spits across two of the tallest rocks so the cleaned and seasoned trout were suspended above the embers. Ten minutes later Nagah and I were pulling flaky but moist meat cleanly from the delicate bones and chewing crackly skin that tasted of wood smoke and sage. I was hard pressed to recall a tastier meal, but November wrinkled her nose when Nagah asked if she'd like a bite.

After dinner, the boy went to bed and I sat on the porch drinking a mug of tea and listening to the burble of the creek that came down the side canyon and the thrum of the Owyhee rolling by in front. November came out as the stars showed themselves.

"Louder Than Wolf will soon find us," she said. "He wants his son."

"It's big country out here," I said. "Someone will have had to tell him where we are for that to happen."

"He can find us wherever we are, for he is both *nuwuddu* and *numu*. I have known him since he came into this world and it has always been so. His father and mother refused to believe it and would not allow themselves to be proud of who he was. It would have been better if they had."

"I didn't know someone could be both first people and second people," I said.

"The few who are walk a special path."

"How can someone be both?"

"Who are we to question who or what someone is? It is like a baby who is both boy and girl when born. They are who they are for that is the way they came into this world."

"Nagah told me his father hears voices and can only talk to them by howling. He called them the others."

"Yes, they are always with him. The *nuwuddu* part of him sometimes gets impatient with the *numu* part because that part cannot fly like Eagle or run fast like Pronghorn. Maybe it would be easier if he were one or the other, but he is not."

"If you're right, what will he do when he finds us?"

"He will take his son."

"I already told Tuhudda that isn't safe. Loud has been in prison a long time. It changes a person. If he is also *nuwuddu*, he could be very angry about having been trapped for so long. Have you ever seen what an animal does when it's caught in a snare?"

"Rabbit will struggle and break his neck trying to get away. Fox will chew off his own leg."

"Exactly. But no matter how changed Loud may be, it's the man he's with that's the greater danger. He has a thirst for hurting and killing people that can't be quenched. I can't let him anywhere near Nagah and you."

"I heard Pudge speak of this man."

"Then you know why I will have to stop him even if it means stopping Loud too."

"You mean killing. Maybe for that man, yes, that would be a good thing, but Louder Than Wolf? That will not be easy for you."

"Because he's both *nuwuddu* and *numu*?"

The old woman had been swaying when she spoke. Now she stood straight and her eyes did not blink when she looked at me. "Who is to say that when you finally meet Louder Than Wolf you won't see yourself in him, for maybe you are part *nuwuddu* too?"

The old healer went back inside. I could hear the door to the bedroom open and close and one of the twin bunks creak. I set my mug down and started walking the perimeter of the river bench. I'd gone on many patrols and walked many perimeters at night when I was in-country, and I'd grown accustomed to walking with death at my side. I'd always told myself that it was my training that made me unafraid of the night and able to stay a squeeze of the trigger faster than the enemy. But now as I patrolled the bench overlooking the Owyhee River, I wondered if maybe November was right.

I SPENT the night on the porch, but no one tried to breach the cabin's perimeter. Dawn broke and the squawk of my pickup's radio competed with the call of mourning doves.

"You all settled in as snug as bugs in a rug?" Pudge greeted me.

"I see why you and Blackpowder like coming here to fish," I said.

"Caught some, did you? Those browns are fighters, all right."

"What's the latest?"

"Why I'm calling, knowing the paperboy won't be throwing the *Burns Herald* on your stoop. Donny Gray woke up."

I was relieved to hear the youngest fugitive was alive. "How's he doing?"

"He's gonna have a limp for life."

"Was he able to provide any information?"

"Nothing that you hadn't already told me. He swears it was Banks who killed the guard and van driver. Banks was planning something all along. He was able to get out of his manacles and shackles. Sounds like he had someone on the inside slip him a key, either a bent guard or a jailhouse trustee. The warden will find out who. Donny says Banks strangled the guard, got his gun, and forced the driver to do his bidding. Donny and Loud were only along for the ride."

"Did they turn south at The Dalles and not north for Canada like we figured?"

"Yep. Loud told Banks he could hide him in Harney County and then help him get across the border to Nevada or Idaho when the dust settled. The driver knowing he was a dead man anyway, slammed on the brakes and swallowed the key. A Good Samaritan driving behind them pulled in to see if they needed help, not knowing it was a prison van."

"Talk about your bad luck. What happened to him?"

"Donny says he doesn't know for sure. Banks forced the citizen to climb into the trunk of his sedan and they took off on a maze of county highways and backroads. In the morning when Donny asked if they should let the guy in the trunk out to do his business and have a drink of water, Banks started laughing like a hyena."

"Banks killed him and dumped him during the night."

"That's about the size of it. Grant County Sheriff's is conducting a search now. Could be some time before they find the body since Donny being a city boy didn't know where they were."

"Did Donny talk about what happened at Clay Barkley's camp? Did he tell you Banks pulled the trigger?"

"That there is a big unknown. See, Donny doesn't recollect much of anything after Banks laughed about the citizen not being in the trunk. Donny says he started crying that he didn't want to be on the run any more. Banks responded by whaling on him and, well, made Donny his personal punch, if you catch my drift. The doc says Donny has the equivalent of combat fatigue. Something you know about, right? He's blanking out most of the real bad stuff."

"He doesn't remember being at the Stinkingwater camp?"

"Nope, the only thing Donny knows for sure is he finally got a chance to run, and took it and got shot and hit by a pickup for his troubles. Not only is he begging us to take him back to prison, he wants to be put in solitary confinement for the rest of his twenty year sentence, he's that scared of Banks."

"Before I drove November and Nagah out here, I read the fax the prison bureau sent about the women Banks murdered."

Pudge's sigh was loud and long. "What gets me is Banks did all those rapes and killings, and they were gonna send him off to a hospital to make log cabins out of popsicle sticks for the rest of his days. Now I'm told, if we catch and arrest him, that's still the worst that's gonna happen to him since he's already been branded loco. That sticks in my craw, I'll tell you that."

"Any idea of where Banks and Loud went after Donny ran off?"

"The tip lines have been lighting up again after Bonnie ran the story about Barkley's murder and you catching Donny. The other two cons have been sighted everywhere but in a jail cell. Most of the tips are garbage, but a couple sound good enough to check out, including one about a sighting of two Indians and a white man riding in a pickup with no plates in Idaho. One of the Indians and the white man match the descriptions of our two fugitives. Maybe the second Indian with them was the Shoshone who killed Loud's wife. Maybe Loud finally caught up to him and was driving him to his grave."

"What about Clay's autopsy? Was Doc able to identify the bullet?"

"That there is another big unknown. Doc moved doing it to the back of the line since we know what happened and haven't arrested a suspect yet. He'll get around to it after he finishes up another mess. A family was using a gas generator to power their house and best anyone can figure, it filled the place with carbon monoxide. Two are in the hospital and two more are on Doc's table. Lawyers and insurance adjustors are raising a stink."

"November says Loud is coming here. She says he's half *nuwuddu*."

Pudge sighed again. "That old woman, her and her ways, she's gonna be the death of me yet. I won't tell you to keep an eye out because I know you already are. Gemma and the Cattlemen's Association boys are still doing flyovers, but they haven't seen anything yet. There's lots of balls in the air here, son. Let's me and you make a habit of checking in first thing in the morning every morning, okay? Til then, watch your back."

22

The nearest payphone to Blackpowder's cabin was at a gas station downriver. I told Nagah and November to stay in the pickup where I could keep an eye on them, and then placed a stack of dimes on the top of the phone and dialed my district supervisor. As it rang, I checked my field watch. It was ten hundred on the nose.

"Where are you presently, Ranger Drake?" he answered. His formal tone signaled the new regional director was on the phone too, although he hadn't been introduced.

"I'm alongside the Snake River islands section of Deer Flat National Wildlife Refuge. I can see lots of waterfowl and other migratory birds using the islands, wetlands, and adjacent fields. It's a beautiful sight."

"Very well. Let's proceed with the performance review, shall we?"

He started by lobbing softballs. As I listened and answered, I watched Nagah and November sitting side by side in the front seat. There was more than a half century between their ages. The old woman had been born at the end of the last century, and the boy, if he was lucky, would live to see the next.

November had risen early that morning and cooked breakfast while I was on the radio with Pudge Warbler. Nagah got up and wanted to go fishing right after eating, but I told him he'd have to wait until after I made a phone call. November argued they could stay behind, but I wouldn't hear of it. When I promised they could touch the Snake River if they went with me, I realized she'd been playing me to get what she wanted.

"Your field work is satisfactory, Ranger Drake," my supervisor said, shifting tone, "but you have a serious deficiency when it comes to conforming with agency policies and procedures. Your reports lack detail. You often submit them long after their due date. You rarely answer the office telephone. You didn't attend the mandatory all-staff meeting here in Portland. You remain three months in arrears submitting your petty cash receipts. Last but not least, there is still the matter of using government script to make an unauthorized purchase of a sixteen-foot skiff, outboard motor, and trailer."

His voice had turned graver with each transgression. He gave a dramatic pause. "Ranger Drake, do you have anything to say for yourself?" It was a fair imitation of a judge about to pass sentence.

I watched as Nagah slid over so he was behind the steering wheel. He pretended to drive. I couldn't remember having set the parking brake, but I knew I'd left the pickup in gear. At least, I hoped I had. If he knocked it into neutral and the rig got rolling, he wouldn't be able to reach the brake pedal. It would coast straight out of the gas station, pick up speed as it crossed the road, bounce over the shoulder, and roll down the embankment into the Snake River.

"I don't make excuses for myself," I told my supervisor. "I learned in the army they don't help bring back the dead. All I can say is, I'll try harder. I like this job. I like it a lot."

"Ranger Drake, this is Regional Director F. D. Powers in

Washington DC. As I've listened to the review of your performance, I've been looking through your personnel file. You've only been with the Service about a year." The line got staticky when he spoke. There were lots of clicks.

"That's true, sir."

"Please don't interrupt ," he said curtly. "I see you patrol six refuges across the entire southeastern part of Oregon. That seems to be an extremely large territory for one man alone. I've also read that on more than one occasion, you've abandoned your assigned duties to help the county sheriff's department with their responsibilities."

The clicking kept up. I could hear papers being shuffled too. "I see you have no formal training or educational background in wildlife sciences or land management," Powers continued. "What makes you think you're up to the task, given the fact that the only reason you have this position is because you benefited from a pet program launched by the last administration to provide jobs to combat casualties?"

Nagah had found the horn in the middle of the steering wheel. He started honking it. The beep-beep-beeps matched my growing impatience.

"Sorry, sir, there's some people saying howdy to each other with their horns. Could you repeat the question?"

Regional Director Powers exhaled loudly. The clicks clicked. I realized it wasn't static on the line. He was clicking a ballpoint pen as he spoke. "I've been entrusted by the president of the United States of America to oversee millions of acres of federally protected land and waterways in the West and a budget of a half billion dollars. Why should President Nixon or I trust you to do this job, an individual with a history of drug abuse and six month's confinement in Walter Reed's psychiatric ward? Is that clear enough for you or do I need to spell it out for you?" He rapidly clicked his pen three times.

"I suppose the same reason the last president trusted me to go fight in Vietnam," I said.

"Are you being flip with me?"

"Only stating a fact. I volunteered and the US government trained me, promoted me to sergeant, and paid me. They got three years of combat duty in exchange."

The clicking pen was at a steady gallop. "Are you denying you were a heroin addict and declared mentally unfit to return to service?"

"Not at all, sir. I made mistakes in 'Nam. I cost good men their lives. It's something I live with every day. I got hooked on *H* after I got wounded. I don't make excuses for it and I don't blame anyone but myself. I'm clean now and I intend to stay that way."

"Am I supposed to find that admirable?"

Nagah was still beeping the horn. The ballpoint pen kept clicking. My impatience was turning into something else.

"Honestly, sir, I don't care if you do or not. Now, you can disrespect me all you want, but don't disrespect the people who gave me a second chance. When you disrespect them, you're disrespecting people who've given more to this country than you'll ever give riding a desk and wielding a ballpoint pen. You want to fire me because I spend my time busting poachers instead of filling out paperwork, have at it. But until I get a pink slip, I'll be outdoors doing my job. And speaking of, I'm late for work."

I slammed the payphone down and wrenched open the pickup's door. "Move over," I growled at Nagah.

The boy smiled back. "Are we going down to the river now, Mr. Nick?"

I took a deep breath. It wasn't nearly enough and so I took another. "You bet," I finally said. "I could use a dunk in cold water myself."

I drove to a boat ramp upriver from the Nyssa Bridge that

crossed the Snake. I backed down and floated the skiff off the trailer, handing the bow line to Nagah.

"Don't let go," I said.

His eyes got as big as when he first saw the river. "I won't."

November got out of the pickup and stood on the ramp staring at the bridge. "It is not the same," she said.

"What's not?"

"The bridge on the road that goes to Pocatello."

"Highway 20," I said. "It runs all the way from Newport, Oregon to Boston, Massachusetts."

"Shoots While Running and Gentle Wind were going to get off the bus in Pocatello. They were going to catch a ride to Fort Hall to see his mother."

I realized this was where their bus tried to cross the Snake. "You're right, this isn't the same bridge. The original was replaced by this one ten years ago."

The old woman kept staring at it. "The bridge has changed, but nothing else has. The river is still the river and my husband and daughter are still gone, and I still grow old without them." She looked tiny standing beside the Snake River that was a thousand feet across.

"If you'd like, I can take you right below the bridge. You can touch the water there."

"I would like that," she said softly.

We loaded into the skiff and I steered toward the span that had replaced the old truss bridge whose guard rail proved no match for a skidding bus that had plunged Girl Born in Snow into the swirling, dark waters below as surely as it had her family.

The boy and old woman sat on the middle thwart and I on the stern with my hand on the tiller. No one spoke. There were no rapids in this section of the river, but the current was strong and fast, boosted by the flows of the Boise and Owyhee. I gave the outboard only enough gas to help hold the course.

Nagah leaned to port and skied his hand atop the water to make a rooster tail. When spray slapped his face, he laughed. November kept her hands folded on her lap, but stared straight ahead and didn't try to duck the spray either.

When we passed under the bridge, I made a sweeping *S* turn so we were pointed upriver. I matched the throttle with the current to hold us in place. It would be a losing battle because the river would never stop flowing and the outboard would eventually run out of gas. Until then, I could give the old woman the time she needed to do whatever she had to do. Pray. Meditate. Listen. Maybe even speak with the dead.

I couldn't see if November closed her eyes, but I could hear her muttering in *numu*. Finally, she leaned over the gunwale, and placed both hands in the water. She said a few more words and then buried her face in her palms. A little while later, she raised her head and turned to me. It wasn't only river water streaming down her cheeks.

"I need to stand in the water," she said. "I need to dance for them."

"Not here. It's too deep. I'll take you to shore over there." I gestured upriver at Bridge Island. "The shore is shallow and you can wade in from there." I didn't add that I would stand right beside her and catch her if she slipped, hold her aloft as the river passed by, keep her from being swept all the way to the great Columbia and the Pacific beyond.

"So take me," she said.

I opened the throttle and the skiff leapt forward and we outmatched the current by tacking. I knew a landing spot from my last patrol of the islands. As I nosed toward it, I called to Nagah. "Take the bow line, jump off, and tie us to that big willow when I say so."

"Me?" he said. "Are you sure?"

"Positive. You can do it. You're fast and strong."

He snatched the end of the line that was coiled in front of him and prepared to spring. The water beneath us grew shallower, the shore grew closer.

"Now," I said as I tilted the outboard and raised the prop.

Nagah timed his leap perfectly and landed on solid ground. He scampered around the trunk of the willow a couple of times, pulling the line taut as he went. I chucked the anchor overboard to secure the stern.

November accepted my hand as I helped her across the deck and over the bow to dry land. She leaned on me as we stood onshore. "It has been a long time since I was on a river," she said. "My husband made a canoe and taught me how to paddle it without making a splash, how to go through rapids without turning over."

The same smile of being lost in reverie I'd seen before gently crossed her lips. "I need to stand in the water now and dance for him and my daughter. I have been waiting a long time to do this."

"I must stand with you," I said. "I can't let you fall."

"I will not fall, but you can stand next to me if that is your wish."

The old woman looped her arm through mine and we waded into the water. The bottom was muddy, the slope slippery, the water cold. When it reached November's shins, I stopped.

"This is as far as we go," I whispered.

November let go of me and started to roll her shoulders and sway her hips. She began humming, then chanting, and then singing. Her voice, her clapping hands, and the water burbling against the back of her legs created a mellifluous song like a wooden flute and drum duet played at round dance. She raised her arms as if they were wings and dipped and soared like a bird as her song grew stronger and louder. Her eyes never left the spot on the river where it passed beneath the Nyssa Bridge.

When she finished, her shoulders slumped. I feared she would crumple and so I put my arm around her waist and turned her back toward shore. She was too weary to climb over the bow of the skiff. I picked her up and sat her on the thwart. Though her skirt and moccasins were soaked, she was as light as a pillow.

"Cast off when I say so," I called to Nagah.

He unwound the line from around the willow trunk and dug his heels in as he held the skiff fast against the pull of the current. When I looked back at Nagah after hoisting the stern anchor and starting the outboard, he seemed bigger and stronger.

23

The pickup's heater was cranking full blast to dry November's skirt and keep her warm as I pulled away from the boat ramp. I started to make the turn to drive back upriver to Blackpowder's cabin when I felt the trailer drag. A check of the side mirror confirmed it was listing. The left tire was half flat. I turned toward Nyssa instead.

A tire store was open on the other side of the bridge. A man wearing a short-billed welder's cap and a denim shirt that had a faded ring on the breast pocket made by a tin of Copenhagen greeted us.

"Looks like you're riding a bit low in the hindquarters," he said with a lopsided grin.

"I must have driven over a sharp rock," I said.

"We got our fair share of them around here."

I joined him as he knelt next to the sagging tire. He ran his hand around it and then behind it. "Yep, I can feel something on the inside sidewall. It's more than a scuff, more like a gouge. Air's leaking out. Sorry to say, but a patch won't hold it."

I didn't want to risk being without a spare. "Do you carry new ones this size?"

"Uh, let's see, it's a sixteen five by six five. That's pretty common, so more than likely. Let me check our stock and see if I can match the brand so you got the same treads on both sides. It'll give your trailer a smoother ride."

That made me think of the tire tread plasters Orville Nelson had taken at Clay Barkley's camp. I wondered if he'd been able to match them and, if so, were they being any help in tracking down the fugitives' stolen car. It would be more evidence against them. Find the car, find them, and nail Barkley's killer for first degree murder.

The tire man disappeared into his shop and was soon back with good news. I told him to go ahead and replace the ruined tire. "Can you jack it up here or do I need to back the trailer into the bay so you can raise it on the lift?"

"I'll swap it out right here. You don't need to unhook the trailer or unload your skiff. I got a floor jack that can hoist a house. Looks like the rim isn't damaged. That's gonna save you a pretty penny. You want, I got a little waiting room inside with magazines. Got the latest issues of *Sports Afield* and *Popular Mechanics*. There may even be some coffee left in the pot."

I stuck my head in the cab and asked my passengers to come with me.

"I am too cold," November said. "I will stay here."

"I'll go. I need to use the bathroom," Nagah said.

I debated forcing November to come with us, but her chills persuaded me otherwise. The boy and I went inside the shop. Nagah found the bathroom and I found the waiting room with the coffee pot. The contents were as thick and black as tires and smelled like burnt rubber. I'd drunk worse. I filled a Styrofoam cup and tried a sip. I was wrong. It was much worse, but I didn't throw it out.

Nagah came out of the bathroom and we returned to the pickup. Another man was leaning against the cab talking through the open window while the man in the welder's cap finished loosening the lug nuts. Old habits didn't break easily. I always held a cup with my left hand to keep my right free. I put it on my revolver's grip.

"Can I help you?" I said.

The man turned around. He was Paiute and looked to be in his midthirties. He glanced at my right hand. "I stopped by to collect my paycheck. I recognized Girl Born in Snow."

"You're Wyanet Lulu's son."

He nodded. "You know my mother?"

"I met her at the hospital. She told me you were on your way. Condolences for your loss."

"I got there in time to watch my father start the journey. A few more minutes on the road and I would've missed it." He turned back to November. "The ceremony's going to take place on the reservation. I came back to fetch my wife and children for it."

"It is a good place for a ceremony," November said.

"Your mother told me you worked at a tire store, but I didn't know it was this one," I said.

"Nyssa is a small town. We're the only place besides the gas station that sells tires."

"And doesn't overcharge you neither," the man in the welder's cap chuckled as he finished loosening the last lug nut.

Wyanet's son stared at Nagah. "You are a Will. I can see it in your brow and jaw line."

"I am Nagah Will," the boy said.

"I knew your father. We grew up together. The last time I saw you, you were..." He held his hand flat by his thigh.

"Now I am bigger," Nagah said and puffed out his chest. "I have caught many trout in the Owyhee and jumped off a boat in the Snake and tied it up."

"I have two sons of my own about your age. One is twelve. The other fifteen. How old are you now?"

"I am thirteen," Nagah said.

Wyanet's son cocked his head. "You are about the age to walk the path."

Nagah shrugged.

"When was the last time you saw Loud Will?" I asked Wyanet's son.

"I have not seen him in many years. Not since..." And he pointed at Nagah and then held his hand flat by his thigh again.

"Your mother told me you and Loud shared the path ceremony at Little Battle Gulch beneath Lookout Ridge. Is that where your oldest son walked?"

He jutted his chin. "Who are you to ask such things?"

"I am a friend of Nagah's and Girl Born in Snow," I replied in *numu*. "I am a friend of Tuhudda Will also."

"Well, I do not know you," he said sharply in English. "Why are you here anyway?"

I switched back to English. "Girl Born in Snow wanted to dance in the Snake River for her husband and daughter."

"And I wanted to fish," Nagah chimed in.

"So you said," he said to the boy. "Why in the Owyhee and not the Snake?"

"Fatter brown trout," I said before Nagah could answer.

Wyanet Lulu's son gave me a hard look before turning back to the pickup's open window. "I am going home now to help my family prepare for the ceremony. Will we see you there?"

November cleared her throat. "Perhaps."

He drove away. Maybe he hadn't seen or spoken to Loud since Nagah was a little boy. Maybe he didn't know that his childhood friend had escaped from prison and wanted to perform the path ceremony for his son himself. And maybe when he was in

Burns watching his father die, Loud hadn't knocked on his door in Nyssa looking for a place to hide after returning from Idaho to hunt down the Shoshone man who'd killed his wife.

That was way too many maybes for me.

The man fixing the flat finished swapping the tire and tightening the lug nuts. "You're good to go," he said. "Are you on your way home?"

"Yes."

I paid him and took a right turn out of the parking lot so we were heading toward Burns. I ran through our options, but after several blocks I turned down a side street and cut back through a neighborhood to rejoin the road to the Owyhee. I tried to tell myself no one noticed, but I couldn't fool myself into believing it.

THE SKY WAS lavender by the time we got back to the cabin and the rhyolite cliffs were turning from firebrick to maroon. An early evening hatch of mayflies billowed over the river as the poking noses of hungry brown trout mushroomed the water's surface.

"I'm going to catch supper again," Nagah shouted.

"Stay on the bank and don't wade into the river," I said. "I have some things to do first, but I'll be down soon."

Nagah ran ahead to collect his rod. I helped November to the cabin. Her breathing was labored.

"Why don't you take a rest. Nagah and I will cook supper," I said.

She didn't argue and went into the bedroom and closed the door.

When I was about Nagah's age, I saved my pennies made from mowing lawns to buy a cap gun. The other boys living around the military bases where I grew up and I would mimic our fathers and play war. The frequency of our battles soon outstripped my income to keep myself in rolls of caps. One day, my old man came home after a long deployment and witnessed one of those skirmishes. I'd run out of caps and was encircled by the other boys who were blasting away at me. I knew better than to cry in humiliation, but I nearly bit a hole through my lip keeping from doing so.

That night after dinner my old man hauled me into the garage and grew red in the face as he lectured me on violating a golden rule of gun battle. "You always shoot to kill, you make every shot count, and you never ever be a bullet short. Never." Afterward, he proceeded to show me how to make my own caps using ground match heads and striker, a strip of paper, and another of tin foil. He took off his shoe and pounded a row of the homemade caps to prove the formula worked.

I scrounged around Blackpowder's cabin and found hammer and nails, tinfoil and paper, and a box of wooden matches. I made several strips of caps and when I was satisfied they banged, I looked behind the stove and icebox and collected mousetraps. I glued strips of caps to the platforms of the traps so they were in line with the hammer when it snapped. I nailed the mousetraps to stakes I made from sharpened pieces of kindling. Then, I grabbed a reel from one of the spinning rods and went outside.

Setting up a trip wire across the single track road that led to the cabin and around the perimeter of the bench didn't take long. I tied one end of a length of clear monofilament line from the reel to a pounded stake a foot above the ground. I ran the end to another stake with a mousetrap nailed to it. I tied the tip of the fishing line to the bait plate and then pulled back the hammer and secured it with the hold bar. I repeated the process until the entire area was secured. The series of tightened lines when stretched by a boot would snap the traps and bang the caps. It wasn't as deadly as a trip wire set with claymore mines like I'd rigged in Vietnam, but the noise would provide precious moments to get ready for intruders trying to sneak up on the cabin in the dead of night.

I walked down to the river. Nagah had already caught and kept two sizeable browns. He'd cleaned them like November had showed him and wrapped them in a handful of wet grass.

"We will eat good tonight," he beamed.

"We still have some time before it gets dark," I said. "Let's follow the creek up the box canyon and see if we can find its headwaters. Blackpowder told me it bubbles out of the ground from underground springs."

The start of the trail was the only gap in my trip line perimeter "Remember this point," I told the boy. "If I give the word, enter the trail here and run up it. You don't go down to the river, understand? You follow the creek into the canyon. Will you do that?"

"Like I did on the boat when you told me to tie it up and cast off?"

"Exactly," I said.

"Why shouldn't I run down to the river?"

I didn't tell him because it was too wide open, that anyone standing on the river bench would have a clean line of fire on me as I guarded him. "Because I said so. I give the word, you come here and run up the creek. You don't stop to ask why. You just go."

We followed the creek into the box canyon. It was narrow and the walls sheer and high. Climbing down them would take ropes and pitons. The floor was jumbled in spots from rocks that had peeled away from the cliffs. I saw them as blinds for shooting behind. I could fall back from one to the next if need be. The creek narrowed into a rivulet and Nagah and I stepped back and forth over it easily. I let him lead the way so he would have a good feel for the trail.

After fifteen minutes of hiking, he stopped. "Look!"

He pointed at a jutting buttress on the canyon wall. It resembled an elongated human head a hundred feet tall from chin to forehead. It was one of rock formations Blackpowder had told me about. An overhang served as the face's heavy brow. Twin grottoes formed the eyes. The nose was a bulge in the rock and ledges formed lips around a smiling mouth.

"Look, another one!" Nagah shouted.

A similarly shaped buttress stared from across the opposite wall. Overhangs, recesses, ledges, and crevices formed the face. The eyes were bigger and the lips were downturned to make a frown. The rock skin of both faces was rougher than the four dead presidents carved in the polished granite of Mount Rushmore, but the pair's expressions seemed more alive.

"Who made them?" Nagah asked.

"Wind and rain and time."

"They make me feel…"

"Frightened?" I said.

"A little."

"Don't be. They will be your friends if you let them."

"Like Dr. Gemma's father? That's what you said about him."

"Yes, like Pudge. We should turn back. Remember this place, okay? If I tell you and November to run, come here. Stay and hide and wait for me, okay?"

"I will."

"Don't be scared."

"I won't," he said.

24

I sat on the porch after dinner checking the weapons the US Fish and Wildlife Service had issued me when I was hired. After the phone call with my supervisor and the regional director, I wondered how long it would be before I had to turn them in along with my badge. I wondered if I'd even get the chance if Loud Will and Banks showed up. The bore of the 12-gauge pump shotgun was spotless. The Winchester's sights were true. The cylinder of the .357 spun easily. An extra box of magnums weighted my pocket.

November came outside. "The boy is in bed," she said. "He told me you took him into the canyon."

I said I had.

She tsked. "That is a sacred place. It is sacred to the Paiute and Shoshone."

"You came here with your husband when you were first married, didn't you? When you were fishing for salmon."

November hesitated before replying. "You think you know everything."

"Then tell me I'm wrong."

"Yes, I have been here before. Shoots While Running wanted to show them to me."

"Who's them?" I asked.

"The Shaming Eyes. They live in the canyon."

"The rocks with faces. Why are they called that?"

"It is from when the old ones walked this land. When someone did something to bring shame, they would be sent to the canyon to be punished or forgiven by the Shaming Eyes."

"The Shaming Eyes are rocks. Was it tribal elders who painted themselves and wore masks that served as judge and jury?"

"It is not our place to question the old ones and their ways." November looked at the weapons surrounding me. "You believe Louder Than Wolf and the other man will come tonight."

"It's possible. Running into Wyanet Lulu's son upped the chances. He learned we've been staying on the Owyhee when we talked to him. There aren't too many cabins up here."

"He is an honorable man. He has no reason to tell Louder Than Wolf where Nagah and we are."

"Unless Loud is holding something over him, like threatening his wife and sons. Maybe when he got home from the tire store, he discovered that while he was in Burns, Loud knocked on his door and is now hiding in the house. All I can do is prepare as if he told him."

"You do not trust men who have honor."

"I respect honor, all right, but I learned it can be a slippery thing to keep when your life is being threatened or the lives of those you love. I've seen brave soldiers—honorable soldiers—do a dishonorable thing because they believed the generals who ordered them to do it were honorable when they weren't."

"If you thought he was going to tell Louder Than Wolf, then why did we come back here? You could have called Pudge on your radio or gone to the Nyssa police and asked them to protect us. You could have taken us home to No Mountain."

"I thought about all those things, but Pudge is too busy supervising the deputies and protecting the people of Harney County to come babysit us. I don't know the local cops, so I couldn't trust they'd believe me. It would take us a long time to drive home. There's a lot of open road between Nyssa and No Mountain. I'd rather be here than out there being chased on a lonely stretch of highway where someone could take the high ground with a rifle and scope."

"You act like you are still in a war." November's brow furrowed. "I think you wanted Wyanet Lulu's son to tell Louder Than Wolf. You want him to come here so you can punish the man who killed your friend."

I hadn't admitted that to myself, but I hadn't denied it either. "It doesn't matter if he told him or not. Loud is half *nuwuddu*, right? You said so. He will find us no matter where we go, either here or back in No Mountain. It's better to end this now."

"Hm." She looked at her moccasins and then back at me. "I can see you are what my husband has been telling me in my dreams."

"What's that?"

"Shoots While Running has been watching you from the spirit world for a long time now. First when you were at war in the green world and now here in the brown world. He said you shoot while you run at your enemies. He said that is why I must teach you our ways so when I join him and Gentle Wind in the spirit world, Gemma and Pudge will have someone to look after them."

"You're not going to be joining your husband and daughter any time soon."

"We shall see."

"I'll keep you safe."

"And the boy?"

"Him too.

November studied me again. "I see you have decided not to shed your antlers. That is good."

"Get some sleep. If I wake you in the middle of the night and tell you to go with Nagah, go. He will lead you to the rock faces. Wait for me there."

"And if you do not come?"

"Then ask the Shaming Eyes to forgive me and to spare you and the boy from punishment."

CAPS BANGED at midnight and were quickly followed by a curse and then hysterical laughter. A wolf's howl drowned out both. I rolled off the porch and pumped a couple of rounds from the 12 gauge toward the voices, ran around to the other side of the cabin and quickly fired two more from the .30-30. I switched to the pistol and pulled the trigger while aiming in the same direction.

If Banks and Loud Will were fooled into thinking they were up against an army, it didn't scare them into turning tail. Gunfire flashed and rounds whistled past. I ran back to the porch and yanked open the door. November and Nagah were already awake. The old woman had pulled dark blankets off the twin beds and draped them over their heads and shoulders.

"Now, Nagah. Like I showed you. Take November's hand and run to the start of the creek trail. Don't stop until you get to the rock faces. Hide and wait."

"Is that my father out there?"

"There is a very dangerous man with him. You must go to the canyon. Run now."

November pushed the boy toward me. "Go," she said to him. "Go now."

Nagah wheeled around. "But you told me I must never run away. That I must always be brave."

"It takes even more courage to know when not to fight," she said.

"You too," I said to November. "Get going."

"I am too old to run."

"No, you're not. You are Girl Born in Snow. Your two feet will carry you. Now go."

The old woman relented and took Nagah's hand. As they left the cabin, I rushed to the window that faced Banks and Loud Will, smashed the glass with the barrel of my rifle, and began laying down cover fire as the pair scurried toward the start of the creek trail.

A volley of shots answered mine. This time they weren't high and wide on purpose like before. They shattered what remained of the glass and thudded into the thick wood planks. I switched windows and emptied the .357 at them. My fire was met with silence. I seized the moment to reload.

I peered out the broken window toward the trail and tried to make out two figures draped in dark blankets. Though the moon was just rising, the pale light was still too faint to reveal anything but shadows. It would help conceal Nagah and November. As long as they didn't trip, they should reach the box canyon undetected.

A wolf howl ended the silence that followed the gunfire. "Nagahhhh. Nagahhhh. Nagahhhh."

"Your son's not here," I yelled back.

"He's lying," a new voice shouted and then squealed with laughter. "Liar, liar, you're going to burn up in a fire."

I couldn't see either man, but I could picture Banks clutching his sides.

"Don't listen to him, Louder Than Wolf," I shouted. "He's like Sonny Stiles. Remember Sonny from Lyle Rides Alone's ranch? He tricked you. Now Banks is trying to trick you. Nagah's not in here."

"Nagahhhh. Nagahhhh," he howled. "Come, Nagahhhh. Come."

"He can't go on the path to manhood with you tonight," I said.

"Liar, liar," Banks started singing again.

As long as I could keep them talking to me, I could buy Nagah and November time. "It's over. Donny Gray is on his way back to prison. He told us everything."

"That little punk," Banks screeched. "I should've—"

"Nagahhhh. I am here. Nagahhhh."

"The sheriff and state troopers are on their way. Give yourself up now. Throw down your weapons."

"You're no cop," Banks said. "I saw what you are. It's plastered all over your truck." Gun shots fired and metal clanged as he put rounds into my pickup.

"Nagahhhh. Here I come."

"Don't be stupid," Banks hissed at him. "He'll shoot you. Time to burn this place down. They'll come running out. You grab your boy and I'll put the rest down."

"Don't trust him, Louder Than Wolf," I called out. "Banks likes killing. You've seen what he's done. He'll kill you and then he'll kill Nagah."

It was too dark to find targets. It would be easier in the canyon from behind one of the jumbles of rocks when daylight came. I started firing at their voices as I ran down to the big river, leaving gun flashes as trail markers as I went. Shots followed me and the bullets ricocheting off granite rocks sent silver sparks flying like the stack of dimes I'd knocked off the top of the payphone when I slammed the handset. Howls and laughter came from the bench above me. I stopped shooting and ducked and ran. I circled back to the creek trail, hoping Banks and Loud would spend the rest of the night searching the riverside for me.

25

Moonlight formed a silvery canopy over the narrow box canyon and made the grains of mica on the sandy floor twinkle. I found November and Nagah huddled in the dark blankets at the base of the rock face with the smiling mouth.

"Everybody okay?" I whispered.

"I heard shooting," Nagah whispered back. "Did you hurt my father?"

"No. I was only trying to scare him off."

"Where are they now?" November said.

"Down along the river. My guess is they'll end up back at the cabin eating our food and resting there until first light."

"Then what?"

"Continue their search when they can see better."

"They will find the trail that leads here. What will you do then?"

"Scare them off again," I said.

"My father will not hurt me," Nagah said. "It would be better if I go to him now."

"Not tonight," I said. "Better would be if you try to get some sleep."

The boy looked at the frowning rock face. The moonlight projected the ominous head's shadow on the wall beside it, distorting the profile so the nose was huge and hooked like a vulture's beak. I flashed on the ones feasting on the dead horses by Clay Barkley's camp.

November followed the boy's gaze. "The Shaming Eyes will protect you."

"They will?" the boy said

"Of course," she said.

The old woman was sitting cross-legged. I was surprised she had that kind of flexibility at her age and weak with sickness. Nagah, exhausted from being forced to flee in the dark, curled on the ground next to her and put his head on her lap. Soon his breathing grew heavy. He sounded like the foal asleep in the Warblers' stable.

"You were not telling the truth about shooting only to frighten them," November said in a chiding whisper.

"What I do tomorrow will be up to Loud and Banks," I said.

She wore the blanket over her head like a hood and gripped it at her throat so her face was framed in darkness. "Tomorrow the boy will see men die. Either them or you. Some believe a boy seeing a man kill another is the path to manhood."

"Is that what you believe?"

"It only matters what the boy believes. Knowing what to believe and what not to believe, what is right and what is wrong, only that will lead him to manhood."

The night air was turning chilly and the more she spoke, the chillier it grew. I didn't want to talk about what I did or didn't believe in, why I had chosen a path that took me to a place where I not only saw men killed, but had to kill men in return. History was filled with boys who'd followed their fathers to war, and I was no exception even though mine had always told me it was my choice whether to become a soldier or not. He never told me stories about his own experiences, never glorified what he'd done in war, never explained why he had made his military service a job for life. He explained the rules to me, like never being a bullet short, but he never challenged me to go out and test them. He never told me how to switch paths either.

"Do you really believe the Shaming Eyes will protect Nagah?" I said.

"The old ones believed it to be so. This land is hard. It has always been so. Yet *numu* have been able to live here since *Mu naa'a* created this world and placed the *nuwuddu* and then the second people here. Our beliefs make that possible."

She stifled a cough. "You still have much to learn. The rocks are as alive as us. The sagebrush, the mountains, the rivers also. We are not separate, but one. That is how to survive in this brown world until we journey to the next."

"But I thought the Shaming Eyes were only used to forgive or punish someone who has shamed?"

"Shame is powerful medicine to help prevent a person from betraying themself or their people. The Shaming Eyes bestow the medicine and protect those who have not shamed. Nagah has not betrayed himself or his people. There is no reason for the Shaming Eyes to punish him."

"Good, because if that's true, they'll protect you too."

The old woman bowed. "I am not without shame."

"You? Everyone respects and honors you. You are a renowned healer, a celebrated dancer. Pudge and Gemma love you. They owe you their happiness."

She muttered in *numu* before saying in English, "I shamed myself. I betrayed my family. I should never have let my husband and daughter board that bus without me. I was blinded by pride when I said they should go and I should stay behind."

"You can't blame yourself for that. You had no way of knowing the bus would get a blowout. It was the tire's fault, the guardrail's, not yours."

Silence passed. A shooting star did too. Finally, November said, "In the morning, the Shaming Eyes might not agree."

We passed the rest of the night sitting beneath the chin of the smiling rock face. It would provide us with cover should the fugitives attempt the arduous hike along the top of the sheer canyon walls and try to shoot down. Nagah dream talked. November hummed to herself. I did what I did before going out on patrol, before marching into battle, or joining a firefight at full run. I shut down my emotions, my memories, my thoughts of family and friends. I concentrated on the welfare of my squad. The old woman and the boy were my squad now. I slowed my breathing. I refused to listen to my heartbeat. I sat. I waited.

AN HOUR before the first touch of gray signaled the night sky was growing old, I positioned myself behind a jumble of fallen rocks. I sighted my rifle at the black maw of the box canyon's entrance. I thought about the unblinking eyes of the rock faces behind me, how they were all-seeing, and I tried to make my own the same.

Dawn broke and the sky grew pink around the paling moon. The canyon's sheer walls turned from black to maroon to firebrick red. Where were George Roscoe Banks and Loud Will? The only way into the canyon was to enter in front of me. Why weren't they flattening themselves against the cliff walls, dodging from shadow to shadow, ducking behind boulders? Had they grown scared and run off? Had I winged one? Had he bled to death on the floor of Blackpowder's cabin?

I had no answers and my thoughts turned to Vietnam and

the questions that hadn't been asked before sending the first GIs over. My training for guerrilla warfare had been an afterthought, usually dismissed with hubris. *Guerrillas are animals with no money for guns and uniforms, men. They're no match for a modern army. Hooah!* A golden rule had been violated, a rule that had existed since cave dwellers fought over hunting grounds: Before declaring war, know who the enemy is, study how they fight, and understand their motivation.

When Banks finally hailed me from behind a buttress at the canyon's entrance, I realized I'd broken the same rule.

"What's your name?" the killer called to me.

"Show yourself and I'll tell you," I replied.

His fingernails-on-a-chalkboard laugh echoed up the narrow canyon. "Take a look behind you."

"How about you step out from behind that rock and point the way?"

Banks laughed louder. "Me and you can stand here trading jokes all day, but the Wolfman, he's got another idea. You underestimated him. See for yourself."

I was well hidden behind the rockpile. The killer would have to jump out and make the equivalent of a bank shot on a pool table to hit me with a ricochet. I stole a glance behind me. Nagah was walking toward me.

"Go back!" I shouted. "Go back!"

"I am sorry, Mr. Nick. My father asked me to come tell you. He is with November now. He says he will have to hurt her if you don't put down your guns."

I didn't have to ask Nagah if he was telling the truth or to explain how his father had done the impossible and scaled down a sheer cliff. A wolf's howl rolled down the canyon. It collided with the echo of Banks's laughter and the sounds of their victory clapped together like thunder over my head.

If I stood unarmed, Banks would shoot me. If I didn't, I might as well shoot November myself.

"Come here, quick," I whispered to Nagah. "Trust me like I trusted you with the bow line."

He pursed his lips as he thought about it and then scurried toward me. I grabbed him and pulled him behind the rocks.

"I saw that," Banks shouted. "Dumb move. I fire off three rounds, Wolfman shoots the squaw."

"Does your father have a gun?" I asked the boy.

He nodded. "A pistol in his belt, but he didn't point it at us. He does not like guns. He never shoots them because of all the noise."

"Now is the time for you to show even more courage. We're going to stand up together. I'm going to hold you close and we'll walk quickly to your father and November. Do you understand? I'll try to talk to him, but if he insists on taking you, be brave and go. I'll come find you later to make sure you're safe. Okay?"

"You will not hurt my father?"

"No."

"You promise."

"I promise."

"Okay, then. I am ready."

"You win, Banks!" I called out. "I'll leave my guns here. The boy and I are going to talk to his dad. Take a shot at me and you risk hitting him. You'll have to answer to Loud then."

I stood up from behind the pile of rocks, clutching the boy close. The Shaming Eyes were sure to punish me for using him as a shield, but I didn't see another choice. We began the long march with the unhinged killer stopping to collect my weapons and then hurrying behind.

26

L oud Will's hair had grown out since the mugshot taken five years ago. He wore it pulled back in a single braid. His skin color was pale despite his Paiute heritage, no doubt a result of being locked in windowless solitary confinement for much of his sentence. The broken arrow tattoos on his throat had also faded and the blue ink was now the color of moss on a river rock. Banks looked little changed from the photo that had been faxed to the sheriff's office. He hadn't bothered to shave off his horseshoe moustache or grow a beard to try to disguise himself. I could sink my fingertips into the hysteria lines that etched his cheeks from the corners of his shiny eyes to the corners of his hungry lips.

"How did you find us?" I asked Loud.

He made some guttural noises as he wrestled with forming words. "Move. Away from Nagah."

"It's okay," I said to the boy and then took a step to the side, careful not to step too far so I could still be able to launch myself and wrest the pistol from Loud's waistband.

"Nagah not your son," he said in between yips and croaks.

"I know that. He's yours, but that doesn't mean he isn't my friend. We are friends, aren't we Nagah?"

The boy nodded. "And she is my friend too." He pointed at November.

Loud howled. "You took him."

"No, your father asked me to keep him safe. When Tuhudda learned you had escaped, he knew lawmen would come to his camp looking for you. He didn't want Nagah to be in harm's way."

"He's lying!" Banks shouted. "Why would your old man give your boy to a white man?" He slammed me in the back with my own rifle. I pitched forward but kept my footing. "Liar, liar, let's build a fire!"

"Your father asked me to take him to Girl Born in Snow," I said. "You know they are old friends. Your mother and she danced together."

"Shut up," Loud said and slapped the side of his head. "Shut up."

I wondered if he was talking to me or the voices inside his head.

November sat cross-legged beneath the chin of the smiling rock face. The blanket wrapped around her looked like a shroud. She didn't take her rheumy eyes off George Roscoe Banks.

"Louder Than Wolf," she said in *numu*. "He tells the truth."

"I decide truth," he replied in English.

"No, they do." She aimed her chin at the Shaming Eyes. "You know them."

"What's she talking about?" Banks said. "Those rocks? They're only big ugly rocks."

"Shut up," Loud said and slapped his head again.

"Tuhudda wants your blessing so he can guide Nagah on the path," I said.

"You know nothing," he said.

"I know your father was there to guide you. I saw the photograph. Your sisters and mother danced for you. You were all laughing. Nagah deserves nothing less."

"Shut up!" he shouted. He slapped his head and howled.

"Wild horses," I said. "Remember them? They came to your ceremony. Now they've come to graze with your family's sheep."

His head cocked. "What?"

"The wild ones are there now. At your family's camp on the reservation. Let Tuhudda guide Nagah on the path there so that your father and son will be safe from the lawmen hunting you. Your daughter and your sisters will dance for him. They will all be among the wild horses. They'll bring Nagah luck."

Banks slammed the Winchester into my back again, this time so hard it brought me to my knees. He followed up by driving the butt to the back of my head. I ducked and took a glancing blow. It still sent me sprawling onto my stomach. Lights flashed, but I didn't black out. I curled my hands around sand.

"Enough!" Loud shouted at Banks. "Not here."

"Because of the rocks? What are they going to do, fall on us?" Banks sneered. "Or don't you want your son to see what real men do?"

"Nagah, come. We go now."

"Hold up," Banks said. "We can't let these two walk out of here. They'll talk to the law."

"You stay. I come back."

"When?"

"Tonight." Loud yipped and croaked. "It is not far."

"What isn't far?" Banks asked.

Loud snorted and grunted. "Wait here."

Banks started to protest, but then switched gears. "Fine, I'll stay. But don't forget our deal. I got you out of prison and you still have to get me out of Oregon. A deal's a deal."

Loud grunted. "Do not kill them." He grabbed Nagah's hand and left.

THE SUN WAS DIRECTLY OVERHEAD and its rays penetrated the narrow box canyon. The walls radiated with heat. So did the ground where I laid. Little air flowed. What few shadows there were, beckoned. Banks kicked me hard in the side.

"Quit playing possum." He laughed. "And drop the sand. You try and throw so much as a grain in my eyes, I'll shoot off your hands." Banks sneered. "Wolfman, he wouldn't shoot at you last night because he didn't want to hit his kid. He doesn't want his kid to see me kill you either."

I pulled myself up to my knees and balanced on my knuckles, drawing deep breaths. The flashing lights dimmed, but a hot poker still burned in my side.

Banks took a seat on a rock. He balanced my Winchester on his knees and waved a pistol between November and me. "Eeny, meeny, miny, moe. Who's going to be the first to go."

"Loud Will won't come back for you." I swallowed pain as I spoke.

"Yes, he will."

"Why? He doesn't need you anymore."

Banks grinned, deepening the lines in his cheeks. "We made a deal. If he goes back on it, I'll kill his son, his daughter, and his father. Maybe not right away, but someday. He knows I will."

"The only way he can stop you from doing that is to kill you himself."

"He doesn't have it in him. Now, sit on your hands and pull your knees up to your chest. Go on." I was slow doing it, so he pointed his gun at November. "One, two..."

I did as instructed.

Banks turned the gun back on me but spoke to November. "What do think of your man now, old woman? He brought you into this trap. Guess he's not too bright."

She called him a pile of steaming cow flop in *numu*.

"That means sweet thing, doesn't it?" Banks chuckled. "You like me, don't you? Can't take your cloudy old eyes off me. How about I do something that'll bring a real shine to them?" He licked his lips.

"The law will find Loud," I said. "He'll tell them where you are."

"No he won't. If Wolfman runs into them, he won't live long enough to talk, even if he could make a complete sentence. He's determined to go to the happy hunting grounds rather than back to the pen. If he's not back here in a couple hours, I'll walk out and take your truck." His teeth showed when he grinned. "You two aren't walking anywhere."

"Do you know what we call the rocks with faces?" November said in English.

Banks scowled. "No, and why should I care?"

"They are the Shaming Eyes. They have powerful medicine."

He snorted again. "It's believing in that kind of crap that keeps your kind groveling in the dirt like gophers. Digger Indians, that's what your tribe is called, isn't it? Always digging around for roots and bugs to eat." He mimicked a shudder, but held the gun steady. "Well, you're going to be digging another kind of hole real soon."

November raised her chin. "If I must dig my own grave, then I will. But before I do, maybe you would like to see me dance."

"Dance? You? What kind of dance?"

"It is called the Shaming Eyes dance."

Banks glanced at the rock faces and then poked the gun at me in case I made a move. "You dance with the rocks?"

"I dance for you. I am a good dancer and it is a very good dance."

"That's right. Your boyfriend here said you used to dance with Wolfman's mother. Maybe you were something back in the day before you got old and grizzled. Maybe if you dance good enough, I'll do something real special to make you feel young again." He traced his horseshoe moustache with the tip of his tongue.

"My dance will shame you," November said.

"What, you're going to take off your clothes and shake your dried-up old dugs at me?" He slapped his knee. It jostled the rifle and nearly caused it to slip off, but he motioned me back with the pistol as I started to pounce. "My old man took me to my first strip club when I was twelve. There's not a titty bar in Portland that doesn't know my name. Shame me? That'll be the day."

Banks waggled the pistol. "Looks like we're going to get a floor show, sport. I'm doing you a favor letting you live long enough to watch it. You might even go out with a smile on your face."

November groaned as she unlocked her knees from sitting cross-legged. She groaned again as she pushed herself off the canyon floor to a standing position. The old woman tottered as she fought to gain her balance. Standing up after having sat for so long must have made her light-headed. I readied to spring at Banks if she toppled, betting that her fall would distract him long enough for me to clamp my hands around his throat.

But November didn't collapse. She pushed the blanket back from her head and left it draped around her shoulders like a shawl. Then she brought her hands together and started clapping, slowly, rhythmically. A chant soon followed, slow at first, then building as her claps grew louder and faster. The chants were not words, but sounds that came from deep within her like the underground spring that burbled out of the canyon floor.

Her feet began to move. Slow at first and then matching the pace of her chanting and clapping. November's dance steps took her closer to Banks. She stopped clapping and took two corners of the blanket so that it formed wings beneath her outstretched arms. Banks was nodding to the beat of her chant. His eyes opened wide as she began to dance in front of him. He grew mesmerized by her supple and elegant moves.

My eyes opened wide too, for each time November twirled around, she seemed more spry, more youthful, not only in the way her body flowed like a river, but in her face and voice. The wrinkles started to smooth and the gray hairs as fine as spider's silk that streaked her braid turned lustrous black. Her thin lips became full and were the color of freshly ground cinnamon as her chants flowed between them. The music rose in power and pitch.

I was spellbound by her eyes. Every time she twirled around, the rheum grew less and less until it disappeared completely, leaving behind brown irises so dark, so deep I felt I could fall in them and never touch bottom.

The years peeled away with each twirl until she was no longer the old healer I knew, but a beautiful maiden who'd been born in a snowstorm and blossomed into the embodiment of springtide. She kept twirling, around and around like a graceful bird soaring on the thermals that rose over the Owyhee. Her chanting soared too, and each time she passed in her twirling, dancing orbit, I could see the allure that had captured Shoots While Running's heart and soul, making him fall so deeply in love that he left his Shoshone home to join her as a Paiute.

As Girl Born in Snow continued to dance, dipping and raising her blanket wings, she drew closer and closer to Banks. She twirled again, and as she passed by him, silver flashed.

"My eyes," he shrieked. "My eyes."

"The Shaming Eyes," she sang. "They see you."

It snapped me back to the moment and I saw a straight red line across Banks's brow. Blood streamed down.

Girl Born in Snow twirled once more, and again, the silver blade of the antler-handled knife flashed. A new red line appeared, this one across the killer's throat. He dropped the pistol to cover the slash with his hands, but blood poured through his fingers, and with it, his life spilled out.

George Roscoe Banks pitched face first into the sand beneath the stony gaze of the Shaming Eyes and laughed no more forever. Girl Born in Snow collapsed too.

27

Her face was still young and beautiful as I rolled her onto her back, her hair black, her lips cinnamon, but her dark brown eyes were closed. I collected my guns and then scooped her up and listened for breathing. I could hear it. It was as soft as a cloud and just as quiet. She was as light as when I put her in my skiff.

Every few steps, I'd look down to see if her eyes had opened. I tried not to dwell on what had taken place in the box canyon as I quickened my pace. What I'd witnessed had no earthly explanation, but after having lived in the high desert for a year now, I'd learned that not everything always did, especially when it came to the ways of the Paiute. It served no purpose to question how November had transformed herself, only to accept that she had.

As I exited the Shaming Eyes canyon, she finally spoke. "You can put me down now. My own two feet will carry me."

Her deep, dark brown eyes opened and were free of rheum, but gray hairs now weaved among the black in her braid like the threads of a cobweb and the wrinkles of time and wisdom etched her face. She was no less beautiful for them.

We walked to my rig. It was the only vehicle parked there. Bullet holes riddled one side. The whiff of leaking gasoline was strong. I yanked open the door to check the police band radio. It was smashed to pieces. My stack of folded topographic maps was still in the glove box. I retrieved them and fanned them out on the hood.

"Loud Will said wherever he's taking Nagah was close by. Little Battle Gulch? Lookout Ridge? They must be somewhere around here."

"Those are *numu* names so they will not be on any white man's map," November said without coughing. "The old ones called them that to honor a battle during the Bannock War."

"But I thought that war was fought in Idaho."

"There was a fight near the Owyhee at a place where a white man was later struck by lightning. His name was Leslie."

One of the topos was titled Leslie Gulch. I unfolded it and saw the gulch ran perpendicular to the eastern shore of Lake Owyhee, the reservoir that had been made by trapping the river behind the dam. The map also showed a ridge running parallel to Leslie Gulch. It was named Bannock Ridge.

"These have to be Little Battle Gulch and Lookout Ridge." I ran my finger over the map as if I were reading Braille. I stopped when I came to a landmark with a familiar name, Three Fingers Rock. I tapped the map. "Gemma told me there is a herd of mustangs near here. Wyanet Lulu said wild horses came to the ceremony for her son and Loud. This must be where he's taking Nagah."

The map showed no direct road from the cabin—dirt, gravel, or otherwise. Loud would have to drive back down to the Snake River, turn south, and then take a dirt road that followed Succor Creek. I got behind the wheel of my pickup and turned the key. The gas gauge hovered on empty.

"There might be a little gas that hasn't leaked out, but not enough to get me there," I said.

November tsked. "No place in this world has only one trail. There is one for the animals to walk, another for the birds to fly, and still another for the fish to swim."

I studied the map again. "It's only a couple of miles to the dam. If I can get there, I can launch the skiff into the lake and reach Leslie Gulch. I'll run the rest of the way."

"What will you do when you find Louder Than Wolf?"

"I'll convince him to let me take Nagah home."

"He may not let you."

"I won't take no for an answer."

She eyed my revolver. "Louder Than Wolf will not let you take him back to prison."

"I know that," I said.

"Then you will have to decide which path to manhood Nagah will take. Will it be the one where seeing a man kill another turns a boy into a man or will it be the one where he can tell what is right and what is wrong for himself?"

I felt myself treading water to keep from sinking into the depths of her dark brown eyes again. "I will make that choice when I get there."

"So be it. I will wait here to learn what it is."

The Shaming Eyes hadn't punished me for using Nagah as a human shield, and now they didn't punish me when I fired the ignition and drove to the dam before running out of gas. I launched the skiff. It was thirty miles up the lake to Leslie Gulch. Loud had a head start and a faster vehicle, but I had to get there before he completed the ceremony and disappeared into the wilds with Nagah. I turned the throttle to full speed and held it there.

No wind blew and Lake Owyhee was still. The river canyon the dam had flooded was deep and made the color of the water as sapphire as the sky. The skiff left a clean, straight line of white wake behind me that stood in stark contrast to the treeless and rugged ridges and buttes that ringed both sides of the man-made lake. Compared to their ancient rocks, my time in the brown world didn't amount to a geological blink of an eye. Yet I felt rooted and didn't want to leave the land or the people who called it home. If Regional Director Powers fired me, I'd find another way to make a living in No Mountain. I'd do whatever it took to stay.

I kept time on my field watch and calculated speed and distance. An hour at full throttle brought me to what should be the end of the dirt road that ran through Leslie Gulch. I steered toward shore, cut the engine, and glided onto the bank. I'd calculated right. The road was there. I tied up the skiff and set off.

I liked running. I always had. I started running track in junior high. Made varsity in high school. Ran cross-country during a couple of years at college before I quit to enlist in the army. No one could keep up with me at basic training, and when I was in-country, neither could the enemy.

Now as I ran, I fell into an easy rhythm. Arms pumping, legs pumping, heart pumping. I didn't grow winded. I could keep up this pace for a marathon race, but the dirt road wasn't as long as the route a fellow soldier had run from a Grecian battlefield to Athens. When I crested a hill, I saw something sparkle in a wide, flat spot north of the road. A thin ribbon of smoke rose beside it.

The sparkle came from the sun striking a windshield and the smoke from a small daytime campfire tended by a father and son sitting cross-legged beside it in a setting I recognized from a black and white photograph hanging on the wall of a single-wide trailer on the Paiute Reservation.

I slowed to a walk as I approached. Loud and Nagah Will held stalks of sage in one hand and braids of bunchgrass in the other. The top of the braids had been lit and smoldered. The smoke smelled sweet, and I knew why wild horses, pronghorn, and cattle alike sought it for graze. Father and son wore breech cloths, leggings, and ceremonial sashes. No pistol was shoved in Loud's waistband. It wasn't on the ground next to him either. The outfits looked exactly like the ones that Tuhudda and Loud had worn in the photograph taken more than twenty years ago. I wondered if they were the same. Had Tuhudda kept them all these years? Had Loud sneaked past the state troopers who'd staked out the singlewide and taken the clothes? Or had father and son secretly met, and if so, where was Tuhudda now?

I didn't join the pair at the fire, but squatted a few feet away and watched wordlessly. Finally, Loud turned toward me. He grunted, barked, and yipped as he struggled to master words.

"Go away," he said.

"I can't," I said.

"Why?"

"I promised your father to keep Nagah safe."

Loud scrunched his face and slapped the side of his head. "Nagah safe with me."

"Not as long as lawmen are hunting you."

Nagah said, "Where is November?"

"She is waiting back at Blackpowder's cabin. She is fine."

He didn't ask about Banks. Neither did his father. Me being there was the answer.

"Has the ceremony begun or is it already finished?" I asked him.

Nagah looked at his father. "Can I tell him?"

Loud grunted and nodded.

"The ceremony is only the beginning. I will always be on the path to manhood, for the journey continues forever, even after I leave for the spirit world."

As he spoke, I could hear something different in his voice. It was like when I saw him holding the skiff against the pull of the powerful Snake River. He not only looked stronger and older, but now he was without shyness.

"It is a path of learning we all take, your grandfather, your father, you, and me, regardless of where we come from," I said.

Loud waved the stalks of sage and a smoldering braid of bunchgrass. "This is so." It was a favorite expression of Tuhudda's and he sounded like his father when he said it.

I glanced at the pickup with its windshield sparkling in the sun. It was black, not green. It had no BLM sticker on the door.

"Where did that come from?" I asked.

Loud made a couple of yips. He barked. "Summit Prairie.

"It was parked at the trailhead of a Forest Service road with some others," Nagah explained. "Loggers leave their pickups there when they go to work. A company bus takes them the rest of the way into the forest."

"Your father told you all that?"

"In so many words. I asked him on the drive here."

"The pickup is stolen."

"Yes, my father takes things. The others tell him to. They say nothing belongs to anyone. The sky does not belong to Eagle, nor the grass to Deer, nor the river to Salmon. They only share it."

"The others told him," I said. "The *nuwuddu*."

"Yes, the *nuwuddu*."

"Do you know if he drove down the Stinkingwater Mountains access road after he shared the pickup?"

Loud shook his head. He snorted and then said some garbled words.

I could understand some, but Nagah translated anyway. "My father says that road is much too slow. He drove into Harney County on the Rattlesnake Road through Call Meadow. It is a better road."

The realization I'd erred again made me reel. I'd jumped to conclusions the same as a war planner who'd never served in the field alongside the grunts his miscalculations sent there. If the fugitives hadn't killed Barkley, who had?

I looked across to Three Fingers Rock. It was still miles away but stood taller than any of the other buttes that rose above the tortured landscape of playas and gulches wedged between treeless ridges. A herd of mustangs grazed in the distance. There were more animals than the group of wild horses that had come to Tuhudda's camp to escape the poisoned saltlicks that had been set out in the Stinkingwaters.

I moved over to the campfire and sat beside Loud and Nagah. Neither scooted away. Their braids of bunchgrass continued to smolder. Occasionally, they'd wave the sage in circles and chant. A peregrine falcon zoomed overhead. A wild stallion's whinny reached us.

"There are things we must talk about, and I am sorry we must talk about them now, but we have no choice," I said. Loud started to howl, but I held up my hand. "With respect, as long as Nagah is with you, the law won't stop hunting you."

"But Father and I can hide in the Owyhee Canyon," Nagah said quickly. "It is deep and rugged and has no trails. We will drink from the river and eat its fish."

"They'll search for you everywhere. You may have started on the path to manhood, but in the white man's law, you are still a minor and that gives them special reason to look for you." I turned to Loud. "They will keep hunting until they find you, and then they will punish you in front of your son. You know this to be true."

He slapped his head. "No prison no more."

"Donny Gray told me Banks orchestrated the escape and killed the guard and driver. He is going to testify to that in court."

"He speaks truth."

"I know he does, but even that won't erase your current prison sentence. Because you're a wanted man, you have to let Nagah go. Let him go home and live with Tuhudda. Now that he is becoming a man, he has responsibilities to his grandfather, his sister, his aunts, and to himself."

"But my father is also my responsibility," Nagah insisted.

"He is, but the best thing you can do for him is to let him go."

"Go where? Not back to prison." Nagah shook his head vehemently. "He'll die first. I can't let that happen. He may have taken things, but he's never hurt anyone. He didn't shoot my mother. He didn't hurt November and you."

We sat. The campfire continued to burn. The wild stallion whinnied again. The thought of turning in Loud for the fifty thousand dollar reward lingered no longer than it took the whinny's echo to fade.

"What about if he goes there?" I pointed to the herd of wild horses grazing between Three Fingers Rock and us. "Your father can live among them."

"Out here, all alone?" Nagah said.

"He won't be alone." I turned to Loud. "Will you?

He seemed transfixed by the wild horses.

"It would be like when you lived at Lyle Rides Alone's ranch. You were good to the horses and they were good to you."

"This is so," he mumbled.

"You can be who you truly are," I said. "A *nuwuddu*."

"*Pooggoo*," he said, using the *numu* word for horse.

"Only Nagah and I will know. It will be our secret. Someday the law will forget about you. They'll have somebody else to chase. But that could take time. Until then, you can't come back. You can't let second people ever see you, only the first people, the animals."

Loud reached down and plucked some sage and gave it to

me. Then he braided a handful of bunchgrass, touched an end to the fire, and handed it over too. I accepted both and the scent of sage and sweet smoke bathed my face.

We sat and watched the mustangs and listened to a male sage grouse drum his chest until the braided bunchgrass burned down to our fingertips. We added the stubs to the daytime campfire along with our handfuls of sage. When the bed of embers turned to ash, Loud stood, kissed his son on the forehead, and started walking. He never looked back.

Nagah and I watched as Louder Than Wolf neared the herd. He held out his palms. Soon he was surrounded by wild horses. We lost sight of him as they bowed their heads and grazed.

28

November sat between Nagah and me as I drove the stolen pickup away from Blackpowder Smith's cabin, along the Snake River, and over the Stinkingwater Mountains. We said nothing about what happened at Leslie Gulch, but I was certain she knew.

Tuhudda Will was sitting on the front stoop of his single-wide trailer as we pulled up to his camp. By now, I had suspended all surprise and so I didn't even blink that he was there or ask where he'd been. He was spooning honey onto a pilot bread cracker.

"Good evening, Grandfather," Nagah said. "I am home."

"So you are," he said, his red bandana headband bobbing as he nodded. "That is good. Do you think we should go to Catlow Valley to be with our family and make sure none of our sheep have become lost?"

"I do," Nagah said.

"Then we shall do as you say."

Nagah patted him on the shoulder before squeezing past and disappearing into the trailer.

Tuhudda looked at me. "Thank you for your gift."

"You're welcome," I said. "Blackpowder's bees make the sweetest honey."

He looked down at the jar and crackers as if it were the first he'd seen them. "Yes, this gift also."

The old man turned to November. "You are no longer sick."

"The sickness season is over," she said. "Now it is spring."

Tuhudda waved the spoon he'd been using to spread the honey. "Will you come to the ceremony for Wyanet Lulu's husband?"

"Of course."

"And will you and Wyanet dance?"

"Of course."

He looked across the darkened meadow wistfully. "When I see you two dance, I see my wife also. Ah, how the three of you can dance."

November reached into her blanket roll and handed him the knife with the deer antler handle.

"You no longer need it?" he asked.

She shook her head. "It is a good knife."

"Yes, the blade is sharp."

The old woman tsked. "What good is a dull one?"

We got back into the stolen pickup and drove through No Mountain. I didn't ask how or when she'd gotten the knife from Tuhudda. It didn't matter, only that she had. I told her that we'd have to tell Pudge what happened so they could retrieve Banks's body and end the manhunt for him.

"It's a clear case of self-defense. You don't have anything to worry about," I said.

"Why should I?" she said. "It was the Shaming Eyes who punished him."

We crossed over the cattle guard. Gemma's Jeep was parked in front of the ranch house. So was Pudge's pickup. The old deputy being home would spare me the drive to Burns, for there was much I needed to tell him. November reached the door first. Pudge was sitting in the dining room. His short-brimmed Stetson was on the table next to him. He was eyeing a shot glass full of whisky. His shoulders were slumped.

"What is wrong?" November asked.

Weariness creased his face. "It's the college boy. He went and got hisself shot and Gemma blames herself and now she's rode off." The old lawman sighed and downed the drink. "If anybody's to blame, it's me."

It happened at night when November and I were hunkered beneath the Shaming Eyes. Gemma, Pudge told us, had been behind the stick of her airplane as part of the air posse searching for the fugitives. She was flying over ranchland east of the Stinkingwater Mountains when she spotted a pair of pickups pulling stock trailers. They were speeding down a gravel road. Suspicious, she overshot them and followed the road. It led to a junction with a bigger road that connected Warm Springs Reservoir with the highway to Idaho. A semitruck hauling a stock carrier was parked there. Two more pickups were transferring cows from their trailers to the one hauled by the big rig.

Certain that she had stumbled across the cattle rustlers, Gemma radioed the sheriff's office. Orville Nelson answered. He was the only one on duty. Burton and two deputies had gone home for the night, and the remaining deputies, including Pudge, were still in the field. Gemma gave him the coordinates.

"I'm running low on fuel and can't stay in the air much longer," she told him. "Can you handle this?"

"I got it," he said. "Go on home."

Orville put out a radio call for help. Pudge responded while on his way back from Lake County where he'd been following up a new tip about the fugitives. He said he'd proceed directly, but it would take him an hour to get there. Knowing the rustlers could make themselves scarce in a hurry, the FBI hopeful grabbed a handheld radio, jumped in his car, and raced east from Burns.

"I am proceeding to where the Warm Springs Road connects with the highway," he told Pudge over the handheld. "If my timing is right, I shall be in position when the semitruck makes the turn for Idaho. I can tail them to wherever they are taking the stolen cattle."

"You will do no such thing!" Pudge thundered. "That big rig could run right over that tin toy car of yours and leave you flatter than roadkill."

"But the driver will have no way of knowing I am with law enforcement," he argued. "My car is not marked."

"They're criminals. They have a sixth sense. Turn around right now and head straight back to the office. That's an order."

Pudge frowned at November and me. "That's when my radio filled with static. Even hitting the squelch button couldn't clear it. That Orville, he cut the connection on purpose."

"What happened next?" I asked.

"I put out a needs assistance even though the college boy wasn't uniformed and hit the gas." The old lawman skated the empty shot glass on the table. "I should've done more to try and stop him."

"Were the state police in the area?"

"Close enough, but they got there too late. I arrived right after they found Orville's car. Best the troopers could make out, rustlers driving a pickup sandwiched him between them and the stock carrier. They rammed him and sent his little car skidding off the blacktop and down an embankment. The impact threw him clean out of his vehicle." Pudge took a deep breath and let it out slowly. "Then one of the sons of bitches got out and shot him in the back while he lay in the dirt."

He slammed his fist on the table. "What kind of no count does something like that? Shoots an unarmed man in the back."

An image of a red rose blooming on Orville Nelson's short-sleeved white shirt flashed. "Maybe he never felt a thing," I said.

"Well, we won't know for sure til he comes to and tells us so."

My head jerked. "What?"

"That is if he wakes up. Didn't I say that already? Sorry. Orville's at the hospital. He's in a coma. I spent the rest of the night there and most of today. The doc who operated on him told me to go on home. Says I'll be the first person he calls if there's any change." His lips tightened. "The bullet nicked his spine. If he makes it, he'll be paralyzed."

November plucked the empty shot glass from Pudge's fingers before he shattered it. "You need to eat. I will see what there is to cook." She pushed through the swinging doors to the kitchen.

"What do you mean Gemma rode off?" I said.

"It's what she does when she gets mad or feels blue. Been doing it since her mother died. She saddled up Sarah and galloped away."

"Where to?"

"Wherever it is she goes to get over whatever riles her."

"I'll go find her."

"I wouldn't if I was you. I learned a long time ago it's best if Gemma runs free of rein. She'll be all right."

"What about you?"

"I'll always feel the burn of blame, but tracking down who shot Orville will make it easier to bear." His shoulders straightened. "Wait a minute. I've been so wrapped up in this, I clean forgot. What are you doing back here and what did you do with Nagah?"

"I would've radioed ahead and told you we were coming, but my rig is at the Owyhee Dam."

I gave him the bare bones of what happened to George Roscoe Banks. As for Loud Will, I shrugged it off by explaining my only choice was to bring Nagah home and not chase after him.

"I doubt we'll ever see him again. He got what he wanted," I said. "He put Nagah on the path and when the ceremony was over, he upped and left. He isn't going to be a problem for anybody anymore."

"You let him go?" I didn't answer. "That was a pretty costly decision you made to forgo collecting the reward."

Again, I didn't reply.

"Well, you may have made that choice, but I can't. It's my duty to catch Loud and take him back to prison."

"Maybe he's already there," I said. "Who says a prison has to have walls with bars?"

Pudge gave me a long look. "Why do I think you know a lot more about where he is than you're telling me or ever gonna tell me?"

"Loud never killed anybody, but there's somebody who did that's still running free." I explained the stolen pickup. "It'll be a match to one reported missing from a logging road trailhead at Summit Prairie. Loud said the fugitives were never at Clay's camp. They were never on the Stinkingwater access road."

"We'll see about that. You need to get that pickup to the department's impound lot pronto for processing."

"I will first thing in the morning. It'll have the fugitives' fingerprints all over it, but the tread patterns of the tires won't line up with the plasters Orville took. You'll see. I've had it all wrong. Someone else murdered Clay, not Banks."

"If not him, then who?"

"That's what I'm going to find out."

"You? Not me?"

"You said you were going after the rustlers who shot Orville. That'll keep you pretty busy, especially if you decide to keep chasing Loud too."

"Well, I suppose he can wait for another day, if what you say is true and he's no danger to anybody but hisself." Pudge rubbed his jaw. "You got any ideas who killed your friend, the BLM man?"

"Some, but I'll need evidence or a confession to make it stick."

29

Gemma didn't call or show up at my place in the middle of the night. In the morning I told myself to heed her father's advice about going to look for her, but I wasn't sure how long I could hold out with a murderer roaming around. I filled a thermos with coffee and put it on the front seat of the stolen pickup before leaning a heavy plank against the tailgate. I rode my motorcycle up the ramp and tied it to the bed. As I pulled out of the drive, the sideview mirror looked pretty empty without my rig, skiff, and the Triumph parked alongside the old lineman's shack. I wondered if I could ever get used to not owning things like the *nuwuddu* had instructed Loud Will.

Pudge was already at his desk at the sheriff's office when I arrived.

"I parked the stolen pickup in the lot," I said.

"What did you do with the key?" he asked.

"There isn't one. They hot-wired it."

"And you know how to do that too?"

I started to tell him about a summer I'd spent joyriding

around Georgia when my old man was stationed at Fort
Benning for a year, but then thought better.

"I'll get some boys to go over it for prints before returning it
to its rightful owner." Pudge puffed his cheeks. "Normally, that's
something the college boy would do with that new evidence kit
we got. He enjoyed that sort of thing."

"Any word from the hospital?"

"Not yet. I swung by on my way in, but he's wrapped up like a
mummy with all sorts of tubes and machines." He let it sit
before muttering to himself, "The son of a bitch shot him in the
back when he was already down."

"I want to go through Clay's personal effects we collected at
his camp and also take a look at the tire plasters. There could be
something there that will help identify his killer," I said.

"You know that's official evidence and you're not official."

"Then swear me in as a deputy. I'm about to lose my job
anyway."

"How so?"

"I may have rubbed the new boss the wrong way."

"Figures, but nobody's swearing in nobody right now. Just
wear some gloves. Everything is still in Orville's office."

"Has Doc got around to the autopsy yet?"

"I just spoke to him. He's gonna start it today. When he
finishes, he'll send a report."

Orville's office was really a file room. A clean white short-
sleeved shirt hung on a hangar on the back of the door. A
calendar was tacked to the wall. He'd been marking off the days
until he left for the eight-week summer program at Quantico.
His makeshift desk sported a pyramid made from empty Shasta
Cola cans, an inbox, and a wire file sorter. Each file was clearly
labeled. I found one marked "BLM Ranger C. Barkley
Homicide."

The FBI hopeful had introduced spreadsheets to the sheriff's department when he signed on as an intern. The one he created for Barkley's campsite listed everything from the clothes inside the tent to the cast iron frying pan and pair of green enamel mugs and matching plates set outside.

I sat at his makeshift desk and read the list from top to bottom, picturing each item. Many things I couldn't recall having seen, like a pair of rubber sandals Barkley probably wore to and from the outdoor shower and a dogeared copy of *One Flew Over the Cuckoo's Nest*. Something nagged when I reached the last entry. Something was missing. Something I'd seen every time I saw Barkley. It was his black and white speckled notebook. I reread the spreadsheet. It wasn't listed. Nor was another item I remembered, the chisel-tip rock hound hammer he used as a paperweight to hold down the notes I gave him on mustang herds.

The foot-long plaster casts Orville had made of tire treads were in a cardboard box set atop a metal file cabinet. A folder with a sheet of typed notes and photographs of the tire tracks was also in the box. I set the folder aside and pulled out the plasters and placed them side by side.

Sticky labels were affixed to their backsides. The first was marked with my name and the make of my pickup. The second had Clay Barkley's name and pickup's make on it. The third was labeled UNO-1. The cast was narrower than Barkley's and mine. The fourth had UNO-2 written on the back. The tread pattern was wide with deep grooves and knobby lugs. It took some head scratching to figure out the three initials until I remembered Orville's favorite TV show. They stood for Unidentified Nonflying Object. It brought a smile until I remembered he was fighting for his life, a life, if and when he woke up, would mean never walking again.

I opened the folder with his notes and photos. The notes were a log, starting with the day Orville had examined the tire tracks through the day he got his film developed and the prints back. There was no entry for having compared the two unidentified plasters to a tread pattern book. Nor did any of the photos have notes written on the back. With all that was going on with the escaped convicts and horse rustlers, he'd never had time to complete his analysis.

Plastic bags filled with Barkley's effects were stored in the file room's broom closet. I searched through them. The notebook and rock hammer weren't there. Pudge poked his head into the file room as I was putting everything back.

"Find anything?" he said.

"It's what I didn't find." I told him about the two missing items.

"What good is the notebook?" he asked.

"Maybe Clay wrote something in it that incriminates his killer. I'll never know unless I find it."

"Well, you can either keep looking here or take a ride with me."

"Where to?"

"The hospital. They called. Sounds like our boy is coming around."

INSTEAD OF RIDING WITH PUDGE, I took my motorcycle. On the way, I made a quick stop at a tire store. A teen in an oil-stained T-shirt was searching for air bubbles leaking from an innertube by dunking it in a drum filled with water.

"Does the shop have a tread pattern book?" I asked.

"Sure does," he said.

I handed him the two UNO plasters. "There's ten bucks in it for you if you can identify the brand and model of these tires. I'll give you another ten if you can match them to the specific make of a car or pickup."

"Show me the ten," he said.

I gave it to him. "I'll be back in a couple of hours. Remember, match the tires to specific makes and models of vehicles earns you the second ten."

"That's a hard one. Whatever tires might've been on when it left the factory or dealer's lot could've been swapped out by now if it's an old car. Happens all the time, people putting on cheaper tires when the originals wear out."

"Go with what was original."

"You're the boss. And twenty bucks for two hours? Thanks, mister. That's more than five times what I get making minimum wage."

I didn't tell him my government salary was the equivalent of a buck sixty an hour too.

They'd moved Orville Nelson from the ICU to a private room right next to it. The redheaded nurse who attended to Donny Gray was coming out.

"I'll tell you what I told the other lawman," she said. "You got two minutes. I hear a beep I don't like from my patient's heart monitor, a line that starts going up and down like a drunk's hand with the shakes, you're out of there faster than I can insert a catheter. And, trust me, you don't want to test me on that one."

Pudge was standing beside the bed. He held his hat. Orville looked pretty much like the deputy had described earlier. It was hard to tell where the bandages started and left off. The young man's eyes were open, though. He blinked twice at me in recognition. An intubation tube prevented him from speaking.

"I'm glad to see you awake, son," Pudge said. "Everybody's

pulling for you. Drake and me stopped by to say, well, get well soon. I also wanted to let you know I'm gonna find the people who did this and clap them in irons."

Orville started blinking. Once, twice, seven times, and then stopped.

"That's okay," Pudge said. "I know you can't talk right now, but don't worry. I'll find them."

Orville struggled to raise his head but couldn't. He tried talking around the tube in his mouth. He couldn't do that either. Frustrated, he started blinking again. The heart monitor beeped louder. That set off an alarm because the redheaded nurse rushed in like a whirling firestorm. Pudge and I didn't need to be told to get out. We stepped into the hallway as a voice over a loudspeaker called for Dr. Goldman. I recognized the man in scrubs who came trotting our way. He was the surgeon who'd operated on Donny Gray, the handsome one the nurse called "Golden Boy."

Pudge and I stood on either side of the door looking at our boots while we waited. A few minutes later, Dr. Goldman came out. "Everything's fine. He got excited seeing you, is all. Any spike in blood pressure or pulse rate triggers the alarm. I upped his sedative. It's like I told you, Deputy. It's going to be a long haul with lots of speed bumps along the way. The fact that he's conscious is encouraging. Very encouraging."

"I'm heartened to hear that. Truly. Uh, does he know yet? You know, about the paralysis?"

"I haven't told him. It's my experience it'll come as a real shock. We need to get him strong first."

"If it's okay with you, I want to be there when you do," Pudge said.

"Of course." The surgeon glanced at me. "We've met before."

"Nick Drake," I said. "It was a few nights go. We talked about serving in 'Nam."

"That's right. You told me you spent time in a MASH. Was it a GSW or shrapnel? Don't tell me it was from a punji stick. Those suckers were mean."

I did have a couple of scars from sharpened bamboo, but told him it was a gunshot wound.

"You standing here means the surgeon was good at his job and you were lucky where you got hit and by what." Dr. Goldman nodded at Orville's room. "Not like your friend in there."

"Being shot in the back, you mean," Pudge said. "Why he's paralyzed."

"Location is only one factor. The fugitive the ranger here brought in had a GSW to the back too, but his wound was high up and, more importantly, the bullet wasn't a hollow point like the one that struck Orville. That's what's caused so much damage. The bullet flattened on impact and fragmented. A piece hit his spine."

"A hollow point?" I said. "Did you keep it?"

"All the fragments I could safely extract without causing additional damage or risking his life, sure, I kept them. They've been logged per the hospital's GSW policy. Now, if you'll excuse me."

Dr. Goldman trotted away.

"We need to take a look at that bullet, or what's left of it, right now," I said.

"What's the rush?" Pudge said.

"Sonny Stiles. I had to take his six-gun away from him at Tuhudda Will's camp. I emptied the cartridges before giving it back to him. He'd carved *x*'s in the noses. I still have them. I think Orville was trying to tell us something. Seven blinks, Seven Fans."

Pudge's jowls reddened. "If that pipsqueak shot the college

boy with a homemade hollow point, he'll be a quarter pint by the time I get done with him."

"And if Doc's autopsy report says Clay was shot in the back of the head with a hollow point, we'll also have him for murder."

The deputy jammed his Stetson back on with a vengeance. "Let's go take a look at that slug."

30

The Seven Fans ranch was a two hundred-acre spread that fronted Stinkingwater Creek on the eastern slope of the mountains. Cutting horses crowded the corral next to the stable. The barn and bunkhouse needed shingling, but the ranch house had a fresh coat of paint. The owners, Darlene and Lester Fanning, watched sourly from the verandah as Pudge and I got out of his rig.

"Did you find our stolen cows yet?" Darlene called. Her cheeks were puckered by a lifetime of scowling.

"Afraid not," Pudge said as we approached the verandah. "It's a safe bet your steers are hamburger by now and the cow-calf pairs sporting new brands."

"Along with every other rancher's stock you haven't been able to protect." She harrumphed. "It's a wonder the taxpayers of Harney County are still willing to pay your salary."

She turned on me. "And what's Fish and Wildlife got to do with stopping rustlers? The only thing your kind ever does is fence off good land and put antelope ahead of cows."

"Drake's lending a hand on a couple of matters since one of

our deputies shipped out to Vietnam and another is, well, reevaluating his employment prospects," Pudge said.

Lester, who seemed content to let his wife do the talking, looked at me. When I stared back, he averted his gaze and started counting the verandah's floor boards.

"If you got nothing to tell me, then why are you here?" Darlene asked.

"Official business," Pudge said.

"This is private property. My deed and property taxes say so. You got an official piece of paper that says you can be here officially?"

"Now, Darlene. There's no reason to go off the handle."

She gave him the stink eye. "I've never forgotten how you and your daughter turned on me about my milk cows. Ranching's hard enough to make a living at and then when your neighbors up and stab you in the back, it's treason. That's what I call it, treason."

"I'm sorry you still feel that way after all this time, but the law's the law and you keeping sick dairy cows and selling tainted milk was breaking it," Pudge said. "Being a veterinarian who's registered with the Department of Ag, Gemma had to call it in."

"I wouldn't let that uppity girl of yours within hundred miles of my ranch again even if my stock was down with blackleg and she had the only vaccine in Harney County."

Pudge tugged his ear. "Despite the fact you ran her off with a shotgun, she'd treat your cows if you called, all right, because that's who she is. Gemma's mother and November brought her up proper."

Darlene's scowl deepened.

"From the look of it, losing your dairy business doesn't seem to have set you back any," he said. "That's a fine herd of cutting horses you got in your corral since last time I was out. Buy those from Lyle Rides Alone, did you?"

"Cattle need herding and cowboys need horses."

"That's a fact. Looks like you got yourself a couple of new vehicles too. That John Deere combine in your front pasture didn't come cheap, I bet. Nor that front-end loader parked up by the barn."

Darlene crossed her arms. "We put in sixteen hour days and never take one off. Idle hands are the Devil's playground."

"That's what the Good Book says." The old deputy let it sit before saying, "As much as I enjoy talking with you, the business that brings me out here is with your foreman. Is Sonny around?"

"He's busy earning his pay. What do you want with him?"

"That's best left said between Sonny and me."

"I'm his boss, so anything you got to say to him, you can say in front of me."

"If that's what you want."

"I do," she said.

"I'll go fetch him," Lester said. Compared to his wife's tart yowl, his voice was a velvet whisper.

Lester's route to the barn took him past a lineup of pickups. I recognized Sonny's four-by-four. It was the same make and model as the teenager at the tire store had identified as a match to the UNO-2 plaster.

"I need to tend to a pot on the stove," Darlene said and went inside the house, leaving Pudge and me standing alone in front of the verandah.

After a few minutes, Lester returned with Sonny Stiles in tow. Another cowboy was following behind. He stopped and stood ten feet away when Lester and Sonny reached us.

"Howdy, Sonny," Pudge said. "Working hard?"

"There ain't no other kind."

"You still moonlighting as a bounty hunter?"

Sonny gave a vigorous shake of his head. "Nope, I gave that up after you and me spoke the other night."

"You mean after the fellas in the pickup you were chasing stopped and started shooting at you."

The foreman jutted his chin. "It's like I told you then, they went off-road and my transfer case was on the fritz. Bad luck for me, good luck for them." Sonny worked his jaw. "I heard they got one, but the other two are still loose. That bounty still up for grabs?"

"I wouldn't bank on cashing in on it, if I was you," Pudge said.

"I'm not. Just curious. I told you, I'm out of that line of work." Sonny hooked a thumb at me. "If the zookeeper here tells you otherwise, he's lying. Sure, I asked him to go partners with me, but we never struck a deal. Did we?"

"Not that I recall," I said.

"So, you're not spending your days and nights bounty hunting?" Pudge said.

"What part of no-I-am-not don't you understand?"

"Just double-checking." Pudge all but yawned. "What I wanted to ask you was about your whereabouts the night before last."

"Night before last? How many times do I got to tell you, I wasn't out hunting that retard redskin. Why, what happened to him?"

"Just answer the question, Sonny. Where were you?"

The foreman hesitated. His face scrunched as he thought. "I don't have to tell you nothing."

Pudge slapped the badge on his chest. "This says you do. You can either answer me right here and now or in a cell in Burns."

"I was here." He glanced over his shoulder at the other cowboy. "Wasn't I, Linc? Tell him."

The cowboy nodded.

"I see you're strapping," Pudge said to Sonny.

"Who doesn't? There's rattlesnakes around here. Big ones." He grinned.

"That six-shooter of yours, is that the Colt .45 Peacemaker commemorative model?"

"What if it is?"

"That's a handsome piece. Mind if I take a look at it?"

"I'm not handing over my gun."

"Why not?

"Because I don't want to. You'll put your greasy fingers all over it. Take me forever to clean 'em off."

"Are you refusing a lawman?"

Sonny hesitated. His face scrunched again.

"Don't give it to him," Darlene called from the back of the verandah. "That fat old deputy can't make you. He don't got a warrant. If he did, he'd've showed it. He's trespassing."

She stepped out of the shadows holding a shotgun. "Now, you've wasted enough of our time. We got work to do. Get off my property."

"Put that thing down before you hurt somebody," Pudge said. "You pull the trigger, you're more than likely gonna fill your husband full of lead."

Lester blanched.

I was keeping an eye on both Sonny and the other cowboy who was wearing a gun too. His hand started to drift toward his holster.

"Don't do it," I said.

Sonny glanced back at him. The cowboy looked at him with a question in his eyes. It was all the time I needed. I drew before he got his pistol halfway out of the holster. He froze.

"Ah, hell," Pudge said. "Everyone calm down. Calm down!"

"Don't give him your gun, Sonny," Darlene said. "You don't have to."

"As a matter of fact, he does," the old deputy said. "I do got a warrant for his arrest. For murder." He let the words hang. "You interfere, Darlene, I'll run you in too."

"For murder!" Sonny screeched. "I didn't murder nobody. It was an accident."

"What was an accident?" Pudge said.

I kept my gun on the cowboy. If he pulled his the rest of the way out, I'd drop him. I'd drop Sonny too if need be.

"Shut your mouth, Sonny!" Darlene shouted.

"It was an accident. Honest," Sonny said. "Tell 'em, Linc. I didn't mean to. I was practicing my quick draw pretending how I'd put a wild horse down when the gun went off. It's got a hair trigger. Tell him, Linc. Tell him what you saw after we ran him off the road."

The cowboy started to open his mouth. He moved his hand far away from his gun and then spun and bolted without saying a word. He jumped in one of the pickups by the barn and took off.

Sonny cried out again. "It was an accident! I swear. Tell him, Mrs. Fanning. Tell him how me and the boys were just trying to scare that kid who was tailing our stock carrier. It wasn't our fault he drove himself off the road and got throw'd out."

Darlene's lips pursed as she glared over the shotgun. "You little runt. Your mother should've drowned you at birth."

"Put that down," Pudge said, this time between clenched teeth. His hand was on his .45's grip.

"Ah, Darlene, it's all over," Lester said, his voice no longer a timid whisper. "I told you we'd never get away with it."

"Get away with what?" Pudge said.

"We got into debt up to our eyeballs last year," Lester said. "Rustling was the only way we could see getting clear of it."

"Shut up!" Darlene screamed. "Shut up before you hang us."

She pulled the trigger. The shotgun blasted. The bb's zinged. The recoil knocked her backward through the kitchen door. I felt a sting on my neck. Blood ran down beneath my collar. Pudge's short-brimmed Stetson somersaulted by me, the crown peppered. He was crouched, but still upright. A couple of beads of blood freckled the side of his head. Sonny was plopped on his butt screaming, but I couldn't see that he'd even been scratched. Lester had taken the brunt of the blast just as Pudge had predicted. He was lying on his back moaning. His left cheek looked as if someone had taken a cheese grater to it. Most of his nose was missing.

"Cover Sonny," Pudge said as he drew his .45. He thumped up the steps to the verandah and across the floorboards. He reached through the kitchen doorway and wrenched the shotgun from Darlene who was trying to pump another shell into the breech. "Get out here and lay face down on the floor. You're under arrest."

I yanked Sonny's gun from his holster. "An accident? You shoot a man in the back and call it an accident? Is that what you call shooting Clay Barkley in the back of the head? Another accident?"

"Who's Clay Barkley?" he whined.

Pudge snapped his handcuffs around Darlene's wrists. "Rustling from yourself to throw me off the scent is one thing, but stealing cows from your hardworking neighbors? Now, that's what I call treason."

31

Lester Fanning was handcuffed to a hospital bed down the hall from Orville Nelson. Darlene was locked in a cell above the sheriff's office, but Pudge and I could hear her cussing as we questioned Sonny Stiles in a room downstairs.

Sonny sat in a chair across a metal table from us. On the table was the plaster cast that still bore the label UNO-2.

"It's a dead match to the front left tire of your four-by, Sonny," Pudge said. "See that little chink in the lug there. Your tire's missing the spitting image."

"I told you, I didn't shoot that BLM man. I may have shot the kid by accident, but I'm no cold-blooded murderer," he wailed.

"But you did threaten Ranger Barkley more than once."

"So what if I did? I told him to pack up and get out, to leave the four-legged pests to me, but that's it."

"And did you?" I interrupted. "Take care of the wild horses by putting out poisoned saltlicks?"

"It ain't against the law. Mustangs are pests. They eat up all the graze. Folks like that BLM man would let them put us out of business."

"But the tire plaster," Pudge said, tapping it with a meaty finger. "This proves you were at his camp right before he was killed."

"Okay, I was there. I went to tell him one last time to leave, that we don't tolerate his kind around here."

"What did he say?" I said.

"Nothing. He wasn't there."

"What did you do then?"

Sonny grinned. "I relieved myself in his outdoor shower."

Pudge groaned. "How many times did you fall off a bronc?"

"What's that supposed to mean?"

"Can anyone prove that's the last time you were there and didn't come back when Barkley returned home?" the lawman asked.

"I don't know." Sonny paused. "Maybe you can take a plaster cast of where I pissed." He grinned again. "I leave a pretty deep hole."

Pudge balled his fist and shook it at him. "You're failing to comprehend the seriousness of this. You're already looking at a long stretch for shooting Orville Nelson. Even if a judge does buy your story of it being an accident, you're still gonna get hit with attempted manslaughter. And then there's the cattle rustling. You admitted to that already. Rustling's a felony. I can't add up all the years they're gonna throw at you. You tack first degree murder on, you're looking at life with no parole. Oregon ever brings back the death penalty, you'll be first in line."

Sonny's grin melted and he caterwauled. "I didn't kill nobody. You got to believe me."

"Then prove it."

"What about the slug? You matched the one they took out of that kid's back to my special ammo. What about the one from the BLM man? Huh? It don't match because it won't match because it can't match because I didn't shoot him. So there."

Pudge and I restrained ourselves from exchanging glances. Right before we started questioning Sonny, the coroner's report came in. Doc concluded that Barkley hadn't been shot. He'd been bludgeoned by something that penetrated his skull and left a wound about the diameter of the head of a rock hound hammer. Trying to get Sonny to admit he'd grabbed Barkley's paperweight and whacked him from behind was proving to be a tall order.

"You told me you wouldn't waste a buck and a half's worth of lead on killing horses, it's why you used strychnine," I said. "What did you use to kill Barkley with if not a bullet?"

"Nothing, because I didn't kill him. I told you. He wasn't there. I took a piss and left. Besides, I wasn't the last person at his camp like you're saying I was."

Pudge leaned forward. "No? Then who was?"

"The person who killed him. Duh!"

The deputy balled his fist again. "Darlene was right about what your mother should've done."

Sonny hung his head. "My mother was plenty mean, I'll hand you that."

"Come on, Sonny. Help me out and help yourself. It'll shave years off the time you're gonna spend in prison. If you didn't kill him, who did?"

"I don't know," he wailed. "You're the lawman. Do your job. Ask that gal who showed up when I was leaving. Maybe she knows something."

Once again, Pudge and I refrained from exchanging glances or showing surprise.

"That gal being who again?" Pudge said in his most laconic way.

"The gal everyone calls Mustang Sally after that song the colored fella sings. It came out a couple of years back. They still play it on the radio. You know, it goes, 'Ride, Sally, ride.' Go ask her."

"What's her real name?"

"I don't know. I never asked."

"Why do you think she'd know anything about Barkley's death?"

"Because she was there after me. I saw her. She drives this foreign car with bumper stickers on it about saving pests, why we call her Mustang Sally. She was hauling down the road when I was going up and I had to pull off to avoid a head-on. Another couple of feet, my rig would've ended up going ass over teacup all the way down the mountainside."

"Did you talk to her when she passed?"

"No, sir. She gave me the finger. I went on my way, but saw in the mirror she was turning into his camp. Ask her what she knows because I don't know nothing."

Pudge escorted Sonny Stiles to a cell upstairs. I collected the folder with Orville's notes and photographs and brought it along with the UNO-1 plaster to the deputy's office. I spread out everything on his desk.

When Pudge joined me, he said, "Sonny's Mustang Sally is that wild horse lover Lily Calla, the one who left the note to Barkley with the *x*'s and *o*'s."

I pointed to the plaster cast. "The kid at the tire store had a hard time identifying this one. It was in an appendix to the store's tread pattern book. He said it came stock on some European models, mostly Mercedes Benzes. It's too wide for a Volkswagen."

"But wide enough for a Volvo station wagon," Pudge said.

I nodded. "Even if we match it to Lily's car, it still doesn't prove anything. We already know she was parked there more than once. The time I met her there and the time she left Clay the note."

Pudge rubbed his jaw. "That's true, and why would she kill him? He's on her side, right? Trying to protect wild horses."

"Clay's job was to conduct studies and make management recommendations. He told me he was pretty realistic about what ranchers and wild horses are both up against. He supported creating special areas where a herd could be managed so as not to compete with cattle for graze."

"Managed, like some kind of crop that needs weeding and pruning?"

"If needed for the area to support them, yes. That's what he recommended down in Nevada. He said it didn't make him Mr. Popular."

"You think Miss Calla might have differed with him on that?"

"Disagreeing with someone's position and killing them over it is a pretty wide canyon to cross."

"Maybe it was something else. Maybe Barkley told her he didn't want to be chummy with her anymore. The x's and o's? Wouldn't be the first time someone lost control after having their heart broke."

"I don't know. When I told Lily about Clay's death, she seemed genuinely shocked. If she did kill him, then she's a pretty good actress."

"You'd be surprised by how often people can make themselves believe they weren't the one who emptied a gun into their mate after they learned they'd been cheated on. I've seen it. I've taken the gun from their hand and slapped the cuffs on while they're still saying why are you arresting me, I didn't do nothing."

"Clay's missing rock hammer has to be the murder weapon. It's possible Lily swung it, but someone else could've too, including Sonny."

"That's why we got to find it and check it for fingerprints," Pudge said.

I started moving the photographs around on his desk to create a panoramic of the pullout in front of Barkley's camp and match the tire tracks to their drivers. "The other thing we need to find is Clay's pickup. What happened to it? Either the killer drove off in it and then came back to collect their own vehicle or they didn't act alone."

"I got to say, son, now you're thinking like a cop, not a ranger. If you do get fired from Fish and Wildlife, you might think about putting in an application here. We got two deputy spots to fill."

I gathered the photos. "I need to go up there and see with my own eyes."

"Good idea," Pudge said. "I'll have another chat with Sonny. He might not be telling us everything. Maybe he and that cowboy Linc were riding together and one of them drove Barkley's pickup somewhere to hide it and throw us off."

I RODE MY TRIUMPH. It was good to feel the wind blowing through my hair and watch the road as it sped past inches beneath my boots. When I arrived at Clay Barkley's camp, I was careful to park the bike off to the side. The Stinkingwater access road was seldom used and the soft dirt in the pullout in front of the BLM ranger's camp was unmarred by new tire tracks.

With the help of Orville's photos, I identified the different vehicles that had used the pullout by their tread marks. Then I examined the tracks more closely and sketched out direction, both coming and going. There was the set made by Sonny Stiles's four-by. They entered, parked, and then exited. The set made by Barkley's pickup ran over the back of Sonny's exit tracks. That.told me the Seven Fans foreman hadn't been lying. Barkley wasn't there; he'd arrived after Sonny had already come and gone.

A short section of the Volvo's tracks had also been overrun by Barkley's pickup, meaning Lily had arrived before him. But then I spotted something else. Barkley's tracks re-crossed the Volvo's. His pickup had arrived and then reversed and left while the Volvo remained parked. I followed Barkley's tracks to determine which direction they went, but they became lost like all the rest when they joined the hardpack of the road. I returned to the pullout and re-examined the Volvo's tracks. When the station wagon had reversed to exit, it crossed a portion of the tracks Barkley's pickup had made when it left, confirming the Volvo was the last to leave.

I took a deep breath. The pain it caused was not from where George Roscoe Banks had kicked me in the side. It was from realizing I'd been wrong again.

The first time I saw Lily Calla, she was scrambling down the hillside behind Barkley's camp. I found the deer trail she'd followed and climbed it to the ridgetop. From there, I looked east. I could see the Seven Fans ranch along Stinkingwater Creek. I slowly turned around. The ridgeline of the mountains ran south to Tuhudda Will's camp. To the west lay Malheur Lake, the Harney Basin, and No Mountain. When I faced north, I saw the draw with the stream running down the middle where I'd first seen Clay Barkley and the poisoned mustangs. I searched for the source of the stream. It ran through a culvert beneath the road and down through a short gorge. A jewel-shaped lake about the size of a baseball field shimmered at the far end.

I scrambled down the deer trail, hopped on the Triumph, and sped toward the draw. All that remained of the foal's family were scattered bones. The vultures and magpies had moved on. I looked upstream and could see the entrance to the gorge. A pair of faint tire tracks ran alongside the stream. I steered onto them and followed. The going was rough. I passed through the gorge. The tracks led straight to the edge of the lake. I turned off the bike and set heel to kickstand, pulled off my boots, and continued on bare feet.

In no time, I was up to my knees in water, and then my hips, and then shoulders. I held my breath and dove. The jewel-shaped lake wasn't so deep that sunbeams couldn't reach the bottom. Clay Barkley's green pickup rested peacefully with its wheels up to their hubs in mud. The driver's side window was open and the water that filled the cab was clear. His long guns rested in the rack in the rear window. His chisel-point rock hammer lay on the front seat as if waiting for someone to swing it and crack open an opal to release the fire trapped inside.

I grabbed it and swam up to the light, up to the truth.

32

Lily Calla peered at me from behind the torn screen door of her bungalow. "I told you last time, I don't need to talk to anybody. I'm fine. Now, if you'll excuse me, I have work to do."

"We need to talk," I said again.

"It'll have to wait. I was just leaving. I received a call about a herd in danger at Riddle Mountain."

I yanked the screen door open. If it had been latched, I didn't hear it snap, nor did I care. "We're going to talk. I'll ask the questions and you'll give the answers. Now sit."

Lily plopped on the couch. Dust rose from the faded flower print fabric. "What are you going to do with that thing?"

I was holding the rock hammer. "You tell me."

"I'll scream. My neighbors will hear and call the sheriff."

"Go right ahead."

She hesitated. "What do you want?"

"Tell me about this." I waved the hammer.

"I don't know anything about it. I've never seen it before."

"Yes, you have. You know whose it is."

"I do?"

"Tell me what happened, Lily. And then tell me why."

Her eyes didn't leave the hammer. "Where did you find it?"

"In Clay's pickup where you left it after you killed him with it. You'd seen the lake when you hiked above his camp. You thought it would be a good place to ditch the hammer. You drove his pickup because it had four-wheel drive to get up the gorge. You weren't used to driving it and hit the gas instead of the brake and sped right into the water. When the pickup settled on the bottom, you rolled down the window, climbed out, and swam to shore."

"You're wrong."

"Okay, you meant to drive his pickup into the lake to hide it too and you tossed his tent to make the whole thing look like a robbery. You'd heard about the escaped convicts and knew they'd be blamed."

"You've got it all wrong!" she shouted.

"What do I have wrong? About tossing his tent? Did you do it looking for your note with the *x*'s and *o*'s or was it his notebook you were after? What's in it that's so important?"

"I meant about Clay. You're wrong about him."

"He didn't die from this breaking his skull?" I shook the hammer. "Or you didn't mean to hit him with it?"

"I meant about *him*."

"What about him?"

"It's all in his notebook. He wasn't going to save the wild horses. He was going to destroy them."

"By recommending they be managed instead of left to starve to death or be slaughtered?"

"At least they'd be free."

"Would they?"

Lily peered at one of the horse posters tacked to the wall. She moaned. "You'll never understand. No one ever does."

"Try me. Why did you kill Clay? Did you hate him that much?"

"Hate him? I loved him. I made love to him and he made love to me. But then that morning after he came back from Steens Mountain, I read his notebook when he left the tent to take a shower." She moaned again.

"What did you read?"

"What he really thought of me."

Her tricolored cat padded in from the kitchen. It paused to lick its paw and then rubbed against Lily's shin. I could hear its purr.

"And what was that?"

"That he felt sorry for me because I'd always be disappointed. That there were so many wild horses and not enough solutions. That he wished he could do more."

"Sounds to me like Clay truly cared about you and the horses. He viewed establishing management areas as a way to protect mustangs like what the refuges I work on do for wildlife."

"He felt sorry for me! Don't you see? He wrote it down." Lily spanked the arm of the couch. The cat arched and skittered away. "I'm not a sorry person. I'm not! I've been called sorry before, and I'm not."

"That's not what Clay said."

"He did too!" She stomped her foot.

"Who called you sorry before?"

"My literature professor, but it doesn't matter anymore because I proved I'm not a sorry person. And I'm not sorry I told his wife about us either. I'm not."

"Your professor's?"

"Yes, but Clay thought I was sorry too."

"No, he didn't. Like I said, he felt sorry for you. That's different. He also felt sorry for the horses. He didn't think they were sorry. He respected and admired them. Clay told me so."

"You're wrong. And guess what? He thinks you're a sorry person too. It's in his notebook. It's all in his notebook. About the horses. About me. About you. About everything. He wrote that if you were around wild horses and took care of one, it could help you get over what happened to you in Vietnam. He wrote that if I spent more time around them, it would help me get over what happened to me too."

"You and the professor?"

Lily's face flushed and her chest heaved. "He wrote wild horses could help kids in trouble and people in jail and people with mental illness." She was racing to get the words out. "Don't you see? He wanted to keep the horses from being wild and free. He was going to turn them into circus animals. He was going to have city people adopt them so they'd have to live in barns and never be wild again." Lily shrieked, "He was! And I couldn't let him do that."

Her sobs came in big, loud gulps. When they started to ebb, I said. "Where's the notebook, Lily? Let me read it."

"Why?"

"To see what he wrote about me."

"Okay, you'll see. You'll see. It's in my bedroom. I'll go get it."

She staggered off. The tricolored cat returned and snaked between my ankles, purring. I glanced around the room. The philodendron with liver spots in the macramé hanger still needed water. The cat box still needed changing. Lily came out of the bedroom. She wasn't carrying the notebook. She was holding Clay's service revolver in a two-handed grip.

"I'm not a sorry person!" she screeched. "And I'm not sorry what I did either!"

I flung the rock hammer. It twirled end over end and struck her shoulder. The blow caused her to jerk her hands. The gun barrel went up as she pulled the trigger. A chunk of plaster fell from the ceiling. I rushed and pulled her into a one-armed bear hug while snatching the revolver away.

"You don't understand!" she wailed, her tears flowing like the stream that ran down the draw where the mustangs died. "Neither did Clay. No one cares about the wild horses and no one cares about me!"

33

A deputy handcuffed Lily Calla and put her in his back seat. I followed them to the sheriff's office. While she was booked and placed in a cell across the hall from Darlene Fanning, I looked for Pudge Warbler. He wasn't there. I gave my report to Sheriff Burton instead.

"What was Deputy Warbler thinking when he allowed you to go to the killer's alone?" he fumed.

"He didn't know. I went on my own."

"I'm going to have to keep your name off anything official. It's for your own good."

I noticed the sheriff was wearing a new tie. "Fine by me. I hope that goes for the *Burns Herald* too."

"That's a tall order, but I'll see what I can do." Burton's moustache made him look like he'd swallowed a cat, not the canary.

"Where's Pudge?" I asked.

"The hospital. He got a call about the intern taking a turn and rushed out of here."

I didn't let the door hit me on the way out as I jumped on my Triumph and raced to the hospital. "Come on, Orville," I shouted into the wind. "Stay in the fight."

I parked and blew past reception and ran down the hall. I paused outside the open door to Orville's room to catch my breath. I looked in but didn't enter. Dr. Goldman, the redheaded nurse, and Pudge had the bed surrounded. I couldn't see past them. The air was somber and I steeled myself for the worst.

Then a familiar voice, though raspy and weak, said, "One day there will be robotic legs for people like me."

"That's the spirit, son," Pudge said.

"It looks like I will not be going to Quantico, after all."

"Maybe not, but as soon as you're ready, your job at the sheriff's office is waiting."

"If Sheriff Burton lets me."

"Maybe Bust'em won't be making the decisions for much longer."

"What do you mean?" Orville said.

"Well, if someone who knows his way around a spreadsheet with all the names and phone numbers of voters who live in Harney County on it would be willing to lend a hand, maybe I'll throw my Stetson back in the ring come election time."

"All right, gentleman," the nurse butted in, "that's enough for now. The patient needs his rest."

I left before Pudge strode out of the room. I had another stop to make that couldn't wait.

It was ten miles from the hospital to the BLM office in Hines. The balding district supervisor was sitting behind his desk pushing paper when I knocked on the door frame and entered.

"I never heard back from you about Clay Barkley's next of kin," I said.

"That's because your office doesn't have a receptionist to answer the phone," he said. "I've tried calling you several times."

He reached into the top drawer of his desk, pulled out a sheet of paper, and slid it toward me. "The names and addresses are all there. The Carson City office notified Barkley's folks by phone. I understand his father was especially broken up hearing about his death."

I read it. I had a hard, sad visit to Albuquerque in store. I folded the sheet and slipped it into my pocket. I placed the black and white speckled notebook on the supervisor's desk.

"What's that?" he said.

"Clay's field notes he kept on the wild horse assessment he was conducting. There's some good information in there. Not only about range science and population estimates, but sketches of potential management areas throughout southeastern Oregon with enough graze on them for mustangs to share with cattle."

"I'll make a point of reading it."

"I'd appreciate it if you did more than that. This notebook is like Clay's last will and testament. It's his legacy. He deserves to be remembered. Make sure it gets to the right people in your agency who can do something about it. You'll find he had some pretty bold ideas for managing wild horses and paying for their upkeep."

"Such as?"

"See for yourself. He says it a lot better than me telling you."

"Then I look forward to reading it," he said.

I took the gravel shortcut from Hines to No Mountain. It was a lot dustier traveling down it on a motorcycle than in my pickup, but seeing the scenery through goggles was no less stirring and the call of wide open spaces no less loud. When I rumbled across the freight train flatcar bridge over Sage Hen Creek and spooked the swallows, I twisted the throttle wide open and let 'er rip for home.

The overhang next to the old lineman's shack still looked empty as I pulled in and parked the Triumph. I'd have to return to the Owyhee to collect my rig and skiff, but not tonight. Dinner needed to be cooked, tea brewed, and bed beckoned.

I turned on the radio and got the college station from Eugene. The DJ was cueing a song from Neil Young's first solo album. As "I've Been Waiting for You" played, I rifled through my stores and came up with enough fixings for a meal. The folk rocker was singing about waiting for a woman to save his life, a woman with the feeling of losing once or twice, when a horse whinnied. I went out to investigate.

Gemma was climbing down from Sarah. She held a long lead line that was tied to Wovoka's halter. Grain bags hung from the buckskin stallion's saddle horn. The filly foal scampered between the two cutting horses.

"Good, you're here," the horse doctor said. "I thought we'd go for a ride."

"Right now?"

Her eyes sparkled as she smiled. "After breakfast."

"What's the foal doing up and about?"

"Turns out she's a high-spirited little thing. She found her way from the stall to the corral and made friends."

"Sarah and Wovoka don't mind she's wild?"

"There's wild in all of us. Horses included."

I couldn't argue with that. "Does this mean you're going to keep her?"

"Only until she's a yearling. Then she'll be big enough to rejoin one of the herds in the Stinkingwaters."

Gemma hobbled the mare and stallion and fitted them with feed bags. "We don't need to worry about the foal. She'll stick close."

"I was making dinner. Hungry?"

"Starving."

We took our time eating, not saying much, just enjoying being together. Finally, Gemma said, "You're not going to ask where I've been?"

"Your father told me you went somewhere that even he

doesn't know about. I figure it's your secret and secrets are important to have."

"And you have secrets that you're not going to share with me too?"

"Some."

"Like where Loud Will is? Pudge told me you wouldn't tell him."

"Everybody needs something that's theirs alone. Holding onto it, well, it helps you be who you are."

"Secrets, huh?" Gemma gave me a sly grin. "I like a man with some mystery about him."

The phone rang. I glanced at my watch, but thinking it might be news about Orville, I answered.

"Ranger Drake? This is Regional Director F. D. Powers."

"It's a little late in Washington to be calling," I said.

"I'm in your time zone. The President sent me to Portland. He has me visiting all the district offices. The American people are going to see some major new policies and laws enacted to protect the environment during his administration. Mark my words, President Nixon is going to be remembered as one of the greatest presidents in history."

The only news I'd heard about him since he took office was his plan for ratcheting up the war. "If you say so, sir."

"The reason for my call is to tell you about some changes that are being made in the region. Your supervisor would have told you himself if he were still with the agency. He is not. I'm taking it upon myself to inform all affected employees about these changes, including field rangers such as yourself. An official letter is on its way to you addressing your particular situation."

"Does that mean I'm fired?"

"It's all in my letter, Ranger Drake. Good night."

I hung up. Gemma said, "What was that about?"

"It looks like my performance review didn't go too well for me or my supervisor."

"You don't seem upset about it," she said.

"Honestly, I'm too tired to care."

Gemma came over and kissed me on the mouth. "Not too tired, I hope."

THE WOOD STOVE sighed as the fire went out and the ashes settled. I was dreaming about drifting down a long river through a twilit canyon whose walls were human faces—some fierce, some forgiving—when Gemma woke me by slipping from my arms and getting out of bed.

"What's wrong?" I said.

"The horses," she whispered. "They're agitated."

"So?"

"It could be a cougar after the foal. I'm going to take a look."

Gemma didn't turn on the lights as she peered out the kitchen window. "Someone's out there."

I sat up quickly. "Trying to rustle the horses?"

"No. He's built a campfire and is sitting by it. I think it's Loud Will."

I bolted out of bed and pulled on my jeans. "Stay inside. I'll have a talk with him."

"Be careful," she said.

I eased open the door and stepped outside. Despite their hobbles, the two cutting horses had gotten the foal between them to protect her. Wovoka's ears were back. He snorted and shook his mane, sending ripples across his withers and down his powerful shoulders.

"Easy boy," I whispered.

A man was sitting cross-legged next to a small fire. I could see he was American Indian, but it wasn't Loud.

"Who are you?" I said.

"The postman." He continued to stare into the fire.

"What's that supposed to mean?"

"You don't know what a postman is?"

"I get my mail at the PO like everyone else in No Mountain. What do you want?"

"To deliver you a letter. Your horses are scared of me. They don't like my scent."

I drew closer to the flickering light cast by the flames. His hair was cut in a long mohawk. He wore no shirt. His biceps bulged. The muscles on his hardened chest and stomach undulated. *Semper Fi* was tattooed across his breast.

"You're not *numu*," I said.

"No. I'm *maklak*."

"Of the Klamath Nation."

"You know of us?"

"I met a *maklak* last autumn in Klamath Falls. He runs the motel where I was staying."

"My cousin, Gordon Loq."

"That's him. What's your name?"

"Loq."

"Is there a first name that goes with that?"

"I don't have much use for it."

"Gordon told me he had a cousin who was a Marine in Vietnam. That must be you. He said when you took the Freedom Bird home, you couldn't stay in town and went to live in the mountains like your family's namesake, the bears."

"That's right, but now it's spring and the *loqs* woke up and so have I."

"Where's the letter?"

Loq shrugged. It sent ripples across his body the same as when Wovoka shook his mane. "I used it to start the fire."

"You burned my letter?"

"I would've used something else if I had it. Your kindling's too green. You need to age it longer."

"Did you happen to see who the letter was from?"

"The man who gave it to me. He said since I was going back to Klamath, I could swing by and drop it off." Loq chuckled. "He's not from Oregon. Thinks every place out here is right next door to each other."

"Who is he?"

"A buddy at the VFW told me the government decided to keep a special program for combat vets. They'll pay me to watch out for my brother *loqs* and other first people. Gordon drove me up to Portland to get hired and then dropped me off here to give you the letter."

"Hired by the US Fish and Wildlife Service to replace me," I said, finally understanding. "Director Powers gave it to you."

Loq added a stick to the fire. "A white man wearing a suit? All you see is the suit. I don't remember his name."

"Did you read the letter before you burned it?"

"I might have."

"Am I fired or not?"

Loq eyed me for a long spell. "Would that matter if I told you poachers were killing first people?"

Stars were telling their last stories overhead before dawn swallowed them. The pale moon had grown bigger since it shined over the Shaming Eyes alongside the Owyhee River. A great horned owl hooted. A coyote howled. The lights turned on in the lineman's shack.

I squatted next to him. "Not at all."

"Right answer," Loq grunted. "I need to know the kind of man who's got my back and whose back I got before I buddy up for a mission. You and me, we got work to do. You know the place white men call Bear Valley?"

"It's near the Klamath Lake Refuge. There's been talk of making it a national wildlife refuge too."

"Someone's killing *loqs* there. Eagles too. That's a sacred place. He's got to be stopped."

"And right away, seeing it's spring and they're raising their young," I said. "We'll move out at first light."

"I didn't see a rig parked out front. Are we going to take your horses?"

"We'll go on my motorcycle. You can ride on the back."

Loq chuckled again and then sniffed the air. His big head rotated back and forth. "I smell coffee."

He turned around. Gemma waved at us from the window.

"Is that your wife?" he said.

"Not yet."

We watched as Gemma started dancing around the kitchen, gliding and soaring like she'd been taught by the girl who'd been born in a snowstorm and grew into a beautiful, powerful healer.

"I love coffee," Loq said. "Does she make it as good as she dances?"

"She does."

"Then you're a lucky man."

"Roger that," I said.

AFTERWORD

In 1971, Congress unanimously passed the Wild Free-Roaming Horse and Burro Act, declaring the animals "are living symbols of the historic and pioneer spirit of the West" and "are fast disappearing."

The Bureau of Land Management manages and protects wild horses and burros on 27 million acres of public lands across 10 western states. In southeastern Oregon, the BLM manages 18 Herd Management Areas with an estimated population of 4,700 wild horses.

Despite the passage of the Act, conflicts remain as the government, ecologists, advocates, and ranchers search for a humane solution for managing wild horses. While the issues are complex, factors include a growing population of wild horse herds, competition for forage with sheep and cattle, and impacts on native wildlife species such as bison, mule deer, and pronghorn.

A source of friction is a practice known as Appropriate Management Level, by which managers estimate the number of animals the land can support, including wild horses, domestic livestock, and wildlife. The result has been the removal of tens of thousands of free roaming wild horses from rangeland across the West and placing them in holding pens for adoption by the public. The adoption program, however, has never kept pace with the number available, and more than half of the BLM's budget for wild horses goes to caring for and feeding animals held in off-range pastures and corrals.

A bright spot is the vital role wild horses are playing in helping wounded warriors heal from physical and emotional trauma sustained while serving the country. Formally known as equine therapy, a growing number of programs have been established for our nation's heroes. Equine therapy is also being used to help people with challenging conditions such as autism, at-risk youth, and prison inmates. You can find more information about available programs in your area by searching online.

GET A FREE BOOK

Dwight Holing's genre-spanning work includes novels, short fiction, and nonfiction. His mystery and suspense thriller series include The Nick Drake Novels and The Jack McCoul Capers. The stories in his collections of literary short fiction have won awards, including the Arts & Letters Prize for Fiction. He has written and edited numerous nonfiction books on nature travel and conservation. He is married to a kick-ass environmental advocate; they have a daughter and son, and two dogs who'd rather swim than walk.

Sign up for his newsletter to get a free book and be the first to learn about the next Nick Drake Novel as well as receive news about crime fiction and special deals.

Visit dwightholing.com/free-book. You can unsubscribe at any time.

ACKNOWLEDGMENTS

I'm indebted to many people who helped in the creation of "The Shaming Eyes." As always, my family provided support throughout the writing process, including a ready willingness to rein me in should I wander too far off the story's trail.

I'm especially grateful to my reader team who read early drafts and gave me very helpful feedback. Thank you, one and all, including Gene Ammerman, George Becker, Terrill Carpenter, Ben Colodzin, Ron Fox, Marcia Lilley, Jeffrey Miller, Kenneth Mitchell, Annie Notthoff, John Onoda, Haris Orkin, and Rhonda Sarver.

Thank you David Jensen for your gorgeous photograph that graces the cover. Entitled "Leslie Gulch Moonrise," it captures the ruggedly beautiful Owyhee River canyon lands. David, who lives in Eastern Oregon, is a top landscape photographer. And kudos to designer Rob Williams for turning it into a stunning cover. Thank you Janine Savage of Write Divas for proofreading and copyediting.

A special thanks to the Northern Paiute Language Project at University of California, Santa Cruz and the Burns Paiute Tribe of the Burns Paiute Indian Colony of Oregon, a federally recognized tribe of Northern Paiute in Harney County, Oregon.

Any errors are my own.

ALSO BY DWIGHT HOLING

The Nick Drake Novels

The Sorrow Hand (Book 1)

The Pity Heart (Book 2)

The Shaming Eyes (Book 3)

The Jack McCoul Capers

A Boatload (Book 1)

Bad Karma (Book 2)

Baby Blue (Book 3)

Shake City (Book 4)

Short Story Collections

California Works

Over Our Heads Under Our Feet

Made in the USA
Monee, IL
11 December 2019